# HISTORIC GARDENS

*Jane Fearnley-Whittingstall*

# HISTORIC GARDENS

A Guide to 160 British Gardens of Interest

JANE FEARNLEY-WHITTINGSTALL

Published in association with the Historic Houses Association and Christie's

Webb & Bower

*Title page*: **Castle Howard, Yorkshire.**

For all those who share my pleasure in visiting gardens,
without whom the gardens in this book could not survive.

*712·50942*

Photographs of award-winning gardens pages 25-67 by
SIMON McBRIDE

First published in Great Britain 1990 by Webb & Bower (Publishers) Limited
5 Cathedral Close, Exeter, Devon EX1 1EZ

Distributed by the Penguin Group
Penguin Books Ltd, Registered Offices: Harmondsworth, Middlesex, England
Viking Penguin Inc, 40 West 23rd Street, New York, NY 10010, USA
Penguin Books Australia Ltd, Ringwood, Victoria, Australia
Penguin Books Canada Ltd, 2801 John Street, Markham, Ontario,
Canada L3R 1B4
Penguin Books (NZ) Ltd, 182–189 Wairau Road, Auckland 10, New Zealand

Designed by Malcolm Couch

**British Library Cataloguing in Publication Data**
Fearnley-Whittingstall, Jane
    Historic gardens: a guide to 160
    British gardens of interest.
    1. Great Britain. Gardens – Visitors' guides
    I. Title
    914.1′04858

ISBN 0–86350–332–2

Library of Congress 89–52086

Text set in Garamond
Typeset in Great Britain by J&L Composition Ltd, Filey, North Yorkshire

Colour and mono reproduction by J Film Process, Thailand

Printed and bound in Italy by LEGO

# Contents

# Preface

It is a great pleasure for both of us to introduce this excellent book by Jane Fearnley-Whittingstall. It celebrates six years of the joint HHA/Christie's Garden of the Year Award. The Award has focused attention on the importance of historic gardens in the private sector. Many of them rely on visitors for their survival.

We are delighted the competition has aroused such interest and support from the public. We look forward to the success of the past six years being repeated many times over in the future.

**The Earl of Shelburne**
President Historic Houses
Association

**The Right Honourable
The Lord Carrington**
KG, GCMG, CH, MC
Chairman Christie's
International plc

# Foreword

The Historic Houses Association and Christie's jointly introduced the Garden of the Year Award in 1984. Despite the tremendous interest the public took (and takes) in going to see gardens not one of the many awards that were bestowed at that time was for simple public enjoyment. We wanted to remedy this and also to recognize the importance of gardens, not only as places of pleasure and beauty in their own right but as the setting for historic houses.

We designed the scheme to operate on minimal resources with the minimum of formality, and we have continued to rely on the voluntary services of Friends and Members of the Association to act as judges throughout the visiting season. Jane Fearnley-Whittingstall's book celebrates six years of the award and demonstrates how well the judges have done their work. Their selections have varied greatly over the years in scale and in kind, but their choice and taste are unified by the common factor of excellence.

The book also illustrates the difficulties of judging fairly. So many wonderful gardens covered in the second section of the book still await their turn to win. I hope that readers will find in all of them the rich delights that exist in such abundance.

All of the gardens illustrated belong to private owners who are members of the Historic Houses Association and who welcome the visiting public, on whose continued interest and support their future depends.

TERRY EMPSON
Director-General
Historic Houses Association

# Introduction

Gardening, the history of gardens and garden visiting generate more interest today than ever before, and in Britain more and more owners are opening their gardens to visitors. This book is intended as a guide for those visitors who make their journey in the imagination from an armchair as well as those who travel to see gardens by road or rail or on foot.

The members of the Historic Houses Association whose gardens are described here have responded to economic pressures by sharing their family heritage with the ever-widening circle of garden enthusiasts. The relationship between owners of and visitors to these gardens is one of interdependence: the financial contributions of visitors enable the owners to maintain, restore and improve their gardens at a time when materials and skilled labour are increasingly costly. The owners and their families, for their part, are fulfilling an obligation to ensure that their gardens, many of which are of great historical importance, are preserved for future generations to enjoy. For most owners, sharing their gardens with fellow-enthusiasts from all walks of life is a pleasure as well as an obligation.

It is almost impossible to exaggerate the difficulty of providing a high standard of maintenance in a large or elaborate garden in the 1980s and 1990s. Trees and shrubs require surgery and pruning as they mature, and replacing when they have passed maturity. Herbaceous plants and bulbs need lifting and dividing every few years, climbing plants have to be tied in, bedding plants set out, hedges trimmed, leaves swept – the list could go on for pages, and we must now add to it the daunting task of repairing the damage caused by the 'Great Storm' of 1987. Although sophisticated machinery can replace manpower to some extent, skilled and knowledge-able workers are essential to operate the machines and to do the jobs that machines cannot do. If the owners and their staff were not dedicated to working long hours in all weathers, many of the gardens described in this book would not survive.

The historic importance of many gardens lies in their buildings, structures, statuary and furniture: the stonework of classical temples, Regency urns and Victorian follies crumbles, the ironwork of gates and gazebos rusts and timber rots. Repairs and restoration are costly items.

It is a privilege for visitors to enjoy a garden which not many years ago was the exclusive preserve of one family and their friends, and a pleasure to know that their contributions are helping to maintain the garden. The

*Opposite:*
The eighteenth-century cascade at Bowood House, Wiltshire designed by the Hon Charles Hamilton of Painshill.

owners, for their part, gladly share their inheritance with a wider group, whose interest and goodwill help to continue its evolution. One of the things that makes these gardens special is that most of them are still family gardens (some have been continuously occupied by the same family for eight hundred years or more), and are therefore living gardens, adapting to change and developing new ideas while conserving the best of the old. In common with their ancestors, today's owners commission work from contemporary designers and craftsmen, and sponsor expeditions to the world's few remaining wild places to collect the seeds of newly discovered plants. By their contributions, garden visitors have a stake in this patronage without which the art of gardening would stand still.

The range of gardens in the Historic Houses Association covers every region of England, Scotland and Wales. It varies from grand showpieces like Blenheim, Castle Howard, Longleat and Bowood to intimate gardens still designed mainly for family recreation, and tended by the owners with little help. Every historically important garden style is represented: Tudor knot gardens and topiary; elaborate parterres, avenues and vistas in the French seventeenth-century style of le Nôtre; the quintessentially English landscapes of 'Capability' Brown and Repton; nineteenth-century collections of rare trees and shrubs; Victorian rock gardens and formal terraces; Edwardian rose gardens; gardens influenced by Gertrude Jekyll and Vita Sackville-West; and, most recently, gardens planted for wild-flower and wildlife conservation.

The descriptions will help the visitor to choose from gardens located in all parts of the country, and students of garden history or seekers after the beautiful and the curious can, by referring to the lists in the book, discover where to find grottoes, mazes, arbours, ice houses, cascades, ha-has, or any other of the built and planted features that make British gardens such a rich and diverse pleasure.

# PART I

CHAPTER 1

# From Medieval Monasteries to Tudor Mansions

The earliest gardens were very practical affairs. Plants were valued as food, as medicine and for their magical properties. The first step towards gardening was the gathering of useful plants from the wild in order to cultivate them in plots attached to dwellings. The 'Wise Woman' brewing herbal remedies from the produce of her plot would in due course become reviled and feared as the 'Wicked Witch' casting evil spells, but it is likely that in pre-Roman, tribal times, anyone with skill in cultivating plants and knowledge of their properties would have commanded respect.

There was almost certainly nothing that we, if we were transported backwards in time through the centuries, would have recognized as an ornamental garden until the Roman Empire's homesick administrators imported the empire's architecture, building their villas around court-yards planted for pleasure as well as usefulness, with evergreen leaves and scented flowers around a pool or fountain. The chaos that followed the withdrawal of the Romans and the collapse of their empire ensured that little evidence remains of these gardens, but their layout may well have influenced the cloistered, courtyard structure of early monasteries; and the fruit, vegetables, herbs and flowering plants imported to Britain by the Romans were given their only chance of survival by members of the religious orders in the relatively safe environment of monastic orchards and walled gardens.

If Henry VIII's quarrel with the Pope had not resulted in the Dissolution of the Monasteries leading to the destruction of many and the conversion of others into private houses, there might be more evidence available from which to reconstruct a medieval garden. As it is, there are tantalizing fragments to stimulate the imagination: monastic stew ponds where the monks bred carp to provide food on Fridays and fast days can still be seen at Dean's Court, Dorset providing a tranquil piscine environment for huge, venerable carp (they are famous for their longevity) which may be the descendants of those pre-Tudor carp which graced the Lenten platters of the monks. At Beaulieu in Hampshire, monastic life is evoked in the cloister garth, one of the surviving parts of

**Topiary at Levens Hall, Cumbria.**

the Cistercian abbey founded by King John, which was planted in 1976 with herbs which would have been in use at that time for flavouring food (sage, thyme, marjoram, lovage and lemon balm among them) and as medicines (lungwort, pennyroyal, stinking hellebore and horehound).

The thirteenth-century undercroft and fourteenth-century well at Chenies Manor House in Buckinghamshire have inspired the owners to construct garden features appropriate to the early history of the house, including a physic garden and a penitential maze, a pattern of turf and paving which penitents negotiated on their knees. Another physic garden of plants known to have been grown in the Middle Ages can be found at Michelham Priory, East Sussex, a moated Augustinian foundation of 1229.

As the Dark Ages receded and domestic life became more settled and secure, manorial households began to extend their outdoor territory. There was still a need for protection from the hostile world outside, and gardens were either walled or enclosed by impenetrable hedges or moats, some of which have survived in whole or in part. Within these enclosures were orchards and gardens of symmetrically laid out raised beds of herbs, vegetables and flowers. Medieval gardens, from the fourteenth century onwards, began to be used for pleasure and leisure for the first time. Illuminated manuscripts show ladies and their swains singing and playing lutes on flowery grass banks with a background of trellised fences and arched arbours planted with roses.

Plants, even trees, are ephemeral, so there is only an occasional venerable mulberry or oak to draw the imagination back to such scenes. It is more often the buildings surrounding a later garden, like the fifteenth-century chapel and outbuildings at Sheldon Manor in Wiltshire, which conjure up a time when the poem *The Romance of the Rose*, which Chaucer translated from the French, was the equivalent of today's best-selling novel, at least for those few who were able to read.

Relative political stability, security and prosperity under the Tudor dynasty encouraged the rich and powerful to build increasingly magnificent houses with elaborate gardens to match. The beneficiaries of the Dissolution of the Monasteries used stone from the buildings that were destroyed to build substantial family houses. Sixteenth-century gardens were laid out in linked, symmetrical enclosures for orchards, herb and vegetable gardens, and knots of clipped hyssop, rue, thyme and santolina. The spaces within were filled with flowers, herbs or, in the case of the more elaborate designs, coloured gravel, crushed brick and coal dust. The knot patterns were designed to be seen from above, either from upper rooms in the house, from a raised walk or terrace, or from an artificial mount which frequently gave views of the surrounding countryside. The pattern of the knot might incorporate the owner's coat of arms or crest, and sometimes it copied an entwined decorative element from plaster-work or panelling within the house. At Helmingham Hall in Suffolk Lord and Lady Tollemache have made a knot garden in authentic Tudor style which can be looked down on from a grass walk along the moat, or seen across the moat from the house. The pattern follows that of the Tollemache 'Fret', a design which is repeated in the fifteenth-century brickwork of the house. One section of the knot includes Lord and Lady Tollemache's initials, and the other is planted with herbs and flowering plants of an appropriate date. The knot garden of herbs at Dalemain in Cumbria follows a pattern from the plaster ceiling in the 'Fretwork Room' of the medieval, Tudor and early Georgian house.

Knots, with their patterns of evergreen and ever-grey foliage, were an important and satisfying element at a time when the choice of flowering plants to provide seasonal colour was very limited. For the same reason the art of topiary which had been fashionable in Roman times was revived, and a positive passion developed for clipping yew, box and other evergreen shrubs into ever more elaborate and fantastical shapes. A practice which continued until the eighteenth-century landscape movement swept away the zoos, chess sets and other eccentric topiary conceits. A rare and famous example which escaped destruction and was set out for James Graham by the French designer Beaumont in 1690 can be seen at Levens Hall in Cumbria.

The fashion for topiary never quite died out, enjoying great popularity in Victorian gardens, and again today. The confident taming of nature by forcing plants to take on architectural and ornamental shapes could be seen, too, in the Tudor technique of pleaching limes and other trees to form tunnels and arbours which gave protection from the heat of the sun. The sixteenth and seventeenth centuries also saw the first maze craze, a theme that was revived by the Victorians (the 1846 maze at Somerleyton Hall in Suffolk is still in excellent condition), and followed by a second maze craze in the 1980s when new mazes were created for several houses including Longleat, Wiltshire and Floors Castle, Roxburghshire.

Tudor and Jacobean gardens developed the art of formal gardening in the domestic surroundings of the house to a sophisticated level. The next stage would begin to push gardens out into the landscape.

# CHAPTER 2

# Leaping the Fence

During the reign of William and Mary, the Dutch influence appeared in English gardens. Formal canals were introduced and, although topiary and patterned beds in the form of knots and parterres, surrounded by raised walks, continued to be fashionable, gardens began to look outwards into surrounding farmland and woods. The view out into a more serene and domesticated landscape than in earlier times could be seen from strategically placed pavilions or gazebos, or through *clair-voyées*: unglazed windows in walls, often ornamented with an open screen of ironwork.

The late seventeenth and early eighteenth century saw the remodelling of many large gardens either in the comparatively intimate and domestic Dutch style, or in the grand French formal style of le Nôtre who created at Versailles vast, elegant *parterres de broderie*, and magnificent displays of water. He also took command of the surrounding forests by driving through them his great canals and avenues.

English garden layouts in this style, although not on the vast scale of Versailles, can still be seen at Boughton House, Northamptonshire, and at Melbourne Hall in Derbyshire, where Thomas Coke took advice in the 1700s from the successful firm of London and Wise. Bramham Park in Yorkshire was laid out in 1725 with *allées* between high beech hedges, *salles de verdure* and a T-shaped canal, all of which can still be seen today.

At Melbourne and at Castle Howard in Yorkshire the importance of garden buildings and statuary becomes clear. Long, straight vistas required focal points to terminate them, and the broad avenues, walks and rides needed incident to relieve the monotony of their length. At Melbourne the famous wrought-iron 'Birdcage Arbour' was made by Robert Bakewell, a local craftsman whose work became much sought after, and erected in 1706 to complete the main vista from the house. From it Crow Walk leads uphill to Van Nost's great lead 'Urn of the Four Seasons', which splendidly punctuates another vista.

Castle Howard's buildings include Vanbrugh's 'Temple of the Four Winds' as the climax to the gently curving terrace walk, and Hawksmoor's Mausoleum, which, wrote Horace Walpole, 'would tempt one to be buried alive,' is the culmination of one of England's finest landscapes. Castle Howard, with Blenheim and Stowe, marks the transition from French landscaping, with its straight avenues and symmetrical stretches of water, to the English landscape of undulating contours, naturally grouped trees and serpentine lakes. The formal terraces and avenues are still there but they overlook informal stretches of water, or lead to paths which meander through woodland from half-hidden temples to carefully placed statues, pools and cascades.

Rhododendrons at
Muncaster Castle,
Cumbria.

Owners like the 3rd Earl of Carlisle at Castle Howard, Lord Cobham
at Stowe and Lord Leicester at Holkham approached landscape gardening as a philosophical subject and an art. Influenced by romantic
literature, European landscape painting and classical buildings seen on
the Grand Tour, eighteenth-century landowners were fortunate in being
able to call on the services of designers of vision to implement their ideas.
The earliest was Bridgeman who, to quote Walpole again, had 'many
detached thoughts, that strongly indicate the dawn of modern taste'. The
invention of the ha-ha, a device of key importance in merging the garden
with the wider landscape, is attributed to Bridgeman, who worked at
Blenheim and Stowe. Subsequent changes have destroyed most of his
work.

Enlightened patronage also ensured work for William Kent, whose
classical landscape at Rousham Park in Oxfordshire is still one of the
most idyllic places through which to wander, for the prolific Lancelot
('Capability') Brown, who must have done more than any one before or
since to change the appearance of the English countryside, and for
Humphry Repton, whose famous Red Books showing 'before' and 'after'
scenes give a fascinating insight into his ideas. Of the gardens described in
this book, at least twenty-six were, in the words of his contemporary, the
diarist Mary Delany, 'modernised by the ingenious and much sought-
after Mr Brown.' Repton's work can be seen at nine or more of the
gardens, and the Red Books have survived for Holkham, Longleat,
Spains Hall in Essex and Woburn Abbey in Bedfordshire.

Some owners, perhaps anxious to be in the vanguard of fashion, called

16

in three of the great landscapers in succession. This happened at Stowe which is perhaps the greatest of all landscape gardens (Bridgeman, Kent and Brown), and at Holkham Hall (Kent, Brown and Repton). At several houses, including Corsham Court, Bowood and Moccas Court, Repton followed Brown.

Much of the impetus of the landscape movement was supplied by the poet Alexander Pope whose *Epistle to Burlington* of 1731 advised, 'In all, let Nature never be forgot ... Consult the Genius of the Place.' He was also to a great extent responsible for the 'grottomania' which gripped makers of fashionable gardens despite the scorn of Dr Johnson who wrote 'A grotto is not often the wish or pleasure of an Englishman, who has more frequent need to solicit than to exclude the sun.' Grottoes and hermitages were part of the romantic Picturesque ideal, relating landscape gardening to literature and painting in a very direct way. At Corby Castle in Cumbria during the 1720s Lord Thomas Howard developed a part of Inglewood Forest which he thought resembled Milton's Eden in *Paradise Lost*. His achievement is described in 1734 by Sir John Clerk. There was, and still is 'A very agreeable winding walk down to the River where there are some artificial grotos ... and statues of the rural deities ... [and] a cascade 140 feet high.'

The hermit's cave at Bowood in Wiltshire is fossil-lined and, with the adjacent cascade which pours with great vigour over rugged moss- and fern-clad rocks, was designed in 1785 for the first Marquess of Lansdowne by Charles Hamilton, taking the scene from a painting by Poussin. The early nineteenth-century turretted flint folly at Houghton Lodge, Hampshire, the mock castle at Hagley Hall, Worcestershire and the general vogue for Gothic buildings such as Brown's bath house at Corsham Court are similarly inspired by the Picturesque ideal.

The landscapers had banished not only parterres, topiary and terraces from many houses, but also the productive parts of the garden. Fruit and vegetables were relegated to positions out of sight from the house, and sometimes a considerable distance from it (at Hartland Abbey in Devon the kitchen garden is a good half-mile away). Many of the walled gardens which today provide rich soil and a sheltered environment for roses and other shrubs and climbing plants are a legacy from this period. Even at the time they were built, walled gardens would have been used to grow flowers for decoration in the house, but priority was given to providing vegetables and fruit for what were, in those days, large households of family, servants and guests. Advantage could be taken of sun-warmed south- and west-facing walls for grapes, figs and peaches. For growing tender plants and for over-wintering evergreens that were susceptible to frost, greenhouses had been in use since the end of the sixteenth century, and by the end of the eighteenth many were heated by hot air, steam or hot water.

Unlike other exotic fruit, oranges and lemons were not consigned to the kitchen gardens, but occupied handsome buildings in prominent positions. Earlier, the sixteenth-century orangery at Margam in west Glamorgan had provided emergency shelter for a cargo of orange trees from a ship wrecked on the coast nearby while carrying the oranges from

Philip II of Spain to Queen Elizabeth. In 1787 it was enlarged to become one of the finest in the country. Orangeries were built in classical, Gothic and almost every other architectural style, but the most eccentric and charming orangery is to be found at Sezincote in Gloucestershire. It forms a long, curving wing to the house, and ends in a domed pavilion. It is built, as is the house, of golden stone in elaborate Indian Mughal style. The owner, Sir Charles Cockerell, was an East India Company nabob, and commissioned his architect brother to build the house at Sezincote in 1805. It is said to have inspired the Prince of Wales to build Brighton Pavilion in the same style.

By the beginning of the nineteenth century trade throughout an ever-expanding known world had led not only to the introduction of exotic architectural styles but also to the discovery of many new plants, especially flowering shrubs (including, in 1763 *Rhododendron ponticum*, an introduction that has resulted in almost as many problems as the export of rabbits to Australia). The need to display the new plants in suitable habitats led to many changes in the design of gardens. Repton had begun the re-introduction of a measure of formality and decoration near the house, so that instead of encountering the Brownian sheep and deer which grazed up to the drawing-room windows, his clients could go straight from their houses into the flower garden, the rosarium or the American garden. Although the rich legacy of landscaped parkland remained and, depending as it does almost entirely upon landform, water and native trees, has proved enduring for a span of over two hundred years, in the nineteenth century the emphasis was to shift from the landscape to the plants which clothe it.

# CHAPTER 3

# A Passion for Plants

From the beginning of the nineteenth century the ideal of the classical landscape composed from the three archetypal landscape elements of water, trees and stone (the latter fashioned into classical buildings, bridges and monuments) receded before a tide of enthusiasm for exotic plants.

Lancelot Brown died in 1783 and Humphry Repton in 1818. By then the insatiable quest for new garden plants had already begun, and with it a taste for botanizing, a hobby that was to become an almost compulsory accomplishment for every Victorian miss. As early as 1787 the first issue of the first gardening magazine was published: William Curtis's *The Botanical Magazine, or, Flower Garden Displayed*, in which the most ornamental foreign plants, cultivated in the open ground, the greenhouse and the stove, are accurately represented in their natural colours. It was a great success and encouraged various rival publications, including John Claudius Loudon's influential *The Gardener's Magazine*, aimed at gardeners rather than land owners.

The plants described in these magazines and coveted by collectors were the hard-won booty of such brave and hardy explorers as David Douglas, whose expeditions to California were sponsored by the Royal Horticultural Society. He met his death in Hawaii in a pit dug to trap wild cattle, into which a bull had already fallen.

The Society which sponsored Douglas was of great importance. In 1801 John Wedgwood, son of the potter Josiah and a keen amateur gardener, began a letter to William Forsyth (George III's gardener) with the words 'I have been turning my attention to the formation of a Horticultural Society.' From this beginning came the Royal Horticultural Society, still today the pre-eminent forum for the introduction of new plants at the Chelsea Flower Show and at its regular monthly shows.

Amateur patrons were able to play their part in the discovery of new plants through membership of the Society or, more directly, by arrangement with traders in the Americas, in Asia and in China, or through friends and relations. Francis Molesworth sent seeds from New Zealand to his brother Sir William who was forming a collection of conifers at Pencarrow in Cornwall and lined a mile-long drive with them. By 1854 he had specimens of all except ten of the conifers known to the Western world at that time.

The introduction of conifers, rhododendrons, azaleas, roses and the vast majority of the flowering shrubs that we grow today completely transformed the design of gardens. The display of plants was the first consideration, and separate plots began to be devoted to particular types of plants. In the 1840s Lord Somers planted a conifer collection at

Eastnor Castle in Herefordshire, and pineta were planted at Scone Palace in Perthshire and at Bowood in Wiltshire. Collectors of Asiatic woodland shrubs had reason to be grateful to their tree-planting ancestors. For example, at Holker Hall in Cumbria, the oaks, beeches and sycamores planted by Sir Thomas Lowther in the eighteenth century provided the ideal environment for nineteenth-century plantings of azaleas, rhododendrons and magnolias.

The understanding that plants from abroad need an environment approaching that which they enjoy in their native habitat led to the construction of elaborate rockeries, water courses and, in some gardens, ferneries. In the eighteenth century rockwork, streams, cascades and grottoes had been constructed for their own sake, as examples of scenery that was 'picturesque', 'sublime' or 'horrid'. In the nineteenth century their purpose was to provide the right setting for newly introduced plants. At Pencarrow the massive granite rockery took three years to construct. Another early example of a rock garden can be seen at Lamport Hall in Northamptonshire, an almost vertical rock face imitating an alpine hillside. Sir Charles Isham, its creator, peopled it with what must have been the very first garden gnomes, the last of which is exhibited in the house.

Improvements in technology for building and heating glass-houses kept pace with the introduction of tender plants (which, until then, were housed in conservatories and orangeries), and provided for the nurture of the flowers and foliage that were used to make elaborate, often garishly colourful patterns of the carpet bedding so much loved by the Victorians. This is such a labour-intensive form of gardening that, although still much used by municipal parks departments, it is seldom seen in privately owned gardens. However, there are good examples at Lyme Park, Cheshire, Harewood House, Yorkshire and Somerleyton Hall, Suffolk.

The Victorian yearning for colourful flowers was matched by the return of a taste for formal pattern around the house, and a revival of terraces and parterres. A rash of 'Italian' gardens and 'Dutch' gardens sprang up to satisfy the taste, and architects and garden designers were employed to plan them. When one considers the numbers of staff required to maintain such elaborate gardens in immaculate condition, it is not surprising that those examples that remain have almost all been considerably simplified. At Ragley Hall, Warwickshire in 1870 sixteen gardeners were employed to look after the formal gardens that the present Lord Hertford's grandfather had restored. Today there are just three full time and one part time.

Prominent among the designers was William Nesfield (1793–1881), a former army officer, who specialized in patterns of box tracery on gravel beds. Rare examples of Nesfield's work are the 1854 parterre at Holkham Hall in Norfolk and the maze at Somerleyton Hall, Suffolk, of 1846. The parterre in the courtyard at Holme Pierrepoint Hall, Nottinghamshire may also be Nesfield's design.

From the middle of the nineteenth century onwards for six weeks in June and July the rose garden was the climax for scent and colour of many gardens. Forward leaps in hybridization coinciding with the vogue for formality led to the construction of symmetrically arranged patterns of rose beds, rose arbours, rose pergolas, pillars and swags. At Warwick Castle the rose garden designed by Robert Marnock in 1864 has been restored to Marnock's original plan, and gives a delightful impression of elegant structure and luxuriant planting. The fashion for giving roses a garden of their own has never died: of the gardens listed in this book, no less than seventy-nine have rose gardens.

Towards the turn of the century the nostalgia which married the Italian style of stone terraces and statuary to the Tudor style of knots and topiary was particularly well expressed by Robert Lorimer, the Scottish architect who laid out gardens at Earlshall Castle, Fife, at Lennoxlove, Lothian and at Torosay Castle on the Isle of Mull. Also to be seen in Scotland are the fine terraces devised in 1909 as a setting for Robert Adam's Mellerstain House in Berwickshire by Sir Reginald Blomfield. Advocating an architectural, formal approach to garden design, Blomfield's book *The Formal Garden in England* (1892) was influential in upholding an alternative to the free 'natural' style championed by William Robinson. In England his design for Godinton Park in Kent survives.

Nostalgia for a bygone period of English history was expressed with a fervour that could perhaps only be felt by an American at Hever Castle in Kent. When Mr W W Astor fell in love with and bought the sixteenth-century home of the Boleyn family, his means fortunately matched his enthusiasm and, as well as restoring the castle and building a Tudor village alongside it, he created a series of gardens including a maze, topiary, a herb garden and Anne Boleyn's orchard. Set apart from these Tudor elements are gardens with other themes, including a spectacular Italian garden of statuary and Roman architectural fragments.

Formality was never entirely banished from gardens where it was appropriate to the architecture of the house, but as the twentieth century began, so too did a new philosophy of gardening.

# CHAPTER 4

# Free-style Gardens

'I think there are as many kinds of gardening as of poetry', wrote Joseph Addison in 1712.

Two hundred years later, this was certainly true. The formal style with its terraces, parterres, clipped hedges and topiary, the landscape style and the plantsman's style, designed to show off collections of woodland shrubs or alpine plants, were joined at the beginning of the twentieth century by two new, interrelated styles of great significance for the future of gardening: the natural style and the cottage garden style. From the Edwardian era until the present, these various kinds of gardening have flourished, often all being represented within the boundaries of one garden.

Two great gardeners were responsible for promoting the new garden philosophy by example in their work, and above all through their writing. William Robinson and Gertrude Jekyll had nothing in common as far as their personalities and backgrounds were concerned, but they shared an appreciation of the natural beauty of wild plants and flowers, and of the luxuriance and artless charm with which the cottagers of English villages planted their gardens.

Their achievement was to free gardens of their Victorian corsets, and persuade gardeners into a looser more natural planting style that was particularly suitable for the smaller country and suburban houses that were being built at that time.

Robinson's book *The Wild Garden* and many of his magazine articles advocated naturalistic planting in woodland and water gardens, and drew attention to the value of native flowering plants to be used among and beneath exotic shrubs and trees. His influence can be seen in the great woodland gardens created between the turn of the century and the First World War in the south of England, in Scotland and in other areas with the benefit of acid soil and native birch and oak woodland. In such conditions rhododendrons, azaleas, heaths and many of the other plants being introduced from Asia thrive.

Gertrude Jekyll shared Robinson's views about wild and woodland gardening, but perhaps her greatest contribution has been to the design of the herbaceous or mixed border. A painter by training, she worked out theories about colour in the garden, put her theories into practise in her own garden and in gardens designed for her clients, and expressed her ideas lucidly in her books. Their recent rediscovery has led to great improvements in many gardens, despite the fact that her planting plans were designed for gardens tended by a large, skilled labour force and therefore need thoughtful adaptation for use today.

Miss Jekyll's immensely fertile collaboration with Sir Edwin Lutyens

led to the happy marriage of the architecture of the garden to its planting. The style they arrived at together, of romantically luxuriant planting within a firm architectural framework of terraces and garden 'rooms', is still today the ideal towards which most gardeners strive.

The High Beeches: a fine example of early twentieth century woodland gardening.

Between the wars country-house entertaining continued and, with the advent of the motor-car and the emergence of 'Bright Young Things', became more hectic. The demand for vegetables and fruit to feed weekend house parties and flowers to decorate the house was, if anything, greater than before. Formerly tranquil lakes became the scene of noisy boating and bathing parties and lawns were adapted to the sporting pursuits of tennis, croquet and badminton. Shrubberies and arbours which had been the scene of romantic trysts were used for childish and grown-up games of hide-and-seek and treasure hunts.

The Second World War brought all this to an abrupt end. Country-house owners, their families and their staff went away to fight or to contribute in other ways to the war effort. Houses were requisitioned as military headquarters or as hospitals. Lawns and borders were ploughed up for food production. Almost without exception every garden described in this book suffered involuntary neglect for a period of five years. It was a salutary lesson that gardens are borrowed from nature and it does not take nature many years to take back her own. By 1945 precious shrubs and young trees were suffocated under a tangle of brambles,

23

nettles and elder. Sycamore and ash saplings sprang up everywhere, lodging themselves in the stonework of walls, steps and terraces and prizing apart the framework of glass-houses.

In post-war years there has been no question of returning to the pre-war system. It is no longer possible for owners to employ teams of ten or twelve gardeners nor, if it was, is the labour available or willing. Nevertheless, beautiful gardens have risen phoenix-like from bonfires of cleared scrub, nettles, bindweed and ground elder. This has come about through adaptation to changed circumstances: through making maximum use of increasingly efficient modern garden machines; through adapting the layout and planting of gardens to suit the machines; and through dedication and hard work by garden owners and their staffs. The adaptation that is required has altered the appearance of gardens, often for the better. Incongruously elaborate and fussy flower-beds have been grassed over, and shrubs, roses and herbaceous plants massed in bold groups which are often more in keeping with the scale of the garden landscape. Trees and shrubs have been underplanted with plants chosen for their weed-smothering quality, which has led to the choice of plants for the sake of their long-lasting fine foliage, rather than for their ephemeral display of flowers. Today, rather than creating special habitats for special groups of plants, gardeners choose plants that will thrive in the existing conditions. So there are, for example, fewer rhododendrons to be seen growing in specially constructed pockets of peat in the Cotswolds, and areas of differing soil and climate each have a stronger regional character.

The post-war rehabilitation of gardens still goes on after nearly fifty years, and an increased interest in garden history has led to the construction of gardens which relate to the architectural style of their houses. This kind of creative development can only take place in privately owned properties, since national organizations which care for houses and gardens on behalf of us all are committed to preservation of what already exists. Projects for renovating neglected gardens and for continuing the tradition whereby each generation contributes to the structure or planting of a garden, are costly. But by sharing their gardens with an ever-widening circle of appreciative visitors, owners will be able to meet these costs.

# PART II

*THE WINNERS OF THE*

*CHRISTIE'S/*

*HISTORIC HOUSES ASSOCIATION*

*GARDEN OF THE YEAR*

*AWARD*

# Heale House

Woodford, Salisbury, Wiltshire (Major David and Lady Anne Rasch)

Gardens 8 acres, park 12 acres

*Christie's/Historic Houses Association Garden of the Year 1984*

IF YOU APPROACH HEALE HOUSE from the north you will cross the tree-less, chalky expanses of Salisbury Plain, where the immemorial monoliths of Stonehenge are inhabited by phantom druids, and the ghostly feet of Roman legionnaires march along the straight roads. A sudden descent will bring you to a hidden landscape in complete contrast to the open plain. The Hampshire Avon flows through fertile water meadows between wooded slopes. In this sheltered valley trees grow to immense stature, sheltering brick and flint cottages with thatched roofs.

Heale House is hidden in this green and comfortable landscape at the end of a double avenue of black poplars and beeches alternating with maples. Meadows on either side are studded with magnificent oaks and massive Spanish chestnuts with deeply grooved trunks of great girth. Streams diverted from the River Avon flow fast and clear and full of trout on the east and south sides of the house, which dates from the sixteenth century and was enlarged with great sensitivity in the 1890s by the present owner's great-uncle, the Hon Louis Greville.

Mr Greville, with the help of the architect Detmar Blow, built to the north and east on the foundations of an earlier wing that had been destroyed by fire. The design and the carefully chosen materials seamlessly unite his additions with the earlier south-west wing. Today the gardens also happily combine an Edwardian with a Tudor style. Much of their layout was planned for Louis Greville by Harold Peto in 1910, and his stone paved terraces and balustraded retaining walls cater for changes of level and create vistas on just the right domestic scale.

Farthest from the house but nearest to the car-park and therefore the first part encountered by visitors, is the walled garden. Originally planned as a rose garden with a pergola over the central lily pond, it became a vegetable plot during the war when the house was requisitioned by Salisbury Hospital. It is now one of the prettiest of kitchen gardens, where fruit, vegetables, flowers and topiary all play their part. On the outside of the west wall red currants are trained as vertical cordons. Reaching almost to the top of the eight-foot (2.4-metre) wall, in July each stem is hung with bunches of translucent scarlet berries in great

*Opposite:*
Heale House: the bridge in the Japanese garden.

profusion. The red-tiled walls enclose the garden on three sides. The fourth is defined by a walk beneath a sturdy pergola clothed with climbers in a predominantly yellow, white and green colour scheme. The yellows include the vigorous climbing rose, 'Easlea's Golden Rambler', laburnum and *Hedera helix* 'Buttercup'. Among the white flowers is the rose 'White Cockade' and *Clematis florida* 'Alba Plena' holds its green rosettes long into the autumn.

The walled garden is quartered by tunnels of apple trees, each a generous thirteen feet (four metres) wide, so that two people can walk abreast beneath them. In the centre where the four paths meet, a small stone-edged lily pond is surrounded by large, satisfyingly solid domes of clipped box planted at the turn of the century. Three quarters of the garden are planted with neat rows of vegetables, flowers to cut for the house or soft fruit, and each bed is edged with bulbs and ground-cover plants such as hostas and pinks. The fourth section is laid to lawn with a circular arbour in the centre, over which newly planted pear trees are being trained, with honeysuckle and clematis. From the seat inside the arbour the view is towards the rounded box domes and beyond them to some of the striking trees in the gardens, including cedars, a fine, tall, wide-spreading copper beech and a magnificent *Cercidiphyllum Japonicum*, one of the largest specimens in Britain, and brilliant in its autumn colour. Beds at the foot of the walls are planted with climbers, shrubs and herbaceous plants that provide colour and scent over a long period. They include the reliable and lovely white rose 'Mme Alfred Carrière', rose 'Lady Hillingdon' of warm apricot-yellow colouring, the pineapple-scented broom, *Cytisus battandieri*, fine irises in the dry south-facing bed, tall hollyhocks and the unusual pink-flowered phlomis, *P. italica*. There is something very satisfying about the fusion of the useful with the beautiful in this garden.

The entrance to Harold Peto's terraced garden to the west of the house is between architecturally shaped yew hedges. The top terrace looks down towards the house, its apricot pink brick and golden stonework softened by climbing roses which complement their colouring: scented 'Alchemist' with its closely packed, very double peachy-yellow flowers and 'Paul Lédé', also scented, a mass of huge, pale, apricot-buff blooms.

Peto's layout remains, but the formal Edwardian planting has been replaced by Lady Anne Rasch with a romantic luxuriance of shrubs and perennials on the top and lowest terraces, and a simple lawn separating them. The top terrace, paved with flag stones, has inviting curved stone seats at either end, and in the centre a large copper bowl planted with cream variegated ivy and white and soft yellow petunias. Plants with purple-red foliage are much used here (and elsewhere in the garden too) to set off roses and other flowering plants and to contrast with variegated and golden foliage. *Cotinus coggygria* 'Royal Purple' and *Philadelphus coronarius* 'Aureus' are interwoven, and the gold-green leaves of a standard wistaria ramble through *Prunus pissardii*. The free-flowering pink rose 'Bourbon Queen' has hauled itself twelve feet (3.5 metres) or more into another purple prunus. Many roses generally described as shrubs of modest size will climb when given the chance. The roses and

shrubs are interplanted with traditional herbaceous plants, many of which are cottage garden favourites: alchemilla, astrantia, crambe, catmint, foxgloves, hollyhocks and honesty (including the prettily variegated form of the latter). The domed shape and graceful wand-like branches of *Pyrus salicifolia* 'Pendula' in one border are echoed by the similar form and habit of *Buddleia alternifolia* in the opposite bed, the branches of the latter a mass of soft, pale, lavender flowers in early summer. Almost hidden in the shade of a large standard wistaria, a small bronze monkey peers at you.

Broad steps lead down to a generously proportioned walk of York flag stones with spacious lawns on either side. The walk is at the centre of a widely spaced avenue of laburnums, but one or two of them died and have been replaced. Laburnums do seem prone to sudden death, and here the young trees will never catch up with the older ones, so that the Raschs now feel that they should have hardened their hearts, taken all the trees out and started again.

The bottom terrace in front of the house is also paved. Twin lily ponds with elegantly shaped oval surrounds of mossy stone are set into the paving, and the beds below the balustraded wall are planted in a style which continues the themes of the top terrace. Shrubs and roses, including the lovely striped 'Rosa Mundi', named after the unlucky mistress of King Henry II, Rosamund Clifford, are underplanted with bulbs which flower in winter and early spring, to be seen from the house on the coldest days. *Cyclamen coum* and *C. neapolitanum* flower from

Heale House: terraced garden on the west front designed by Harold Peto.

**Heale House: honeysuckle and roses frame the entrance to the walled garden.**

August till April, and other early bulbs include *Iris reticulata* and *Fritillaria meleagris*. On either side of the steps height is given, and the view back to the upper terrace framed, by two tall trellised pyramids, their structure almost completely hidden beneath the spectacular roses 'Rambling Rector', 'Spek's Yellow' and 'Wedding Day'. Clematis 'Nellie Moser' climbs with them and wanders forwards through the purple leaves of a cotinus.

On the north side of the house dense drifts of aconites, snowdrops and, later, daffodils, cover the orchard beyond the tennis court. From here a walk runs between the house and the river which flows just beyond a stone balustrade draped with 'Albertine' and other rambling roses dating from the 1920s. There is a delightful little boat terrace reached by balustraded steps opposite a broad, paved terrace filling an angle in the house walls. In the paving *Alchemilla mollis*, rue, sisyrinchium, stonecrop and mimulus spread themselves liberally. Lady Anne Rasch is tender-hearted towards self-seeding plants, and there is a generous profusion of such reliable and familiar friends throughout the gardens. On the house walls there are two fine *Magnolia grandiflora* and the lovely rose 'Paul Lédé' again.

In June and again in late summer the sweet scent of hybrid musk roses draws you across the croquet lawn to a dense hedge of 'Penelope', 'Cornelia', 'Buff Beauty', 'Moonlight' and 'Felicia', with sedums planted at their feet to attract the butterflies. The grass walk beside the hybrid musks finishes at one end under the splendid copper beech which dominates the garden from most viewpoints, and at the other under a whitebeam – one of the loveliest of English trees. At a lower level a long border of shrub roses, delphiniums, pale apricot foxgloves and other herbaceous plants with the startling silver-grey thistle *Onopordium acanthium* rising above them, leads to a wrought-iron gate entwined with honeysuckle. The opulent pink climbing rose 'Mme Grégoire Staechelin' embraces one of the brick piers. The gate leads through an old, tiled cob wall, perhaps one of the garden walls of the original house. Beyond it a lawn leading down to the river is planted with apple and plum trees and a mulberry survives from Louis Greville's time.

From the lawn the eye is caught by a flash of scarlet. It is the first intimation of a garden which must once have seemed a little incongruous in this most English of scenes, but today is fully integrated into the gardens as a whole. The scarlet that stands out so vividly above the river is a small version of the famous Nikko Bridge, and part of an authentic Japanese garden made for Louis Greville who had spent some time in the diplomatic service in Tokyo. Four Japanese gardeners came to England to create the garden, and the bridge, a huge stone temple lantern and a delightful tea house still remain. The thatched tea house bestrides an intersection of two streams and has a fretted timber balcony and sliding rice paper shutters. Much of the original rockwork has gone, and the planting is softened, with roses climbing into trees and waterside plants growing more luxuriantly than might be acceptable in Kyoto. But the water crossed and recrossed by little bridges, the magnolias, the shapely acers and the outline of a gnarled walnut tree looking like a giant bonsai specimen all contribute to an oriental atmosphere in this part of the garden.

As with so many successful gardens, that of Heale House has been adapted to today's conditions without losing its timeless atmosphere. All the work of maintaining it is done as a labour of love by the owners with a staff of two gardeners, and the fact that it is not too immaculately manicured contributes much to its charm and romance.

# Hodnet Hall

## Market Drayton, Shropshire (Mr and the Hon Mrs A Heber-Percy)

Gardens and park 60 acres

*Christie's/Historic Houses Association Garden of the Year 1985*

IT WAS THE PRESENT OWNER'S FATHER, Brigadier A G W Heber-Percy who had the vision to flood the valley below Hodnet Hall, thus creating the series of pools which contribute so much to the beauty and tranquillity of the gardens. It is hard to imagine the scene without water, but before 1922 the massive red-brick mansion, designed by Salvin in the Elizabethan style and built in the 1870s, presided grandly over nothing more than a broad terrace with steps leading down to a marshy hollow between wooded slopes. The terrace is still there but it now looks over the main lake surrounded by a rich and diverse landscape of trees, shrubs and waterside plants.

In the 1920s the late Brigadier, then a young officer in the Grenadier Guards, set about his ambitious project with the permission of his father, given somewhat grudgingly. The water supply was provided by a small stream which flowed from west to east into the marsh below the house and, fed on the way by numerous springs, flowed into the horse wash pond, which was probably used to water horses at the end of the working day long before the present hall was built. Mature stands of beech and oak on both sides of the valley provided a fine framework for the chain of seven pools which were to descend through dammed cascades to a main pool below the house.

He was helped by teams of Grenadiers who dug out the pools and, on one occasion, by an engineer from the Italian army who pointed out that a pool with perpendicular sides could not be guaranteed to hold water. The engineer obligingly supervised the construction of one dam with its sides sloped to the correct angle, and this is said to be the only one which never leaks.

Having accomplished the orderly flow of water from an anonymous top pool through paradise pool, Heber pool, pike pool, the water garden, main pool and horse wash pool, the brigadier devoted himself to planting the pool margins and the slopes above them. Over a period of about forty years, he created the landscape which we see today. The acid loam overlaying clay and the moist and benign microclimate provided by the pools gave scope for planting rhododendrons, azaleas, camellias and

*Opposite:*
**Looking across Main Pool in May.**

Hodnet Hall: Pike Pool and
Heber Pool in spring.

other calcifuge plants. The choice of rare and interesting plants was influenced to some extent by E A Bowles, the distinguished amateur botanist and gardening writer, whose own garden at Myddleton House in Middlesex was one of the most remarkable in England. He was the great-uncle of the present owner, and visited Hodnet in the early days of the garden's development, offering encouragement and donating plants. From the 1960s onwards the Brigadier's original planting has been extended and modified by his son and daughter-in-law, with a view to providing colour and interest from early spring to autumn. One of their aims is to achieve softer colour schemes as old plants are replaced. Many plants were lost in the drought years of the 1970s and in the winter of 1981–82, when this part of Shropshire suffered twenty-six degrees of frost. But the Heber-Percys treated these disasters philosophically in the knowledge that a fine garden cannot remain static, but must evolve. The loss of cherished plants is a sad affair, but it does open up new opportunities.

After his father's death, in order to be able to continue living at Hodnet, Algernon Heber-Percy made radical alterations to the house, removing entirely its top storey and demolishing a wing. The result is a well-proportioned building which presides over but does not dominate the gardens below it.

The visitor to the gardens following the route suggested in the guide book comes first to the north forecourt of the hall. From here the vista down the drive, sadly interrupted by the A442 road, terminates with a tall stone portico on the skyline. It came from Apley Castle in Shropshire when it was demolished in 1956 and, erected here as a memorial to Brigadier Heber-Percy, gives an eighteenth-century touch to the landscape. From the forecourt a path leads through a woodland garden newly planted with specimen trees and rhododendrons, with a carpet of spring bulbs. By descending a gentle slope you can follow a route which skirts the pike pool and Heber pool. Here the gardens merge with the Shropshire countryside. The refreshing expanses of clear water reflecting the sky are wide enough to be in scale with the great forest trees on the banks which in spring are carpeted with bluebells. Groups of trees are underplanted with generous drifts of narcissi, some white, some yellow, and grassy banks are studded with anemones, bluebells and primroses in spring, followed by campion and other wild flowers. This simple, calm, idealized landscape is both a contrast to and a preparation for the richly varied and colourful planting around the lower pools.

The water garden below pike pool is crossed by paths and stepping stones which invite the visitor to wander through the pools for closer inspection of each group of plants. The water's margin is planted to great effect with boldly massed groups: gunneras are here not in twos or threes but in dozens. In May their knobbly flower spikes rise out of a debris of dead leaves and stems and the new season's leaves begin to unfurl from huge, gnarled brown dragons' fists. White- and yellow-flowered lysichitum, hostas and ligularia are grouped with the same conviction, their clumps of bold foliage linked by great drifts of candelabra primulas and the feathery foliage of astilbes which will flower later in interlocking masses of white, pink and red. On the bank, with a background of massive forest trees, are groups of Exbury hybrid azaleas, *Rhododendron impeditum*, 'Blue Tit' and *R. williamsianum* and a bed of yellow and white azaleas presented to Mr and Mrs Heber-Percy by Hodnet Women's Institute on their marriage in 1966.

On the north side of the water garden the path leads on to a spacious lawn above the main lake. There is a fine view across the lake to the house, with central, broad, stone steps descending by stages to the water's edge. The slopes on each side of the steps are planted with rhododendrons and brooms followed in flower by berberis, rose species and heathers. Mounded acers provide architectural form. At the bottom of the steps on each side a large *Exochorda macrantha* 'The Bride' spills out over a retaining wall. The lakeside planting is simple and bold, with fine weeping willows, large clumps of iris and ornamental grasses, and groups of purple hazel.

On a more intimate scale, a series of small pools at the eastern end of the main lake are connected with little streams and cascades, their margins planted with irises, rodgersias, astilbes, candelabra primulas and ferns. The banks of the horse wash pool are planted with *Primula* 'Postford White', white astilbes and Ghent, Mollis and Japanese azaleas. Nearby are lilacs, philadelphus, a *Davidia* and a venerable walnut tree. Here too are groups of *Hydrangea sargentiana* and *H. villosa* with their bold foliage and lacecap flowers in late summer.

Above the horse wash pool there is a small, enclosed garden, its entrance flanked by two rough stone pillars. At its centre is a massive glacial boulder, removed from the horse wash pool in 1960. This garden, bordered on two sides with oaks underplanted with bamboos, bergenia, pulmonaria and *Cornus canadensis*, is planted for summer with rose species and shrub roses, including *R. moyesii* 'Geranium', *R. hugonis*, 'Maigold', 'Golden Wings', 'Scarlet Fire' and 'Nevada'. The under-planting is of the long-flowering shrubby potentillas, catmint, hardy geraniums, dicentras, hostas and day lilies. Philadelphus mingles its scent with that of the roses, and hydrangeas and fuchsias flower from later summer into autumn. Beyond 'The Stone Garden' the grove of oak and bamboos encircles a curious kiln-shaped little building of brick with a conical dome. This peacefully situated summer-house was formerly a smoke-house, used to preserve the produce of the estate. The bamboos here were planted at a later date than those elsewhere in the gardens, which recently all flowered in the same season and seemed, as bamboos do after flowering, to die. The flowered stems were cut to the ground, and now many are showing signs of life again. Behind the smoke-house the russet trunks of Scots pine soar up out of a mown grass sward, marking the transition between the gardens and the rural landscape beyond.

Across the drive from the smoke-house and behind the old stables (now the tea-rooms) there is a garden of shrubs which enjoys the shelter of a light canopy of mature forest trees. Camellias, rhododendrons and pieris are followed in flower by cornuses, hydrangeas, eucryphias and fothergillas. Rarities include *Hydrangea xanthoneura wilsonii*, *Viburnum wrightii*, *Syringa josikae* and *Acer senkaki* with pinky-orange bark. Beneath the trees and shrubs are red-flowered trilliums, euphorbias, *Meconopsis grandis* and *Smilacina racemosa*. A seventeenth-century Italian well-head provides a focal point at the centre of the lawn.

On the east side of the glade a path leads to the magnolia walk, a broad walk descending through several short flights of shallow steps towards the beech avenue. This formal walk, the beech drive and the circular rose garden, are relics of the earlier garden of the Elizabethan house of which only the stable block remains today. Planted in 1956–57, the magnolias are now handsome and flowering well. Among them are *M. mollicomata*, the fragrant white-flowered *M. officinalis*, *M. sargentiana* and *M. lennei*, its flowers rose-purple outside and white within. The graceful form of *Magnolia* 'Heaven Sent' and a large specimen of *Magnolia obovata* are also striking. Just beyond are more remarkable trees and shrubs, including the handkerchief tree, *Davidia involucrata* with its spectacular fluttering white bracts, and an unusually large-flowered form of *Halesia monticola vestita* which bears its lovely white bell-shaped flowers in May.

At the end of the magnolia walk there is a junction of paths. To the south are the old stables, a black and white timbered building which is all that remains of the original family house. Inside are the shop and tea-rooms, the latter decorated with an amazing collection of big game trophies: not just heads and horns, but also an entire snarling tiger. The walls of the old stables are planted with camellias, the scarlet climber

*Eccremocarpus scaber* and *Schizophragma integrifolia*. Around a lawn, where refreshments can be taken in fine weather, there are borders of tree peonies, roses, viburnums, the blue-podded *Decaisnea fargesii* and eremuruses, or foxtail lilies.

Beyond the stables a drive leads through a wrought-iron gate to a handsome seventeenth-century tithe barn and beyond it to the walled kitchen garden, laid out in about 1860, where vegetables and flowers for the house are grown in neat box-edged beds. In the kitchen garden plants, fruit, flowers and vegetables are for sale.

If you return past the old stables you will find yourself facing down the beech avenue. Its ancient trees were planted long before the Elizabethan house was demolished. The present owner's ancestor, the missionary Bishop Heber, enjoyed their shade, where every prospect does indeed please, and walked there while he was composing his stirring hymns in the early nineteenth century. At the beginning of the avenue on the east side there is a glade planted entirely with pale yellow and soft flame-orange azaleas carpeted with bluebells, a colour combination breath-taking in its purity.

At the south-west end of the beech avenue there is an intensively gardened area which includes a circular formal garden: all that remains, with the magnolia walk and the beech avenue, from the gardens of the earlier house. Known as the lower rose garden, its concentric beds are ingeniously planted to provide a succession of flowers. The outer ring is planted with mixed herbaceous peonies, the inner ring with the flori-bunda rose 'Korresia' and the centre with *Hydrangea paniculata* 'Grandiflora' edged with caryopteris and old English lavender. In the middle there is a large stone statue of an angel with a beard.

A path ascends the red sandstone cliff behind the lower rose garden, through the camellia garden. Large, flourishing specimens of camellias 'St Ewe', 'Rosemary Williams', 'Lady's Maid', 'Donation' and 'Cornish Snow' are interplanted with small rhododendrons including the scarlet 'Britannia', blue-purple *R. russatum* and mauve *R. scintillans*. From the rustic summer-house here you can look down over the rose garden to the pools and the wider landscape beyond.

Walking west, towards the hall from the summer-house you pass beds of red, pink, orange and cerise azaleas and cream and yellow brooms, the high colour softened with underplantings of shuttlecock ferns and blue *Scilla campanulata*. This brings you to the broad walk, a wide, gravelled terrace below the house which commands the main view to the south. In the foreground the hectic colours of rhododendrons and azaleas are moderated by the graceful domes of *Acer* 'Dissectum Atropurpureum' and *Acer palmatum* 'Palmatifidum'. Later in the summer kalmias are in flower. Below is the calm expanse of the main lake and beyond, framed by majestic trees, an agricultural landscape fading to blue, distant hills. Perfectly positioned to catch the eye in the middle distance is a pretty dovecote built in 1656. Between the house and the broad walk there are generously wide herbaceous borders, providing an air of Edwardian formality between the hall's south-facing terrace and the banked shrubs below.

Hodnet Hall: azaleas, acers and brooms frame the view from the terrace to the dovecote.

Looking out over the gardens from the broad walk you can choose which parts of the garden to revisit. I have chosen to describe a route which begins beside the upper pools in the peaceful idealized English landscape of water, native trees, grassy banks and wild flowers. As you progress towards the ever more varied and colourful planting near the house, your eye and imagination are increasingly stimulated. Yet even in May when the rhododendrons and azaleas are in full flower, the eye is never dazzled and sated with their rich and sometimes garish colours. Careful planning ensures that colour groupings are always pleasing. Yellows and oranges are separated from magentas and mauves, and the eye finds relief in the cool underplantings of ferns and bluebells, in white canopies of cherry blossom and in the majestic backdrop of the forest trees which set the scale of the gardens and settle them comfortably into the landscape. Above all water is the theme which unites the various areas of the garden, reflecting impartially the simple wooded banks of the upper pools and the intricately balanced colours and textures of the water garden.

A more leisurely exploration in reverse, starting from the broad walk and taking the narrow grass path to the summer-house above the circular rose garden will invert the experience and take you from excitement and stimulation towards tranquillity. It provides an opportunity to savour contrasts between shaded and sunlit spaces and between intimate paths enclosed by dense and colourful planting and open lawns studded with fine trees. You will also have the chance to enjoy the plants in detail, and to appreciate the positioning of the buildings in the gardens and the rough-hewn stone gateposts that mark entrances to paths. Other pleasing details include the little stone bridges which cross and recross the water, and the cascades which link the pools, some with a gush, some with a trickle. As you go round you cannot help noticing that this is a garden which is loved and cherished, that the owners like sharing it with you, and that your enjoyment and that of other visitors contributes to its happy atmosphere.

# Newby Hall

## Skelton-on-Ure, Ripon, North Yorkshire (Mr Robin Compton)

### Gardens 25 acres

*Christie's/Historic Houses Association Garden of the Year 1986*

CELIA FIENNES IN HER DIARY for 1697 described Newby Hall as 'The finest house I saw in Yorkshire'. Today it also has one of the finest gardens in England. The garden makes a perfect setting for the beautifully proportioned house, which was built of mellow brick in 1690 for Sir Edward Blackett, Member of Parliament for Ripon.

A Kip drawing of about 1710 shows the gardens as Celia Fiennes would have seen them, laid out with the symmetry that was then fashionable. The house was approached from the west by a drive leading between lawns flanked by plantations of closely regimented trees into a walled forecourt decorated with statuary. A promenade on the south front of the house descended to a great lawn quartered by paths and sheltered by trees set out in straight rows. To the north were 'squares full of dwarfe trees both fruites and green'. Straight avenues radiated from the house into the landscape beyond. One of the avenues running diagonally from the house to the river was rediscovered amid much excitement in 1981. During clearance of overgrown woodland and scrub a fine mature lime tree was revealed, then another, then a third and a fourth, all on the same line. All work elsewhere in the gardens ceased until the entire avenue had been reinstated. Plans are now in hand for the restoration of a second avenue which is aligned with Ripon Cathedral.

In 1748 Newby was sold to William Weddell, ancestor of the present owner, Robin Compton. He was a man of great taste and commissioned the neo-classical architect John Carr to add the two east wings of the house and Robert Adam later to complete this work and to decorate much of the interior. Adam's work can be seen in the sculpture gallery built for William Weddell's collection of classical statuary brought back from the Grand Tour in 1766, and in the room he designed to display a beautiful set of Gobelins tapestries. Thomas Chippendale made the frames for the chairs and sofas and all the contents are intact today, which makes the room unique. Weddell's cousin Lord Grantham succeeded to the property in 1792. He added the Regency dining-room on the north-west corner of the house and it was probably at this time that much of the

formal garden was swept away bringing the landscape up to the house in Brownian style, as shown in an etching of this period. From this time onwards many of the fine trees which form the framework of the gardens would have been planted.

Lord Grantham gave Newby to his daughter, Lady Mary Vyner. In 1870 she commissioned William Burges to build the church in the park in memory of her son Frederick who tragically met his death at the hands of brigands while travelling in Greece. The church is one of Burges's finest works. As you cross the park you can see it framed by fine specimens of weeping beech. Burges also laid out the statue walk which defines the east–west axis of the gardens. Graceful Venetian stone figures carrying flowers or fruit stand in alcoves formed by Irish yews. The bases of their plinths are softened by *Cotoneaster horizontalis* which fans out on to the gravel walk. Handsome curved stone seats terminate the walk at each end, and from it vistas open up at intervals through the gardens to the south and towards the house to the north.

Mary Vyner's grand-daughter, another Mary and the grandmother of the present owner of Newby, married into the horticultural aristocracy. Green blood in the veins of the Compton family can certainly be traced back to 1632 when Henry Compton, the youngest son of the 2nd Earl of Northampton, was born. Henry Compton became Bishop of London and made the garden at Fulham Palace famous for his collection of trees and shrubs from North America. Stephen Switzer wrote of him as 'Not only a Father of the Church, but likewise on Gard'ning'.

Certainly the green blood was inherited by Mary's son, Major Edward Compton. The garden he inherited in 1921 consisted of the statue walk, a large kitchen garden, a rock garden and a nine-hole golf course. He transformed the layout of the garden to what it is today. The areas around the house combine stone terracing and balustrading, uncluttered lawns and substantial, well-kept yew hedging. The scale and proportion of each area is exactly right, and the whole is completely integrated with the fine architecture of the hall and with the landscape beyond.

The pivot of Major Compton's plan is the formal main axis through the garden which runs from the south front of the hall to the River Ure below. This axis is crossed by the statue walk and by other symmetrical secondary paths which in turn are crossed by walks parallel to the main axis. The series of connected rectangles provide vista upon vista, each view emphasized by a carefully placed stone urn, seat or specimen tree. Areas between and beyond the formal gardens are richly planted with trees and shrubs, making a harmonious counter-balance between formality and informality. Major Compton's son Robin and his wife Jane have retained the layout and modified and strengthened the planting, simplifying some areas so that the gardens can be looked after by a team of five gardeners instead of ten, and adding to the woodland areas to create an atmosphere of romantic mystery.

The planting of the several gardens-within-a-garden is planned so that each area reaches its climax of colour at a different time of year, making this truly a garden for all seasons. Separate leaflets have been thoughtfully prepared for spring, summer and autumn to guide the visitor towards

*Opposite:*
Newby Hall: *Embothrium lanceolatum* flowering above rhododendrons in the woodland garden.

Newby Hall: a seat designed by William Kent. *Rosa banksiae lutea* on the wall.

those parts of the twenty-five-acre gardens which are at their seasonal best. At all seasons the central point of the garden is the intersection of the statue walk with the north–south axis. Standing at this point you can appreciate the symmetry of the house in one direction and the long vista between the herbaceous borders in the other.

In spring the 'good bones' of the garden are clearly visible. Clipped yew hedges and groups of tall conifers beyond make a strong architectural framework and form a background against which the fine stonework of the two curved seats at each end of the statue walk (one from Italy, the other from Caen in France), and the four urns on the lawn below the lily pond can be appreciated. The walk from the lawn to Sylvia's garden leads through The Wars of the Roses where in June the striped 'Rosa mundi' will be in flower, keeping the peace between *Rosa gallica officinalis*, the red rose of Lancaster and the white rose of York, *Rosa alba semiplena*. Sylvia's garden is named after Robin Compton's mother. Her initials are on the iron gates brought there by Mrs Robin Compton which, like all the ironwork here, is painted a deep and subtle shade of blue which has come to be known as 'Newby Blue'. A square enclosure surrounded by yew hedges, Sylvia's garden is entered beneath the branches of the pale yellow Japanese cherry, *Prunus ukon*, beside a bank of the species rose, *R. woodsii fendleri* smothered in bright lilac pink flowers in June and bright red hips in autumn. It is an intimate and peaceful garden, paved with brick and stone on three levels, with a Byzantine carved stone corn-grinder in the centre. It has been replanted by Robin Compton's wife Jane with an unerring eye for colour and form. A spring display of species tulips is followed in early summer by brilliant blue delphiniums contrasting with pale yellow irises. The planting is on a small scale and rewards detailed inspection, for there are some very special plants here. Good foliage plants add interest for late summer and autumn.

Sylvia's garden and the paved, sunken rose garden are places to sit quietly and enjoy the colours, forms and scents of flowers. In the rose garden alba, centifolia, damask, gallica and moss roses bloom against an unusual background hedge of copper beech, with loose domes of *Pyrus salicifolia* 'Pendula' in each corner. Philadelphus varieties mingle their scent with that of the roses, and the soft pinks and purples of the roses are complemented by the foliage and flowers of *Geranium renardii*, *Veronica perfoliata*, *Erodium pelargonifolium*, baptisias, violas, and many unusual herbaceous plants including the best form of ajuga, *Ajuga reptans* 'Metallica'. In a sunny corner two excellent Convolvulus, *althaeoides* and *mauritanicus*, surprisingly defy the Yorkshire climate.

Elsewhere in the gardens, although there are seats strategically placed for rest and contemplation, the predominant mood is one of movement. A glimpse along a vista or the sight of the flaming flowers of *Embothrium lanceolatum* glowing in the distance against a dark background of conifers leads you on in exploration. The rose pergola invites you down a tunnel of 'Albertine', 'Maigold', 'Veilchenblau', 'Blairii No 2' and other climbing and rambling roses, Victorian and modern. Emerging at its southern end, it is the sound of running water that intrigues. It brings you to the rock garden where a series of cascades falls down a mossy cliff-face beside a tall arched stone bridge. The bridge conceals the conduit that originally carried the water up from the river. The rock garden with its massive mossy stones, pools and maze of narrow paths through mini gorges, was designed by Ellen Willmott, the distinguished amateur gardener, at the turn of the century. Today, under the shade of acers and other trees, it is dark, cool and mysterious.

You are lured from the rock garden into a curving pergola covered with *Laburnum vossii*, its pillars clothed with different varieties of chaenomeles underplanted with the bold foliage of bergenia. To the left of the pergola a blue carpet of *Scilla sibirica* is spread under a handsome lime tree in spring, and to the right there is an ancient stone well-head brought from a Vyner property in Cheshire. The path leads on past a memorial commemorating the Newby ferry disaster. In 1869 Sir Charles Slingsby and five others were drowned trying to cross the River Ure in flood while pursuing a fox. Beyond the memorial, towards the river the graceful white stems of a group of Himalayan birch, *Betula jacquemontii*, are underplanted with weed-smothering, interlocking drifts of pale pink and saffron primulas, *Polygonum campanulatum*, astilbes, hostas, *Geranium macrorrhizum* and Solomon's seal. In a glade close by, other trees remarkable for their bark are grown, *Acer griseum* and *Prunus serrulata*, its polished stem the colour of fresh conkers. Most of the trees and shrubs in this quiet corner of the garden, which include *Davidia involucrata*, the so-called pocket-handkerchief tree, and *Magnolia sargentiana robusta*, were introduced by the great plant collector E H Wilson – so it is aptly called 'Wilson's Corner'.

In these informal, wooded areas you are led by the nose: in spring and early summer it is the scent of azaleas which draws you from one green

**Newby Hall: olive jars flank a long vista through the sunken rose garden.**

glade to the next. The fine collection of azaleas and rhododendrons includes the vibrant orange azalea 'Gloria Mundi', the late-flowering *Azalea occidentale* 'Superba' with pink-buff buds opening to white flushed with pink, and rhododendrons 'Williamsianum', 'Blue Tit', *R. fictolacteum*, and the scented *R. Loderi* 'Pink Diamond' and 'King George'. Whatever path of exploration you take, you will find yourself sooner or later crossing the broad grass walk which is the central axis of the gardens.

The vista along the walk is framed by herbaceous borders designed by Mrs Compton to display colour and form throughout the summer. To save the labour of staking tall and floppy plants, wide mesh nets are stretched horizontally for the stems to grow through. The borders are backed by yew hedges and punctuated where paths cross them by *Viburnum plicatum mariesii* or substantial groups of shrub roses. Beyond the hedges tall trees of varied shape and textures form a dense background and frame the view northwards to the hall and south across the river. To the east of the herbaceous borders are the circular garden, tropical garden, orchard garden, white garden and autumn garden, each providing a different experience. With typical thoughtfulness, Robin and Jane Compton have planned a clearly but unobtrusively sign-posted route round the gardens for wheelchairs and provided a paddling pool, adventure gardens and miniature railway to entertain children, whose restlessness and boredom can so easily spoil garden visiting for their parents.

Twenty-five acres make a lot of garden, specially when they are filled with such a wide variety of rare and beautiful plants. Yet there are no signs of a struggle to keep up the high standard of maintenance. This is due to the hard work and dedication of the head gardener and his team of four, and also to Robin Compton's life-long love of gardening and knowledge of plants. The rich and subtle planting schemes are worked out not only with an eye to their beauty by Jane Compton, but with a view to providing plants with their ideal habitat by Robin Compton, and to arranging them so that weeds stand little chance. He is generous in sharing his expertise, as President of the Northern Horticultural Society, as a member of the National Trust's Gardens Panel and as Chairman of the National Council for the Conservation of Plants and Gardens, for whom he holds the national collection of *Cornus* at Newby.

Robin and Jane Compton's son James has inherited their love of and talent for gardening, and was head gardener at the Chelsea Physic Garden for nine years, the unique botanical collection begun in London in 1673 by the Society of Apothecaries. He is also the author of the excellent book *Success with Unusual Plants*. So it seems as though the future of the gardens at Newby is assured.

# Arley Hall

## Northwich, Cheshire (the Hon Michael Flower)

### Gardens 12 acres

*Christie's/Historic Houses Association Garden of the Year 1987*

THE AFFECTION FELT by five generations of the same family for their home and its surroundings has led to the continuous enrichment of Arley Hall's gardens within a framework that has remained virtually unaltered since it was laid out by Rowland and Mary Egerton-Warburton between 1840 and 1860.

Rowland Egerton-Warburton, whose life (1804–91) spanned a period of great prosperity for the English landed gentry, was a Victorian romantic with a creative passion for architecture, poetry and gardening. His beautiful wife shared his enthusiasms and took an active interest in his projects for the house and garden. He rebuilt the house in the Jacobean style with elaborate brickwork, curly gables, oriel windows and ornamental chimneys, employing a local architect to implement his own ideas. The enlarged house catered for the needs of the large numbers of guests and servants that were part of country-house life in the Victorian era. The gardens too were in need of expansion to produce vegetables, fruit and flowers for a large household, to provide recreation for the family and their guests, and to make an appropriate setting for the house. Rowland's ideas for the garden were ahead of his time. In order to protect it from the strong winds that scour the Cheshire plain he extended the walled enclosures of an earlier garden and planted yew hedges which divide the gardens into a series of further enclosures. The result is a series of gardens within a garden which predates Sissinghurst and Hidcote by one hundred years. By 1846 when a detailed plan of the gardens was drawn he had also planned and planted the famous double herbaceous border which is probably the first to be made in England, and is still one of the finest.

The hall faces south and looks out across a balustraded forecourt to parkland studded with fine trees with woodland beyond. The gardens are laid out in a wedge-shaped area to the south-west of the hall, bounded on the north side by a carriage drive. The drive runs between a short avenue of magnificent pleached limes which soar to the roof height of the two fine old brick and timber barns flanking the arched entrance. Above the arch is a Bavarian-style clock tower and the drive runs under the clock tower to the courtyard on the south front of the hall.

*Opposite:*
Arley Hall: willows and ferns overhang the water in the Rootree.

From the courtyard there is a broad gravelled walk set at an angle of forty-five degrees to the hall. Known as the furlong walk (its length is one-eighth of a mile), it divides the gardens from the park with a low wall above a ha-ha, and provides a series of vistas into the garden from east to west which give a strong impression of its overall symmetry. Sadly, Rowland Egerton-Warburton became blind towards the end of his life, but continued to take his exercise along the furlong walk, using his stick to follow a wire stretched from one end to the other. The wire was connected to a bell which rang a warning when he reached the steps at the end.

The first area which the visitor enters is the flag garden, named for the flag stones with which it is paved. It is also laid out more or less in the pattern of a Union Jack. The flag garden was made on a reclaimed rubbish tip in 1900 by Antoinette (née de Saumarez), the wife of Rowland's son Piers. An intimate, sheltered area, walled on two sides and hedged with yew on the other two, it is planted today in a style which reflects her gentle personality. Lavender-edged beds are filled with floribunda roses in soft colours: 'Apricot Nectar', 'Inner Wheel', 'Sea Pearl', and 'United Nations'. A central figure of a boy with a dolphin is surrounded by white petunias, lime helichrysum and santolina. Climbing plants on the south- and west-facing walls include *Akebia quinata*, *Lonicera tragophylla*, a passion flower and the crimson-flowered jasmine, *Jasminum beesianum*. In August the delicate flame-coloured flowers of *Tropaeolum speciosum* ramble through the yew hedges, and earlier in the summer large-flowered clematis varieties, soft pink 'Hagley Hybrid', blue-purple 'The President', lavender 'William Kennett' and the pure white 'Henryi' clothe posts connected with chains and underplanted with violas 'Bowles Black' and 'Moonlight'.

If, on leaving the flag garden, you pause and look to your right before turning towards the furlong walk, you can enjoy a long vista between yew hedges through three arched openings in the walls of the kitchen garden and walled garden. Looking to the park from the furlong walk, you will see an exceptionally fine Turkey oak in the foreground and a majestic avenue of limes centred on the south front of the hall. On the garden side of the walk pink, red and mauve rhododendrons flower in the shelter of holm oaks, yews and a red-flowered horse chestnut. A large group of creamy and coppery brooms conceals until the last minute the entrance to the herbaceous borders between walls of yew with handsome topiary finials.

The twin herbaceous borders are contained by a high brick wall covered with a magnificent ceanothus, *Solanum crispum* 'Glasnevin' and roses 'The New Dawn', 'Arthur Bell' and 'Grand Hotel' on one side and a yew hedge on the other. A wide grass walk runs between the borders and the long vista is terminated by the Alcove, an elegant brick and stucco summer-house with a wide arched entrance and a tiled floor. The walls of the Alcove are hung with photographs, one of Rowland and Mary Egerton-Warburton taken in 1870, one of the team of gardeners who look after the gardens today, and a useful display of colour photographs identifying the flowers to be seen in the garden in different months of the

year. In June the colour scheme is dominated by the blues and mauves of delphiniums with their cobalt, turquoise and Mediterranean blue spires, thalictrums, alliums, *Cynoglossum nervosum* and geraniums, and the yellows of achilleas, *Cephalaria tartarica* and *Geum* 'Lady Strathden'. Accents that contrast with the cool blue and yellows are provided by Iceland poppies and the deep crimson of *Cirsium rivulare*. Colours change as the season continues, and salvias, anthemis, eremurus and tall campanulas are succeeded by crocosmias, phloxes, sedums, herbaceous clematis, *Lysimachia clethroides*, the glowing scarlet *Lobelia cardinalis* with its beetroot-coloured leaves, and two other seldom seen lobelias, the crimson-violet *L. × vedrariensis* and clear blue *L. syphilitica*. The kaleidoscopic borders are given structure by grey foliage and by domes of the purple-leaved berberis, *Berberis thunbergii* 'Atropurpurea nana', and divided at intervals by substantial, curved yew buttresses, which provide an architectural framework and a sober background to the bright colours.

Immediately around the Alcove there is a simple and effective planting of *Geranium* 'Johnson's Blue' with the delicate yellow turk's cap lily, *Lilium pyrenaicum* beneath a wall supporting *Magnolia grandiflora*, a ceanothus and *Fremontia californica*. In 1889 George Elgood painted the herbaceous borders, and in 1904 his paintings were used to illustrate Gertrude Jekyll's book *Some English Gardens*. Three of them are hung in Arley Hall and show how little this part of the garden has changed in a hundred years.

Arley Hall: heraldic beasts guard the pool in the walled garden.

The main north–south axis of the gardens crosses between the herbaceous borders and the Alcove, providing a vista looking north through the walled garden or south along the famous ilex avenue. The ilex trees (*Quercus ilex*), which just survived the bitter winds and frosts of 1981–82 are clipped into immense tall cylinders. Their unusual shape and size is fortuitous: originally they were intended to form pyramids of moderate size, but they were left unclipped during the First World War, and their shape today is the result of a salvage operation when life returned to normal. The view beyond the avenue is framed by two large and handsome stone urns, and takes the eye far into the park to the wooded horizon touched with colour from a group of rhododendrons at the edge of the wood.

If you turn left at the beginning of the ilex avenue, you will see, half hidden by shrub roses planted in informal, curving beds, the Tea Cottage. Inside the little half-timbered building you receive a strong impression of the personality of Rowland Egerton-Warburton. There are painted inscriptions round the walls of some of his verses. They were moved here from an octagonal room at the top of the hall tower when it was demolished. Each verse refers to a neighbouring family and was placed over the window which faced towards their house. For example:

Of daughters four is NORTON reft.
How blest who, bent on further theft
Shall win the only daughter left.

The central inscription over the fireplace is addressed to his wife Mary:

If thou wouldst a form behold,
Cast in beauty's rarest mould,
Every virtue there enshrin'd
Which a husband's heart can bind
Such the cherished BRIDE whose bower
Midway lies within this tower.

The serpentine beds of old roses were planned and planted by Lady Ashbrook, the mother of the present owner, who has known and loved the garden all her life and, with the head gardener who has worked at Arley since 1940 with an interval when he served in the air force during the Second World War, is responsible for the evolution of the gardens for the past few decades. The rose beds replaced a formal rose garden with elaborate topiary. The shrub and species roses do better than the hybrid teas that they have replaced, and, with ground-cover plantings of foxgloves, hardy geraniums, *Viola labradorica*, *Claytonia* and golden creeping Jenny, require much less upkeep. With a background of buddleias, purple-leaved cotinus and a vast old cedar tree with low sweeping branches that have rooted into the ground, the soft pinks and dusky purples of such roses as 'Fantin-Latour', 'Mme Isaac Pereire', 'Reine des Violettes' and 'Mme Legras de St Germain' make this an area through which to wander slowly, savouring scent as well as colour. An unusually comprehensive collection of species roses, so different in character from most of the hybrids, is planted in separate beds where the simple charm of the flowers and fresh, delicate foliage of these incomparable shrubs from all over the northern hemisphere can be appreciated.

The ilex avenue and the furlong walk both terminate in the sundial circle on the southern boundary between garden and park. The circular lawn is also at the lowest level, reached by broad flights of steps. The beds here prepare you for a style of planting and colour schemes that are different from anything that you have seen in the more formal parts of the garden. The vibrant sky blue of the Himalayan poppy, *Meconopsis grandis* contrasts with peachy-orange and yellow azaleas and pink kalmia. Later the hybrid musk rose 'Erfurt' will open its lovely single pink flowers, white at the centre, in front of a bank of philadelphus. The central sundial stands on a paved sunray pattern of flag stones and cobbles. It is inscribed 'Shine not for one but for all'. To the south of the lawn a ha-ha gives on to the park, and on the west side a path leads to the Rootree.

The Rootree is where the gardens change their character completely. This area started as a rock garden, built from sandstone and ancient tree stumps, hence its name. Its construction was recorded in 1875 in a photograph of Mary Egerton-Warburton standing beside a gardener on bare rock among newly planted trees. The growth of these trees to maturity has completely altered the micro-climate, so that after post-war clearance of undergrowth, it became clear that it was no longer a suitable site for a collection of alpine plants. Some survivors thrived, notably the royal fern, *Osmunda regalis*, a handsome red-leaved Japanese maple and, beside the pool, *Peltiphyllum peltatum* with its fine round leaves. Today the pool is surrounded by species rhododendrons, pieris and scented azaleas, of which one is particularly striking: unnamed, it grows to about seven feet (two metres) high and as wide, and is smothered in dense clusters of salmon-peach, funnel-shaped flowers, each petal with a darker central stripe, and the upper petal of each funnel pale gold shading to apricot at the centre. The overall effect is of brilliant but soft orange, set off by neat, bright green leaves. Its scent is heady. The pool margins are planted with dramatic foliage plants: peltiphyllum, lysichitum, ligularias and bergenia, which contrast with delicate candelabra primulas of pale to dusky pink and coral. Bronze-red acers overhang the pool and the whole area is shaded by oaks, limes and yews. Narrow paths wind along and cross over the serpentine pool in this intimate, secret pocket of woodland, the paths lined with ferns and hostas, bluebells, red campion and willow gentian. Mossy rocks and gnarled roots surface here and there, and on the north side a mysterious little brick-lined cave nestles under a picturesque tree stump.

Standing in the shade of the west side of the Rootree you can look down over a sunlit pool framed by the giant leaves of *Gunnera manicata*, with wide drifts of magenta primulas, pale pink *Polygonum bistorta* 'Superbum' and pale foxgloves beyond the water. The play of light and shade contributes to the charm and mystery of the Rootree. Looking back over the pool, the sunlight catches the transparent red leaves of the feathery acer, and turns the green ferns to gold.

From the Rootree you can reach the fish garden, skirting 'The Rough'

Arley Hall: Rowland Egerton-Warburton's herbaceous borders were made before 1846.

where cream, peach and white azaleas are grouped with a young *Cornus controversa* 'Variegata'. Part of an earlier bowling green, the fish garden was made in 1930. A sunken square pool with creamy water-lilies is set in stone paving with sentinel junipers at each side. The planting is on an intimate scale, with pinks, London pride, dwarf phlox and grey-leaved helianthemums with orange, yellow and pink flowers sprawling over the low walls. A quiet seat looking down over the pool is flanked by two creamy-white flowering cherries, *Prunus ukon*, planted in 1959. Ranged at the foot of the holly hedge behind them are seven memorial stones commemorating in verse Rowland Egerton-Warburton's favourite horses. One reads:

> Restored to life were Marigold my mare
> Mid all the flowers which deck this
>    garden fair
> Not one in Beauty could with her compare.

Returning past the Alcove you reach the walled garden, a complete contrast in scale. Once part of the kitchen gardens and used during the Second World War to feed the inmates and staff of the hospital that was housed at Arley Hall, it has high brick walls with fruit trees trained against them. From the end of the war until 1960 it was run as a commercial market garden, but today it is entirely ornamental. The central stone-edged pool was moved from the east side of the house, and the heraldic beasts that stand at its corners surrounded with *Alchemilla mollis* came from part of the house which was demolished in 1968. Four fastigiate 'Dawyck' beeches, tall enough to suit the scale of this spacious garden, and suitably formal in their habit, complete the central pattern. The wide borders are planted with large flowering shrubs, many with golden foliage, and herbaceous plants with striking foliage such as *Euphorbia wulfenii*, *Macleaya cordata*, *Onopordium acanthium* (the giant silver thistle) and rhubarb. At the south end a fine wrought-iron gate half smothered in honeysuckle gives on to the ilex avenue and the vista to the park. At the north side a stone seat is surrounded by roses in all shades of red edged with catmint.

The adjacent walled garden is still used to grow vegetables and flowers for the house behind hedges of roses 'Belle Poitevine' and 'Blanc Double de Coubert'. The greenhouse or vinery dates from the mid-nineteenth century, but the roof was replaced in 1921. It houses beautifully trained fig trees which were planted in about 1860.

On the right as you leave the kitchen garden, and through a yew arch is the herb garden. It was laid out in 1969 with simple rectangular beds surrounding a stone pinnacle from a building in Piccadilly Circus. The pinnacle is charmingly copied in box topiary on either side of a stone seat. Rose 'Mme Alfred Carrière' and *Lonicera brownii* grow against the wall and angelica, sweet cecily, fennel and other culinary and sweet-smelling herbs spill out of the beds. The tiny scented garden made in 1977 is hidden in a corner beyond, filled with circular stone beds of different heights and radius planted with wallflowers, pinks, philadelphus, *Lilium regale*, species lilacs and *Clethra alnifolia*.

Each generation has contributed to the gardens and the present owner, Michael Flower is no exception. He has reclaimed an overgrown wilderness to the east of the hall, on the site of a garden of shrubberies and informal walks dating from the 1750s. Selected oaks, birches, yews and hollies were retained to provide shelter, visual screening and back-grounds to a new collection of trees and shrubs. This woodland garden is still being developed, but an interesting range of unusual trees can already be seen, particularly birches, maples, magnolias and sorbuses, many of them chosen for their spectacular autumn colour. There are large groups of rhododendrons and azaleas, and in spring drifts of narcissi, especially white and pale yellow varieties.

Towards the end of the twentieth century the gardens at Arley Hall are planned very much with the pleasure of visitors at all seasons in mind, yet they still have the atmosphere of a family garden, and in that respect have changed little over more than a hundred years.

# Barnsley House

Barnsley, Cirencester, Gloucestershire (Mrs Rosemary Verey)

Garden 4 acres

*Christie's/Historic Houses Association Garden of the Year 1988*

A CLUE AS TO WHAT to expect in the garden at Barnsley House can be gleaned from the titles of some of Rosemary Verey's books: *The Scented Garden, Classic Garden Design, The Garden in Winter, The Flower Arranger's Garden.* All these themes are woven into the complex tapestry of her garden. Other threads used in the pattern have their origins in her library, which houses her collection of rare old gardening and botanical books.

Today, thirty years after David and Rosemary Verey began to make it, the garden epitomizes his architectural expertise and sure eye for the enclosure of space and the structure of axis and cross-axis, and her knowledge and experience of plants and their history. The garden wears this erudition lightly, and although it is full of complex and subtle ideas, plants chosen for their historic or literary associations are always arranged with a view to the effect their texture and colour has on the entire composition.

The Vereys had lived in the house, which dates from 1697, for ten years before they started to make a garden of what had been, during those years, a place for cricket, croquet and ponies for their children. Even then they were in no great hurry, and careful deliberation from the start about the layout of the garden and the positioning of each plant is surely one of the secrets of the garden's success. Some years before making a start Rosemary Verey, with typical thoroughness, set about acquiring the knowledge that she felt she needed. Books, particularly those by Vita Sackville-West and Christopher Lloyd, visits to other people's gardens, and regular attendance at the Royal Horticultural Society's shows at Vincent Square framed her ideas and fed her interest in the colours and textures of plants. Visits to Hidcote, Sissinghurst and Great Dixter convinced her of the value of dividing the garden into interlocking spaces, each expressing a different mood, and at Barnsley this is achieved not by totally enclosing each area, but by using paths and tall mixed shrub planting to create divisions.

The result is a garden of formal vistas and richly varied planting. As soon as you enter it your eye is caught by some hitherto unknown plant or un-thought-of juxtaposition. Your awareness is heightened, making

*Opposite:*
**Barnsley House:** *Vitis coignetiae* intertwined with a cream-variegated euonymus behind one of the strategically placed seats.

Barnsley House: Simon Verity's stone figures mark the path leading to the *potager*.

you alert, expectant and determined not to miss any of the surprises and treats that are in store.

The entrance to the drive, overhung by yews, is flanked by eighteenth-century stone gateposts, and the drive shaded by majestic plane trees, limes and chestnuts. The Cotswold stone house stands on a level terrace, the ground falling away in a grassy slope towards the entrance from the road. Planting on this side of the house is formal and restrained, influenced by Russell Page. A row of columnar *Chamaecyparis* 'Ellwoodii' stands sentinel at the base of the terrace. In summer there is nothing to distract from the architecture of the house, but in winter and spring carpets of aconites and snowdrops followed by scillas, grape hyacinths and crocuses are spread under the trees along the drive, and in the autumn hardy cyclamen take over.

The visitor enters the garden through a yard where the practical business of greenhouse, potting shed and plant sales goes on. The first view of the garden is towards a vista between bushes of golden philadelphus, weigela and privet pruned to loose domes. The golden theme is carried through with conviction, the gold forms of lonicera, elm, marjoram, euphorbias and hostas mingling in unity of colour and contrast of texture and density. Blue *Clematis macropetala* grows over golden privet, and blue *Viola cornuta* beneath *Spiraea* × *bumalda* 'Gold

56

Flame'. The view is to a pretty stone Gothic summer-house. It was built in 1771 when the house was the rectory, by the Rev Charles Coxwell who also built the fine stone wall that encloses the garden. The summer-house is known as Mrs Coxwell's Alcove. It is set at an oblique angle to the vista rather than directly facing it, so that it gives a view not only of the walk by which you reached it, but also across the open lawn to the stone loggia in front of the house and directly down the slope to the entrance gate. The Alcove is flanked by the bold foliage of *Euphorbia wulfenii* and *Ligularia*. On one side an arch covered in the rich golden-yellow, scented rose 'Lawrence Johnston' frames a narrow path leading to a low stone column. Its inscription, engraved by Simon Verity, reads 'As no man be very miserable that is master of a Garden here: so will no man ever be happy who is not sure of a Garden hereafter. . . . Where the first Adam fell the second rose.' A stone seat against the wall behind provides an opportunity to sit and contemplate this message, or gaze beyond along what must be one of the most photographed features in any English garden: the laburnum tunnel.

Barnsley House is not the only garden with a laburnum tunnel, but there is something very special about this one. Even when it is not lit by the pendulous yellow racemes of the laburnum's flowers, it makes an intimate, enclosed walk of just the right scale. The floor of the walk was paved by David Verey in patterns of cobbles set in mortar, and the beds on either side are planted with the soft purple drumstick heads of *Allium aflatunense* to coincide with the laburnum's flowering, and with scarlet tulips to precede it and hostas to follow. The line of the tunnel is continued in an *allée* of pleached lime which meets at right angles the second famous vista: pairs of clipped Irish yews line a broad stone path which is almost hidden in summer by a tapestry of white, pink and rose-coloured helianthemums. This path and the lime and laburnum walk form the two strongest axes of the garden, with secondary vistas echoing and crossing them. At one end of the path is an arched doorway into the house, and at the other a wrought-iron gate in the boundary wall leading to the potager. The point where these walks meet is marked by two weeping cherries underplanted with yellow erythroniums. On either side of the gate stand stone figures carved by Simon Verity of a garden boy and a gardening lady in a startling hat. Another of his distinctive statues, an Edwardian Diana in riding habit and veiled hat, accompanied by a stone hound, provides the distant focal point for a cross-vista half-way down the laburnum walk. A seat against the wall, with *Lonicera* 'Dropmore Scarlet' planted behind it, tactfully invites you to observe this view which otherwise you might miss.

If, emerging from the laburnum and lime walk, you follow the path ahead of you, you will come to a small enclosed paved garden where you can sit in a handsome classical temple and look across a stone-edged lily pool back along the main axis. The eighteenth-century temple at Fairford Park was given to David Verey by the owners, the Cook Trust. Today it looks as if it were made for its present site. Enclosed on three sides by walls and divided from the garden beyond by Georgian wrought-iron gates and railings, this is the most secret and enclosed part of the garden.

Shaded by a silver birch and a quince, it has a satisfying air of tranquillity. The ironwork is painted a deep, rich shade of blue and interwoven with the hairy red stems of the Japanese wineberry, *Rubus phoenicolasius* and *Clematis durandii* with its deep blue flowers. Around the pool there are marsh marigolds and yellow *Primula florindae*, rosemary climbs the walls and tree peonies add colour, scent and handsome foliage.

From the pool garden a broad grass walk between mixed borders runs the whole length of the garden, parallel to the lime and laburnum walk, to a delightfully eccentric fountain where four giant stone frogs squirt water up at two embracing sheep. Around the fountain angelica has seeded itself with abandon. Rosemary Verey is kind to self-seeding plants, and it is one of the pleasures of the garden to find shady corners inhabited by honesty and sweet cecily, or feverfew, forget-me-nots, violas and sweet rocket rubbing shoulders with more aristocratic plants.

There is a third parallel walk between the laburnum tunnel and the boundary wall. Here a patterned brick path is lined with rows of box balls, giving a firm structure to plantings of dark hellebores and deep crimson polyanthus, ferns and foxgloves at the foot of the nine foot (2.75-metre) high wall. Roses, clematis, kolkwitzia and *Buddleia fallowiana* are trained against the wall. Here too are *Ribes speciosum*, 'the most beautiful of the gooseberries' according to W J Bean, with its graceful rich red fuchsia-like flowers in April and May; and *Prunus glandulosa* 'Sinensis', a neat shrub with many-petalled double pink flowers in May.

In front of the Gothic loggia on the south side of the house the knot garden expresses Rosemary Verey's love of pattern and knowledge of garden history. Based on designs from *La Maison Rustique* (1583) and Stephen Blake's *The Compleat Gardener's Practice* (1664), the pattern is woven in threads of box in two colours and *Teucrium chamaedrys*. Phillyrea and four clipped hollies, both much valued as 'greens' in Tudor times, add a vertical dimension. On the opposite side of the spacious lawn 'the wilderness' is planted with a collection of unusual trees, including several sorbuses. In winter *Sorbus* 'Embley' has dark red buds, sharp as needles. In autumn the light red berries of *Sorbus vilmorinii* fade to pink and then to white. Serpentine mown paths wander through the long grass between the trees, and in spring the grass is spangled with snakes-head fritillaries, lily-flowered tulips and hundreds of daffodils.

On the other side of a farm track outside the garden wall, and easily missed if it were not so famous, is the kitchen garden. A *Petit Villandry*, it is both an ornamental pleasure garden and an area for food production. Paths laid in different patterns of red brick, blue engineering brick and concrete define square-and diamond-shaped beds edged with box, lavender, alpine strawberries or chives. The corners of the beds are decorated with pyramids and globes of clipped box and golden privet, and in the beds neat rows of onions, lettuces and carrots are in contrast to the dramatic forms of silver artichoke foliage or scarlet-stemmed beet. Standard gooseberries march along a lavender walk, apple trees trained as goblets decorate the centre of each bed, and at the heart of the garden the apple 'Jester' is surrounded by the pretty mop-heads of standard rose 'Little White Pet' underplanted with golden box, oxlips and *Viola*

'Bowles Black'. Over the central path a metal tunnel is hung with sweet peas, scarlet runner beans and trailing marrows. At the far end domes of clipped, standard hawthorn trees screen the farmyard. Throughout the garden at Barnsley House there are seats placed strategically, so that you can pause for a longer look at the garden pictures that are composed with such loving care. In the kitchen garden the two seats face each other in small, trellised, pedimented arbours with a medieval look to them. One is covered with golden hops, the other in the purple-leaved *Vitis vinifera* 'Brandt'.

Throughout the garden much pleasure can be derived from the orderly symmetry of patterned beds and plants clipped to formal shapes. They are a reassuring antidote to the disorder of the world outside, and the satisfaction that they give is heightened by the contrast with free, exuberant planting around them, in soft, harmonizing colours. Beds are densely planted so that plants follow each other in flower on the same spot, early spring bulbs giving way to tulips which fill almost every bed in May. Then come polemoniums, pale hollyhocks, francoa, penstemons, nicotianas and mallows including the garden's own *Lavatera* 'Barnsley'.

**Barnsley House: the solid shapes of clipped golden-foliage plants frame the vista to the 1771 Gothic alcove.**

The changing harmonies of flower colour are underpinned everywhere by plants chosen for their dramatic foliage, such as acanthus, *Crambe maritima* and *Phormium tenax*; and evergreen and ever-grey shrubs to provide the contrast of solid form and dense texture.

The garden at Barnsley House is full of inspiration at all times of the year, for its intricate formal patterns, its sense of history, its subtle colour combinations, and the wit and charm of its statuary; but above all else for the beauty and distinction of its plants. Many are charming and unusual forms of familiar favourites, like the variegated philadelphus near the frog fountain. Others have flowers which repay the closest inspection, such as the bronze striped yellow *Crocus* 'Gipsy Girl', or *Rehmannia elata*, a tender oriental plant with rose-purple, trumpet-shaped flowers, their pale yellow throats maroon-spotted.

It is worth returning to Barnsley again and again, and worth going round twice each time, the second time with your eyes firmly fixed to the ground in case you miss some unobtrusive treasure.

# Brympton d'Evercy

Yeovil, Somerset (Mr and Mrs Charles Clive-Ponsonby-Fane)

Gardens 9 acres, park 80 acres

*Christie's/Historic Houses Association Garden of the Year 1989*

'THERE ARE GREATER, more historic, more architecturally impressive buildings in grander scenery; but I know of none of which the whole impression is more lovely. None that summarises so exquisitely English country life.'

These words were written by the late Christopher Hussey in *Country Life*, and today it might be added that Brympton also summarizes the ability of the English to adapt to changing circumstances. The house and gardens have seen many changes since the fifteenth century, but none of these changes has involved such determination and dedication as that which Charles and Judy Clive-Ponsonby-Fane brought to the Herculean task of restoration of the house and gardens in 1974. The property had suffered the inevitable neglect and reductions in staff of the two world wars, followed by nearly twenty years of institutionalization as a boys' public school. Now, after fifteen years of incredibly hard work, the house is once more a home, full of the life of an energetic young family, and the gardens are once more a tranquil and beautiful setting for it. There cannot be many owners of historic houses who have rolled up their sleeves and got on themselves with the paint-stripping, the painting, the curtain-making and, outdoors, the hacking out of brambles and forking out of nettles, ground elder and bindweed. The Clive-Ponsonby-Fanes' total personal commitment to Brympton is one of the things which gives it its unique atmosphere.

The bones of the gardens immediately round the house are little changed from the layout shown in a seventeenth-century engraving by Knyff, with a walled forecourt on the Tudor west front of the house. A central path leads between lawns to the porch. The broad terrace on the south front, then newly built, with steps down to the bowling green and the walled kitchen garden can also be seen in the engraving. The kitchen garden is still used for food production, but today the produce is meat, rather than vegetables and fruit, since it is grazed by beef cattle.

Since 1731 when the Fane family came to Brympton, its most influential gardeners have all been women. The first was Lady Georgiana

61

Fane, daughter of John, 10th Earl of Westmorland and his second wife Jane Saunders. The marriage was not a success and the Earl is said to have been delighted when his wife and daughter retired to Brympton leaving him to enjoy the peace of other Westmorland properties. Lady Georgiana never married, but carried a torch all her spinster life for a young ADC of her father's who later became Duke of Wellington. After her mother died in 1857 she devoted her time to running the estate at Brympton. She planted thousands of oak trees, some of which can still be seen in their full maturity, and made the pond below the south lawn, which adds greatly to the tranquillity of the scene.

Lady Georgiana left the estate to her nephew, Sir Spencer Ponsonby-Fane. Sir Spencer had a passion for cricket which has been shared by his male descendants. Co-founder of the I Zingari Cricket Club, he was also Treasurer of the MCC and played for the Gentlemen v Players. His grand-daughter Violet Clive was a distinguished gardener and such planting as survived Brympton's period as a school was her work. Mrs Clive's unmarried brother who had inherited the estate spent much of his time in Japan, and she herself travelled widely during her thirty years of widowhood, bringing home in her sponge bag plants that at that time were rare. Many of her plants have since become universally valued and cultivated.

She was one of a small sorority of talented Somerset gardeners; Margery Fish at East Lambrook Manor and Mrs Reiss of Tintinhull being near neighbours and close friends. The three women were in the vanguard of the reaction against the elaborate formality of Victorian gardening, and at Brympton Mrs Clive replaced brightly coloured bedding schemes in complex beds with wide borders of shrubs and herbaceous plants in drifts of subtle colouring.

In the 1980s the replanting and maintenance of the gardens has been the responsibility of Judy Clive-Ponsonby-Fane helped by Debbie Stabbins who first came to Brympton on a young workers' scheme. The planting style is modern in that it is geared to low maintenance, with no bedding out or staking. It relies for colour as much on foliage as on flowers and attention is paid to dense planting and to ground-cover plants in order to suppress weeds. As with other successful gardens that are planned to give pleasure to visitors, great importance is attached to providing interest at all seasons. This philosophy still gives scope for the use of many unusual plants and for carefully worked out colour schemes designed to complement the golden Ham stone of the buildings.

The entrance courtyard is framed on one side by the parish church and priest house, built in the thirteenth century and now a museum of country life and distillery; and on the other by a delightful clock tower and the old stables where teas are served. The lower storey of the clock tower may have been the original entrance to the house and is now put to practical use as a log store. The dovecote in front of the stables is perched on a stone pillar moved here by Violet Clive when Yeovil Town Hall was demolished. Under its base are coins and a copy of *The Times* placed there to celebrate the ending of the First World War. The wide borders surrounding the forecourt are planted with yellow and white flowers.

*Opposite:*
Brympton d'Evercy: stone steps lead from the south lawn to the balustraded terrace.

Many of the plants have the bold foliage that large-scale planting demands: *Crambe cordifolia* with its dark green rhubarb-shaped leaves and great cloud of honey-scented white flowers; acanthus; the Chinese gooseberry *Actinidia chinensis*; tree peonies; and the giant thistle *Onopordium acanthium*, its huge silver-white stems soaring above its neighbours. Against the house the hybrid musk rose 'Buff Beauty' reflects the honey-coloured stone and climbing 'Iceberg', smothered in flowers throughout the summer, reaches to fifteen feet (4.5 metres). In spring daffodils, hellebores and *Fritillaria lutea maxima* flower. Later *Cytisus battandieri*, the pineapple-scented broom, *Piptanthus laburnifolius*, the Californian poppy *Romneya coulteri*, exochorda and *Fremontia californica* thrive on the sunny side. In the damp shade of the north-facing walls there are hydrangeas, epimediums, hostas, Solomon's seal and *Kirengeshoma palmata*, a graceful Japanese plant with smooth, clear green leaves on arching stems and sprays of cool yellow flowers in early autumn. Height in the border is provided by the green-yellow foliage of *Robinia frisia*.

From the north side of the forecourt curved steps made by Violet Clive from stone fragments and urns found around the estate lead to the vineyard on an upper terrace. Two grape varieties, Muller Thurgeau and Reichensteiner are planted on American 5BB root stock from Guisenheim in Germany. In a good year they produce 2,500 bottles of a light dry wine with a fruity flavour, which can be bought in the shop at Brympton. This is the one labour-intensive part of the gardens, as the vines have to be sprayed against phomopsis, oidium and botrytis every fourteen days from May until October. The wall behind the vineyard is planted with large-flowered clematis varieties, honeysuckle and a banksia rose. Beyond is a mini-arboretum with a Japanese stone lantern in front of a yew semi-circle as the focal point. The emphasis is on silver and gold foliage, including a golden elm, the new golden-leaved birch, and *Catalpa bignonioides* 'Aurea'. Other young trees include a liquidambar, magnolia and *Cornus kousa*. *Paulownia tomentosa* is pollarded to encourage its huge leaves to grow to even greater size. In years when late frosts do not prevent it flowering, it bears large lavender-blue flowers like foxgloves.

A path leads back to the forecourt between the stables and the vineyard. On one side of it a bed is planted with massed *Crinum powellii*, the crinum lily, a spectacular sight in flower. If you cross the forecourt and go through the gate in the corner between the house and the priest house you will find yourself on the south terrace.

The balustraded terrace is planted to set off the famous, generously fenestrated south front built in 1678. It terminates in the east wall of the priest house at one end and in a classical temple with pillars salvaged by Mrs Clive from Yeovil Town Hall when it was demolished in the 1920s. The unusual stone ornaments on the balustrade are planted with house leeks. Among them is a rare Georgian example of a four-sided sundial. The colour scheme is mainly pink, with shrub roses, escallonia, hibiscus and cistus billowing out over the gravel from a bed not more than eighteen inches (forty-five centimetres) wide. Against the wall in a sheltered corner, slightly tender plants thrive, including silvery-leaved,

Climbing rose 'Iceberg' on the wall of the house.

rosy-mauve *Buddleia crispa*, *Teucrium fruticans* and the lobster-claw climber, *Clianthus puniceus*. The house walls are clothed with the lovely apricot pink rose 'Albertine', wistaria, *Robinia hispida* 'Rosea' looking rather like a rose-pink laburnum, abutilon and a creamy variegated euonymus. A huge yucca spills on to the terrace.

Steps lead down to a terrace below the retaining wall where the pink theme is continued with *Weigela florida* 'Variegata', kolkwitzia, deutzia and phloxes. The seldom seen rambler rose 'Phyllis Bide' is amazingly floriferous in June, spilling dense clusters of orange and cream flowers through the balustrade on to the top terrace. In the bed below, coral alstroemeria and orange lilies associate well with golden feverfew.

65

Violet Clive's curved steps, flanked by urns found on the estate, lead to the vineyard on the upper terrace. The delightful clock tower overlooks this peaceful scene.

The view from the terrace takes the eye across the lawn, the pond and the ha-ha between garden and park to a fine copper beech tree on the horizon. White water-lilies float on the pond; its small island with a Japanese lantern as an eye-catcher is inhabited by ducks and a lead heron. Clumps of gunnera and tall iris punctuate the pond's margin, and beyond the pond trees and shrubs chosen for their foliage are arranged in groups of purple and silver or green and gold. Purple forms of cotinus, berberis, weigela and prunus contrast with the silvers and greys of caryopteris, lavender, senecio, atriplex and *Stachys olympica*. The green foliage of *Garrya elliptica*, ruscus and escallonias offsets golden philadelphus, spiraea, euonymus and *Robinia pseudoacacia* 'Frisia' and a ground covering of variegated vinca suppresses weeds.

A walk round the pond to an inviting seat on its far bank takes you through a shady grove out of which, in a few years time, a herd of topiary elephants will charge on to the lawn. The idea is the result of a holiday in Thailand. At the moment all that can be seen are sixteen privet legs and one privet trunk, but in the fullness of time they should be a spectacular sight. Mature trees conceal the garden's boundary on the south-east side of the pond, among them oaks and yews, fine specimens of acacia and *Liriodendron tulipifera*, one of the earliest and most beautiful introductions from North America, and a golden-leaved poplar in sunlit

66

contrast to a copper beech. Beneath the trees evergreen shrubs (choisya, fatsia, *Lonicera nitida* 'Baggenson's Gold' and *Prunus lusitanica*) form a background to the water and provide cover for the ducks. The wall retaining the east side of the pond is softened by overhanging branches of senecio, rosemary, bergenia and prostrate juniper.

An area south of the pond has been planted to commemorate the Japanese connections of Violet Clive's brother, Richard Ponsonby-Fane. The early sixteenth-century stone lantern here and the others in the garden came from his garden in Kyoto, and those plants of Japanese origin that will tolerate the soil here with a pH of 7.5 have been planted around it. A camellia and an azalea do not appear to be struggling, and there are also junipers, peonies, chaenomeles, and *Stephenandra tanakae*. The leaves of the latter turn a spectacular orange-yellow in autumn. New trees have been planted to the south-west of the pond, to balance those on the south-east side. Among them are acers with purple and variegated leaves and *Quercus rubra*, the fast-growing red oak.

The view back across the pond to the house stirs the emotions. The south front has an air of inviting friendliness, and the golden stone seems to have absorbed centuries of sunlight and to give out its warmth. You can see at Brympton that the gardens, trees and landscapes that surround historic houses are not merely embellishments for fine architecture; the buildings and their gardens are part of an integrated whole and together they summarize, as Christopher Hussey wrote, English country life. Such houses and gardens are imbued with the history of architecture and plants. They have also absorbed over the centuries, and continue to reflect today, the histories of their owners: some have been great and distinguished families which have played their part in national and international history. Others have been content with closer horizons, serving their local communities and conscientiously caring for their homes and their land so that future generations might enjoy them. They all have in common a capacity to adapt to changing circumstances, and nothing illustrates this more clearly than the renaissance of Brympton.

# PART III

## REGIONAL GAZETTEER

For opening times and additional attractions, see the current edition of
*Historic Houses, Castles and Gardens Open to the Public.*

### Cumbria

**CORBY CASTLE**, Great Corby, Carlisle, Cumbria (Mr J P Howard)
*Park 15 acres*

Thomas Howard laid out the River Walks at Corby in 1720. The grounds with their handsome trees follow the River Eden for about a mile and are a fine surviving example of an early romantic landscape. The most dramatic feature is the cascade which falls in steps from the lawns down to the river. In the basin there is a statue of Lord Nelson, put there soon after the Battle of Trafalgar. The massive stone figure of Polyphemus on the path down to the river is known locally as 'Belted Will', a nickname given to Lord William Howard who bought Corby Castle in the early seventeenth century. From the foot of the cascade a long green walk leads to a small temple.

**DALEMAIN**, Dacre, by Penrith, Cumbria (Mr and Mrs Bryce McCosh)
*Gardens 8 acres*

The gardens, like the house with its twelfth-century pele tower, medieval hall, Tudor fretwork room and Georgian facade, has evolved over the centuries. The knot garden

and the gazebo commanding views down to the Dacre beck and along the old coach road both date from the Tudor period. In 1679 Sir Edward Hasell bought the house and his descendant, the gardening writer Sylvia McCosh, lives there today, and has done much to enrich the gardens. Sir Edward employed James Swingler in 1685 to lay out and supervise the building of walls round the garden, and almost every subsequent generation has left its mark. Himalayan blue poppies grow well here, and there is a good collection of shrub roses.

House open. Lunches, teas. Guided tours. Plant sales.

*Below:* **Dalemain: the Himalayan blue poppy,** *Meconopsis betonicifolia.*

*Opposite:* **Warwick Castle: aerial view of Robert Marnock's Victorian rose garden.**

## HOLKER HALL, Cark-in-Cartmel, Grange-over-Sands, Cumbria
### (Mr R H Cavendish)
*Gardens 25 acres, park 125 acres*

The framework of the landscaped gardens and park between Morecambe Bay and the Lake District was made to replace formal gardens in c1760 by Lord George Augustus Cavendish, who also began the distinguished collection of rare trees and shrubs. The 7th Duke of Devonshire added many plants with the help of Sir Joseph Paxton including the large monkey puzzle *Araucaria araucana* which Paxton raised from seed brought from Chile by William Lobb in 1844. Other notable trees include a fine collection of cut-leaved beech, *Laurelia serrata*, *Oxydendrum arboreum*, *Gingko biloba* and *Cornus controversa*. Around the house Thomas Mawson modified the Victorian terraces in the 1920s for Lady Moyra Cavendish, who was a talented gardener and added many rare and beautiful shrubs to the collection. Its enrichment was continued by her daughter-in-law and by her grandson and his wife, Mr and Mrs Hugh Cavendish, the present owners. They have altered and extended the formal gardens and replanted the charming rose garden with its stone dovecote with old roses chosen for their scent and opulent colouring.

House open. Lunches, teas. Plant sales, including seedlings of Paxton's monkey puzzle.

Holker Hall.

## HUTTON-IN-THE-FOREST, Skelton, Penrith, Cumbria (the Lord Inglewood)
*Gardens 5 acres, park and woodland 10 acres*

Seventeenth-century terraces remain to the south and west of the house which was built at that time around a medieval pele tower. The lake and the layout of the park date from the eighteenth century and further alterations to park and gardens were made in the 1820s by William Sawrey Gilpin, admirer of the Picturesque style of Uvedale Price. There are outstanding specimen trees in the park and woodland, which is rich in wildlife. On the edge of the park a seventeenth-century octagonal dovecote contains 450 nesting boxes reached by a revolving ladder. On the terraces the four early eighteenth century Van Nost statues were probably placed at that time and the topiary added later by Lady Vane who was involved with the Arts and Crafts movement. She also laid out the formal rhododendron garden designed in the shape of two interlocking stars which has recently been cleared with the help of the Countryside Commission and replanted. The 1736 walled garden is being restored to its original layout with the help of Ursula Buchan.

House open. Teas.

## LEVENS HALL, Kendal, Cumbria
### (Mr C H Bagot)
*Gardens 8 acres, park 250 acres*

World famous for its ancient yew topiary, Levens Hall has scarcely changed since its formal parterres and beech circle and *allées* were laid out between 1689 and 1712. M Guillaume Beaumont, who worked for King James II at Hampton Court, designed the Levens Hall gardens and park for Colonel James Grahame, whose family still live there

Levens Hall.

today. The family archives include lists of the plants and seeds that were used, receipts for their purchase and a drawing showing the plan of the gardens in 1730. The park shows the early beginnings of the English landscape movement and is separated from the gardens by the first ha-ha ever to be constructed. The extraordinary sense of continuity which pervades Levens Hall can perhaps be accounted for partly by the obvious affection which succeeding generations of owners have felt for it and partly by the fact that in three hundred years there have only been ten head gardeners: an average tenure of thirty years in the post. The family's own rare breed of Bagot goats with immense horns roam the park.

House open. Lunches, teas. Guided tours. Plant sales.

**MUNCASTER CASTLE**, Ravenglass, Cumbria (Mr and Mrs P R Gordon-Duff-Pennington)
*Gardens 45 acres, park 50 acres*

The fine collection of rhododendrons, magnolias, camellias, maples and hydrangeas is mainly the work of Sir John Ramsden who inherited the estate in 1917. With the help of John Millais he created the informal gardens in the shelter of woodlands planted in the 1780s by John, Lord Muncaster. Sir John Ramsden was a keen hybridizer of rhododendrons and added many of his own breeding to the original collection of species. His hybrids include 'Katerina', named after his beautiful and charming daughter-in-law, with large, buff flowers, 'Muncaster Mist' with pale mauve flowers and fine leaves, 'Jo Ramsden' and 'The Muncaster Hybrid'. The first Lord Muncaster's terrace constructed in 1783, stretches for three-quarters of a mile and commands lovely views over Eskdale, Ruskin's 'Gateway to Paradise'.

House open. Lunches, teas. Guided tours if booked in advance. Plant sales.

| *East Anglia* Essex, Norfolk, Suffolk |
| --- |

**ELTON HALL**, Peterborough, Cambridgeshire (Mr and Mrs William Proby)
*Gardens 8 acres, park 300 acres*

The gardens have been developed in three phases. Before 1860 the house, dating from

Elton Hall.

1475 but with later, part Gothic, part classical facades, was surrounded by parkland, with little in the way of gardens. In 1860 the 3rd Earl of Carysfort laid out formal gardens and planted hedges, and in the 1920s Col Douglas and Lady Margaret Proby altered the layout to what we see today. During the 1980s the present owners have carried out extensive restoration and improvements, Mrs Proby using her own skills, but also taking advice from today's distinguished experts: Alan Mitchell has designed the arboretum, Peter Beales the rose garden and Ursula Buchan the herbaceous borders. A conservatory and formal garden are planned for 1990, and two pairs of wrought-iron gates have been commissioned.

House open. Lunches, teas and suppers by arrangement.

### EUSTON HALL, Thetford, Norfolk (His Grace the Duke of Grafton)
*Pleasure grounds 70 acres, park 1,000 acres*

John Evelyn, the distinguished tree and gardening expert, advised the Earl of Arlington on the layout of the pleasure grounds and avenues in 1670. A generation later, however, the 2nd Duke of Grafton (his father, Charles II's son by Lady Castlemaine, had married Lord Arlington's daughter) employed William Kent to draw plans for a less formal landscape. Kent designed characteristic clumps of trees and transformed a formal canal into 'a very pretty rivulet cut in a winding and irregular manner with now and then a little lake'. The landscape's focal point is Kent's Palladian stone temple with an octagonal banquetting room above a basement storey. Further alterations to the landscape were made by 'Capability' Brown towards the end of his life.

House open. Teas.

Helmingham Hall: the Saxon moat.

Haughley Park.

### HAUGHLEY PARK, Stowmarket, Suffolk (Mr A J Williams)
*Gardens 6 acres, park 100 acres*

The general layout and the brick walls have survived since the house was built by Sir John Sulyard in 1620, and the Sulyard family's occupation which lasted until 1809 is pre-dated by a magnificent one thousand-year-old oak tree with a girth of over thirty feet (nine metres). The present owner added the drive approach and a small lake stocked with golden orfe and planted with pink, white and yellow water-lilies. From 1960 onwards he has carried out extensive planting of trees and shrubs within a series of enclosed gardens and

in the woodland dell where rhododendrons, camellias and bamboos are underplanted with aconites, cyclamen, hellebores and toad lilies. Spring and summer flowers throughout he garden are followed by bright berries and glowing leaf colour in the autumn.

## HELMINGHAM HALL GARDENS,
Stowmarket, Suffolk (the Lord Tollemache)
*Gardens 10 acres, park 400 acres*

These romantic gardens are listed Grade I by English Heritage. Nineteen generations of Tollemaches have cared for them over a period of five hundred years and the present Lord and Lady Tollemache have continued to enrich them. The brick house dates from the 1500s and is completely surrounded by a moat spanned by two drawbridges which have been raised every night since 1510. The smaller moat around the walled garden probably dates from Saxon times and was intended to protect stock from marauders. The walls were built in 1740 and protect cruciform herbaceous borders which are screened from productive beds of vegetables and fruit by fences clad in old-fashioned climbing roses, many of them rare varieties. At the east end of the walled garden a parterre of box filled with *Viola cornuta* is surrounded by beds of magnificent, scented hybrid musk roses interplanted with campanulas and lilies. A walk outside the walls leads through an apple walk, meadow garden, spring border and shrubbery. In the park herds of red and fallow deer, a herd of Highland cattle and a flock of wild Soay sheep roam among nine hundred-year-old oak trees.

Teas. Plant and produce sales.

## KENTWELL HALL, Long Melford,
Suffolk (Mr Patrick Phillips)
*Gardens 15 acres, park 100 acres*

The moated Tudor manor house, little altered since its completion at the end of the sixteenth century, is surrounded by tranquil gardens rescued from dereliction by the present owners and restored to preserve elements from different periods of their history: a seventeenth-century lime avenue, espalier fruit trees, yew walk, dovecote and walled garden; the park c1800 reputedly designed by Humphry Repton; and the yew bank planted by Sir Connop and Lady Guthrie in the 1930s. Recent work includes a brick paved maze representing a Tudor rose in the courtyard, a herb garden with over 160 different varieties, and much new planting with the emphasis on plants of the Tudor period.

House open. Teas. Guided tours.

## LAYER MARNEY TOWER, Colchester,
Essex (Major and Mrs Gerald Charrington)
*Gardens 5 acres, park 5 acres*

The spectacular eighty-foot (twenty-four-metre) tower which dominates the site was built in the days of Henry VIII, and in 1579 Queen Elizabeth stayed with the owner Mrs Tuke for two days. The formal garden was laid out by Walter de Zoëte in 1904. He made the wide steps on the south side and placed the Italian lion statues there. The Charrington's ownership is marked by the Portland stone griffins (their family crest) on the brick gateposts, carved by John Shuffleton in 1969. The terraced, yew-hedged gardens include roses, lilacs, herbaceous plants and rare trees including a loquat. Dexter cattle graze the park.

House open. Guided tours.

## MANNINGTON GARDENS, Mannington
Hall, Norwich, Norfolk (the Lord Walpole)
*Gardens 10 acres, park 17 acres*

The romantic moated hall with its flint and terracotta turrets, battlements and chimneys is little changed since it was built in 1460. Horatio, 1st Baron Walpole and brother of Sir Robert Walpole, England's first prime minister, bought the house in the early

Mannington gardens.

eighteenth century, and it has remained in his family since. The walled garden within the moat was probably the original garden for the fifteenth-century house, and is now planted with colour-planned herbaceous borders backed by climbing roses and honeysuckle. There is a modern rose garden, an intimate scented garden, its beds laid out in the pattern of the dining-room ceiling, as it might have been in Tudor times, and informal pleasure grounds with unusual trees, shrubberies and a walk to the ruined thirteenth-century church. The temple by the lake and the horses' graves surrounded by rhododendrons were put here by the 4th Earl, an eccentric misogynist. In the former walled kitchen garden is an interesting and instructive heritage rose garden, laid out in plots which show changes in the design of rose gardens and the rose varieties used from medieval to modern times.

Lunches, teas. Plant sales (Peter Beales roses). Nature and farm trails.

Otley Hall: wistaria.

**OTLEY HALL**, Otley, Ipswich, Suffolk
(Mr John Mosseson)
*Gardens 10 acres*

The moated hall, listed Grade I, is a rare and beautiful example of fifteenth-century architecture. The gardens with the moat, two fish ponds and large mount form an authentic setting for a house of this period. In 1915 a plan for the garden was drawn up by Inigo Thomas, a colleague of Sir Reginald Bloomfield and fellow protagonist of the formal garden style. Only part of his plan was carried out. Today the visitor to the garden can experience a series of linked spaces of different scale and character including formal and informal lawns, woodland, an orchard and two nutteries. The whole is dominated by tranquil stretches of water inhabited by stately black swans.

House open. Lunches, teas. Guided tours.

## THE PRIORY, Lavenham, Suffolk (Mr and Mrs Alan Casey)
*Garden 1 acre, meadow 2½ acres*

The gardens have been created from a wilderness of rubbish and nettles in the 1980s by the present owners who undertook the restoration of the ruined medieval and Tudor house. The medieval pond and cattle walk have been restored and a paved courtyard and herb garden introduced in the Tudor style. The

**The Priory, Lavenham.**

centre-piece in the herb garden, laid out in flint, is a five-pointed star, the emblem of the de Vere family, Lords of the Manor of Lavenham from 1066. There is a walnut orchard and current projects include a knot garden, mount, pergola and orchard.

House open. Lunches, teas.

## RAINTHORPE HALL, Tasburgh, Norwich, Norfolk (Mr George Hastings)
*Gardens 3 acres, park 30 acres, woodland 80 acres*

The well-preserved Tudor house is haunted by the spirit of the luckless Amy Robsart, wife of Queen Elizabeth's favourite Robert Dudley, Earl of Leicester. She stayed here often as a child and would have known the garden which runs down to the River Tas. The long narrow knot of clipped box in a flowing pattern of circles and curves remains from this period, and the nuttery of coppiced hazel dates back to the Middle Ages, as does an ancient yew tree beyond the formal lily pond.

House open. Garden centre.

## ST OSYTH'S PRIORY, St Osyth, Essex (Mr Somerset de Chair)
*Gardens 17 acres, park 400 acres*

Ancient monastic calm still prevails at St Osyth's Priory, eight centuries since the foundation of the abbey, four and a half centuries since its dissolution and three and a half since Cromwell's men sacked and looted the house. The unique and beautiful gatehouse, restored by the present owner, leads to spacious lawns bounded on all four sides by ancient buildings. The 3rd Earl of Rochford, who added a Georgian wing to the house, brought the first Lombardy poplars to England, and planted them and other fine trees here. A topiary garden and a rose garden laid out as an open knot reflect the earlier history of the place, and the water garden was made by Lady Cowley early this century.

House open.

## SOMERLEYTON HALL, Lowestoft, Suffolk (the Lord and Lady Somerleyton)
*Gardens 12 acres, park 300 acres*

The gardens as well as the 'Princely residence with solid magnificence' (as Somerleyton was described in 1861) are a remarkable example of the high Victorian Italianate style. They were laid out in 1846 for Sir Morton Peto by William Nesfield and include an exceptionally fine yew maze with a pagoda in the centre, and a three-hundred-foot (ninety-metre) long iron pergola planted with white, pink and mauve wistaria and many other climbing plants. In the walled kitchen garden there is a remarkable range of ridge-and-furrow glasshouses, probably designed by Paxton. Paxton also designed the winter garden, of which the loggia remains, surrounding a formal

sunken garden. The clock tower was originally designed by Vulliamy for the Houses of Parliament for the position now occupied by Big Ben. The gardens are planted with splendid specimen trees and shrubs, rhododendrons and azaleas being followed in the summer by formal bedding displays and herbaceous borders.

House open. Teas. Guided tours.

## SPAINS HALL, Finchingfield, Essex (Colonel Sir John Ruggles-Brise)
*Gardens 3 acres, park 17 acres*

Humphry Repton designed the gardens and park for the red-brick Elizabethan house in 1807, and the surviving kitchen garden, lake and fence palings can be compared with his drawing and with two watercolours made by John Adey Repton in 1824. Traces of a thirteenth-century moat and seven early seventeenth-century fish ponds represent earlier phases in the garden's history. The fish ponds are said to have been made by William Kempe who took a vow of silence after

**Somerleyton Hall: the maze.**

wrongfully accusing his wife of unfaithfulness. He kept his vow for seven years. In the flower garden, laid out about a hundred years ago, a cedar of Lebanon, planted in 1670, has a spread of 186 feet (fifty-seven metres). The sundial was made by Adams in 1799 and is flanked by the continuous flowering pink China rose, 'Hermosa', brought from Sir Walter Gilbey's vineyards in France. The prayer house at the end of the Elizabethan wall of the kitchen garden was rebuilt in 1839. Bougainvilleas in the greenhouse came from the owner's sister's garden in Kenya.

House open. Teas.

---

**East Midlands**  Derbyshire, Leicestershire, Lincolnshire, Northamptonshire, Nottinghamshire, South Humberside.

---

## BELVOIR CASTLE, Grantham, Leicestershire (His Grace the Duke of Rutland)
*Gardens 40 acres, park extensive*

The mid-nineteenth century gardens are integrated with the architecture of the castle, forming a series of narrow terraces and slopes descending from the hilltop site with its spectacular views. On the opposite side of a small valley is the Duchess's garden, locally known as 'Spring Gardens'. As well as a mass of early flowering shrubs and bulbs, there are ground-covering plants which have been added since 1970 by the present Duchess. Peacocks are very much a feature at Belvoir, not only strutting on the terraces but also represented in the stonework and tapestries of the castle.

Castle open. Lunches, teas.

## CHATSWORTH HOUSE, Bakewell, Derbyshire (His Grace the Duke of Devonshire)
*Gardens 105 acres, park 1,100 acres*

Chatsworth House: the baroque Cascade Pavilion.

The vast gardens at Chatsworth, set in a very beautiful landscape, must rank among the finest anywhere. Many historic styles are represented. The layout around the house was designed for the 1st Duke by London and Wise in the formal French style in the late seventeenth century. The parterres and terraces were swept away by 'Capability' Brown some seventy years later, but the famous stepped cascade with its baroque pavilion, the canal, and the 1st Duke's greenhouse which shelters rare camellias and other half-hardy plants, are all still to be seen. The willow-tree fountain, a unique water-joke, dates from 1692. Brown's naturalistic landscape and trees formed the framework for developments during the famous partnership between the 6th Duke and Joseph Paxton. Paxton's genius for designing glass buildings is seen in the Conservative Wall completed in 1848. The slender glass panels are stepped up a slope for a distance of 331 feet (one hundred metres). He also designed the emperor fountain in the canal with its spectacular single, gravity-fed jet spurting to nearly three hundred feet (ninety metres). Paxton's rock-work, including the Wellington rock, is also spectacular. In this century the present Duke and Duchess

77

have added the pleached limes on the south lawn, the serpentine beech hedges, and a parterre setting out the ground plan of Chiswick Villa in golden box. New projects include a kitchen garden and a cottage garden.

House open. Lunches, teas. Garden centre.

## DODDINGTON HALL, Lincolnshire (Mr A Jarvis)
*Gardens 5 acres, park 30 acres*

The Elizabethan house, designed by Robert Smythson, is externally unaltered since its completion in 1600. The layout of the formal walled gardens around the house also dates from this period, and is shown in a Kip engraving of 1700. The east garden, through which the house is approached from the gatehouse, is a simple pattern of lawns and gravel, and by contrast the west garden has an elaborate box-edged knot laid out in 1900 with advice from Kew and *Country Life*, and today luxuriantly planted with old-fashioned roses. In this century Mr and Mrs Ralph Jarvis and their son Antony Jarvis have greatly improved and extended the gardens, adding a maze in 1986 and enriching the planting in the four-acre wild garden.

House open. Lunches, teas.

## ELSHAM HALL COUNTRY PARK, Brigg, South Humberside (Captain J Elwes)
*Park 1,000 acres*

The park dates mainly from 1740 to 1760 with its lakes incorporating earlier medieval fish ponds, and with Victorian additions. Today it is organized primarily with the conservation of plants and wildlife in mind. There are educational programmes for school parties and other visitors based on a choice of nature trails, an arboretum trail, a children's animal farmyard, a bird garden and an outdoor butterfly garden, the first in Britain with an overwalk. In spring the blossom and bulbs are

Doddington Hall: the west garden.

spectacular, and there is a wonderful display of snowdrops in the dark walk.

Lunches, teas. Guided tours. Garden centre.

## GRIMSTHORPE CASTLE, Bourne, Lincolnshire (Grimsthorpe and Drummond Castle Trust)
*Gardens 21 acres, park 3,000 acres*

The gardens retain much of the formal layout in rectangular enclosures that is shown in a Kip engraving of the house in the 1660s. The formality was modified in Stephen Switzer's alterations in the early eighteenth century to complement Sir John Vanbrugh's alterations to the house. Switzer opened up the garden to the wood beyond and surrounded it with a terrace walk. Today there are formal lawns, a parterre, a rose garden, and a superb formal kitchen garden laid out by the late Countess of Ancaster and Peter Coats in 1965. The park and lake were designed by 'Capability' Brown.

House open. Teas.

## HADDON HALL, Bakewell, Derbyshire (His Grace the Duke of Rutland)
*Gardens 2½ acres*

The hall is a remarkable example of Tudor domestic architecture, and the terraced gardens with their massive buttressed walls and fine stone balustrading have remained intact since 1641 when John Manners transferred his household to Belvoir Castle. The planting on the terraces, which had become derelict and overgrown, dates from the 1920s. In spring there are masses of bulbs. The great glory of the gardens is its profusion of roses covering the walls and descending in cascades of scent and colour from terrace to terrace. Many of the roses date from the 1920s and are now rare. They are supplemented by clematis and herbaceous plants including a magnificent border of delphiniums.

House open. Lunches, teas.

## HOLDENBY HOUSE, Holdenby, Northamptonshire (Mr and Mrs James Lowther)
*Gardens 20 acres*

The house was built in 1583 by Sir Christopher Hatton, Queen Elizabeth I's Lord Chancellor, and was then the largest house in England. King Charles I was imprisoned here in 1547, and parts of the house were demolished after his execution, leaving the handsome wing and entrance arches that we see today. The surviving Elizabethan garden layout for such a grand house is a rare and important piece of garden history. It has been planted in the 1980s by Rosemary Verey, using plants that were available in 1580. The nineteenth-century gardens have also been restored and include a fragrant border and a silver border.

House open on bank holidays. Lunches, teas. Plant sales.

## HOLME PIERREPONT HALL, Nottingham, Nottinghamshire (Mr and Mrs Robin Brackenbury)
*Gardens and park 30 acres*

The Victorian parterre in the enclosed courtyard of this medieval manor house was restored in the 1970s by Mrs Brackenbury who took 1,500 cuttings of box and meticulously followed a detailed drawing of 1875. The pattern in box is strongly indicative of Nesfield's work. Appropriate permanent planting has replaced the bedding plants which the Victorians would have used, but rose beds shown on the plan are being reinstated. To the east of the house a garden was laid out in 1973 with some advice from John Codrington. A formal framework including a yew circle and avenue of yews is planted with luxuriant informality with flowering shrubs, shrub roses and ground-cover plants.

House open. Teas. Guided tours.

## LAMPORT HALL, Northampton, Northamptonshire (Lamport Hall Preservation Trust Ltd)
*Gardens 5 acres, park 140 acres*

An insight into the history of the garden gnome can be had at Lamport Hall. Sir Charles Isham, the 10th Baronet, imported gnomes in great numbers from Nuremberg to people his rockery, built from the 1850s onwards. Ninety feet (twenty-seven metres) long, forty-seven feet (thirteen metres) wide and twenty-four feet (seven metres) high, the rockery faces north towards the windows of the house and is built against a wall which conceals it from the garden. The scenery of this miniature alp included moats, caves and canyons as well as a collection of alpine plants. The gnomes were to be seen at work mining crystal in the caves and canyons, and indeed they were seen by large numbers of tourists coming in charabancs from London. Sir Charles, a convinced spiritualist, believed that other gnomes besides those purchased in Nuremberg were at work. He published an article entitled *Visions of Fairy Blacksmiths at Work* and wrote in *Notes on Gnomes*, 'Seeing and hearing gnomes is not mental delusion, but extension of faculty'. Alas only one gnome is still in residence at Lamport, and he is on display inside the house. The stone walls, raised banks and terraces of the garden date from 1676–1679, and form the framework for later developments carried out by Sir Charles including an Italian garden and yew walk. Restoration of this Victorian phase is going ahead throughout the gardens.

House open. Lunches, teas. Guided tours.

### MELBOURNE HALL GARDENS,
Melbourne, Derbyshire (Lord Ralph Kerr)
*Gardens 16 acres, park 350 acres*

A rare and valuable example of a late seventeenth- early eighteenth-century garden in the French style, Melbourne was laid out by Thomas Coke, Vice Chamberlain to Queen Anne, assisted by Henry Wise. The garden is a classical *petit Versailles* with a touch of English romanticism. Green alleys and vistas lead to formal pools, fountains and other focal points, such as the magnificent lead urn known as the Four Seasons Monument by Jan Van Nost and given to Thomas Coke by Queen Anne. Van Nost also made the charming *putti* which flank the paths of the cross-axes in pairs, and the statues of Mercury, Perseus and Andromeda. The main vista from the hall to the great basin follows the line of an ancient yew arbour or tunnel two hundred yards (183 metres) long which predates the rest of the gardens. Above the great basin stands 'The Birdcage', a modest name for the handsome and elaborate wrought-iron arbour made by the great Derbyshire craftsman Robert Bakewell. Hidden in woodland there is a grotto or wishing well fed by a

Melbourne Hall: Robert Bakewell's 'Birdcage'.

natural spring and bearing a verse inscribed by the volatile and highly strung Lady Caroline Lamb, who was married to Queen Victoria's first prime minister the 2nd Viscount Melbourne and infatuated with 'mad, bad and dangerous to know' Lord Byron.

### ROCKINGHAM CASTLE, Market
Harborough, Leicestershire (Commander Michael Saunders Watson)
*Gardens 20 acres, park 500 acres, woods 400 acres*

Built by William the Conqueror, modernized by Edward I from 1276 to 1291, the moated castle commands views across four counties. The development of the gardens reflects that of the buildings since the fortified castle became a Tudor family residence. The terraces, mount and extraordinary elephantine double yew hedge are the legacy of Lewis Watson in the 1660s who restored the castle after much was destroyed in the Civil War. The front park was laid out by his son Edward. The 1820 rose garden on the site of the old keep follows the keep's circular form, and is intersected by paths which echo its layout. Richard Watson's wild garden of 1840 was replanted in 1960 and selective felling and replanting to ensure a succession of fine trees in future centuries continues today.

House open. Teas.

## WHATTON GARDENS, Loughborough, Leicestershire (the Lord Crawshaw)
*Gardens 15 acres*

Situated in a commanding position with fine views to the Soar Valley and Charnwood Forest, Whatton is approached by three drives, one of which, Long Whatton Drive, runs through a fine avenue of limes. Two stone cassowaries on pillars mark the drive from

Hathern. There are many exceptional trees, a number of them planted in about 1800 when the gardens were first laid out, others in the late nineteenth century by the 1st Lord Crawshaw. He also made the delightful and eccentric Chinese garden. It is enclosed by laurel hedges and entered through an art nouveau gate. Inside are all manner of Chinese ornaments including pagodas, one of which shelters the ancient Buddha Gautama sitting on a lotus, brought from the Summer Palace in Peking. In the woodland there is a rocky canyon garden, a Doric temple faced with bark strips, and a stream and ponds planted with water-loving plants. Rhododendrons, azaleas and magnolias, primulas and meconopsis thrive here. Near the house there is a long-established herbaceous border and a pretty rose garden with beds edged in scalloped stone. During the Second World War the house was a maternity hospital. Over two thousand babies were born at Whatton, and many have revisited their birthplace.

Teas. Garden centre. Guided tours by arrangement.

**Rockingham Castle: the rose garden.**

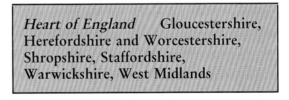

*Heart of England*    Gloucestershire, **Herefordshire and Worcestershire, Shropshire, Staffordshire, Warwickshire, West Midlands**

## ARBURY HALL, Nuneaton, Warwickshire (the Viscount Daventry)
*Gardens 19 acres, park 250 acres*

The gardens are much as they were in the mid-eighteenth century, when Sir Roger Newdigate (founder of the Newdigate Prize for poetry at Oxford University) altered the Elizabethan formal gardens at the same time that he altered the house to the splendid example of the Gothic style that it is today. Water is the chief component of his landscape, the gardens being embraced on three sides by a canal and lakes linked by a cascade devised by Sanderson Miller, the architect

who worked on Gothicizing the house. Plant lists in the archives at Arbury dated 1748, 1753, 1757, 1770 indicate that although the garden was informally landscaped, it contained a great wealth of flowering shrubs and herbaceous plants as well as specimen trees. Some were planted 'upon the Terras Border', some 'In the Clump next to the American' and others 'In The Great Clump before ye Greenhouse'. George Eliot was born on the Estate in 1819 and described Arbury as 'Cheverel Manor' in her novel *Mr Gilgil's Love Story*.

House open. Lunches, teas.

**BARNSLEY HOUSE**, Cirencester, Gloucestershire (Mrs Rosemary Verey). See page 54

Left: Arbury Hall.

Below: Batsford Arboretum.

**BATSFORD ARBORETUM**, Moreton-in-Marsh, Gloucestershire (Batsford Foundation)
*Arboretum 50 acres*

Lord Dulverton's arboretum is one of the most distinguished in Britain, containing exceptionally fine specimens of familiar trees and many rarities. The framework was begun by Lord Redesdale, grandfather of the talented Mitford sisters, who built the mansion at the end of the nineteenth century. A former attaché at the British embassy in Tokyo, his aim was to create a picturesque landscape with a Japanese feeling. His legacy consists of a rest house, a bronze Buddha, bronze animals, a rock and water garden and numerous bamboos. Lord Redesdale's plantings of conifers provide a benign microclimate for the less hardy species in the collection, to which Lord Dulverton has added steadily since he inherited the property from his father in 1956, always positioning the trees so that they enhance the landscape. Thus, Batsford is not only a place of pilgrimage for tree connoisseurs, but also a place of delight at all seasons for lovers of beauty.

Garden centre with tea-room. Falconry centre.

**BERKELEY CASTLE**, Berkeley, Gloucestershire (Major R J Berkeley)
*Gardens 5 acres*

Gertrude Jekyll wrote of the castle '. . . it looks like some great fortress roughly hewn out of natural rock. Nature would seem to have taken back to herself the masses of stone reared seven and a half centuries ago.' Like the castle, the main terrace and bowling green probably date from the twelfth century. Further terraces were added in the 1920s by the 8th Earl of Berkeley, and the plants, many rare and tender, which soften the massive south-facing walls, were mainly planted by Major Robert Berkeley whose other garden was at Spetchley Park. The Berkeley family have remained here since Saxon times, and the

castle and its terrace gardens have settled into a state of imperturbable tranquillity.

Castle open. Lunches, teas.

**CHILLINGTON HALL**, Codsall Wood, Wolverhampton, Staffordshire. (Mr and Mrs Peter Giffard)
*Garden 2 acres, park 300 acres*

The Giffards have lived at Chillington since 1178, but the present house and 'Capability' Brown landscape were made by Peter Giffard who inherited in 1718. The fine oak avenue of the original approach to the house predates Brown's work. Brown's ninety-acre lake inspired James Paine who designed the stone bridge at its lower edge to write 'In this park is confessedly one of the finest pieces of water, within an inclosure, that this kingdom produces: the verges of which are bounded by fine plantations, intermixed with groves of venerable stately oaks.' The landscape is punctuated by a larger bridge by Brown, a Grecian temple and a Roman temple. A modern problem has been the accommodation of the M54 which involved moving 420,000 tonnes of soil to preserve the view to an 'eye-catcher' outside the park known as the 'Whitehouse' or 'Sham House'.

House open.

**EASTNOR CASTLE**, Ledbury, Herefordshire (Mr James and the Hon Mrs Hervey Bathurst)
*Grounds 76 acres, park 300 acres*

A very remarkable collection of coniferous trees marries the imperious grandeur of the massive grey stone castle to the gentle, pastoral Herefordshire landscape. The castle seems like a giant toy. It was designed by Sir Robert Smirke, R A in the romantic medieval style for the 1st Earl Somers and built between 1812 and 1818. Tree planting began at the same time within the framework of the ancient

Eastnor Castle.

Lobel's maple in Europe, and a rare Mexican pine. New planting is in progress to replace specimens past their maturity. To improve the overall landscape this includes underplanting of great sweeps of magnolias, viburnums and other appropriate shrubs to create different moods. Distinguished relations and family friends who have visited Eastnor include Elizabeth Barrett Browning, Maria Edgeworth, the pioneer photographer Julia Margaret Cameron, Alfred, Lord Tennyson, the painter G F Watts and Queen Mary.

House open. Lunches, teas.

natural oak forest which supplied much of the timber for the house, and for British ship building for the Napoleonic Wars. The 2nd Earl continued the collection, raising the first *Cedrus atlantica* in Britain from seed that he collected at Téniet-el-Hâad. It is unusual to find conifers thriving so exceptionally on alkaline soil, but treasures at Eastnor include the tallest Santa Lucia firs, Dragon spruce and

**ECCLESHALL CASTLE**, Stafford, Staffordshire (Mr Mark Carter)
*Gardens 2 acres, park 15 acres*

The history of Eccleshall dates back to Roman times, and the castle was a seat of the Bishops of Lichfield from St Chad (664–672)

Eccleshall Castle.

to Bishop John Lonsdale who died there in 1864. After the castle was sacked by Cromwell's men, the existing house was built. It was Bishop John Hough who laid out the grounds in the early eighteenth century and planted trees, some of which survive, including the lime avenue. Other trees, particularly yews, may be even older. The 650-year-old walls of the moat garden (drained, together with the surrounding lake and marsh in the eighteenth century) are planted with espalier apples. Other interesting features include a two-hundred-year-old wistaria on the south front of the house, a fine pair of wrought-iron gates attributed to 'Capability' Brown, and an exceptional cut-leaved beech tree.

Teas.

**HERGEST CROFT GARDENS**, Kington, Herefordshire (Mr W L Banks)
*Gardens 20 acres, park 30 acres*

A great treat for the seeker after rare and beautiful plants, the collection at Hergest Croft has been formed by three generations of the Banks family, having been started by W H Banks, grandfather of Lawrence Banks, the present owner. Many of the trees and shrubs were grown from seed sent back from the Far East at the beginning of this century, and are now in the splendour of maturity. The gardens near the house including the traditional kitchen garden have an Edwardian formality. The rest of the garden, mainly in a woodland setting, follows closely the principles of naturalistic planting advocated at the beginning of this century by William Robinson and Gertrude Jekyll. The result is a richly varied landscape in which the shapes, texture and colours of the plants are chosen for harmony or contrast to give pleasure at all seasons. The national collections of maples, birches and zelkovas are included in what is one of the finest collections of trees and shrubs in the British Isles.

Lunches, teas.

**HODNET HALL**, Market Drayton, Shropshire (Mr and the Hon Mrs Algernon Heber-Percy). See page 32

**HOW CAPLE COURT**, How Caple, Herefordshire (Mr P L Lee)
*Gardens 5 acres, woodland 6 acres*

A major restoration project is under way to restore these gardens to their Edwardian splendour. The formal terraces descending towards the River Wye are in keeping with the late seventeenth century architecture of the house. They were laid out in Edwardian times by Lennox Bertram Lee, an amateur garden planner who advised on the design of the royal gardens in Bucharest. The south terraces are strongly architectural with walls, steps, ponds and statuary. To the west is a series of water features and a sunken Florentine garden leading to informally planted areas of fine trees, flowering shrubs and old roses. There is a rose garden and herbaceous borders planned by Alan Bloom.

Teas.

**MISARDEN PARK**, Misarden, Stroud, Gloucestershire (Major and Mrs M T N H Wills)
*Gardens 11 acres, park 100 acres*

Although the house dates from 1620, the most fruitful period of development in the gardens was between the two world wars. Lutyens designed the wistaria-covered loggia on his east wing, and may have planned the butler's walk with its mushroom-shaped hornbeams. Unusual features include double borders of the white rose bay willow herb, broad, finely detailed grass steps, and yew topiary 'sentry boxes' housing stone urns. Among the remarkable plants are a fine specimen of *Magnolia x soulangeana*, a huge *Catalpa bignonioides*, a vast sycamore growing out of a stone wall and martagon lilies naturalized in grass along the drive. The whole area of the gardens which once claimed the attention of ten gardeners is now maintained by just two, and careful planning and planting have resulted in no loss of beauty in the overall effect.

Teas in the village. Plant centre.

## MOCCAS COURT, Hereford, Herefordshire (Mr R T G Chester-Master)
*Gardens 8.7 acres, park 30 acres*

'Capability' Brown drew up plans for landscaping the gardens during the building of the house to plans by Robert and James Adam. He was paid £100. Humphry Repton also gave advice but his Red Book has not survived. The house is in a fine position on the River Wye, and although the pleasure grounds have reverted to agricultural use, elements of the eighteenth-century landscape survive, including trees, a ha-ha and an icehouse. Later features, such as a water garden and fernery in a rocky ravine, are being restored.

## PAINSWICK ROCOCO GARDEN, Painswick, Gloucestershire (the Lord Dickinson)
*Gardens 6 acres, park 30 acres*

A remarkable restoration project began in 1984 in the overgrown, wooded grounds of Painswick House. The aim was to restore the hidden combe below the house to the garden shown by Thomas Robins in 1748 in his delightful, detailed paintings. They show views of a garden in the 'rococo' style combining formal vistas with the informality of serpentine paths, strategically placed areas of water and small buildings of great charm in classical Gothic and rustic architectural styles. The Doric seat, the Gothic alcove, the red house, pigeon house and eagle house all survived, though in various states of dereliction, and as the woodland was cleared, traces of the old paths were revealed. The orchard

Painswick Rococo Gardens: the Red House.

and shrubberies have been planted with varieties that were available in the mid-eighteenth century. The restored garden already evokes that light-hearted, pleasure-loving era. In late February and early March the woods and the banks of the stream are completely carpeted with snowdrops.

Lunches, teas. Guided tours.

## RAGLEY HALL, Alcester, Warwickshire (the Marquess of Hertford)
*Gardens 27 acres, park 400 acres*

The Marquess of Hertford's family, the Seymours, have been closely connected with English history for many centuries. It was Sir Edward Seymour who built the house in 1680, and the 5th Marquess who, having inherited the estate after a period of neglect, laid out the gardens in High Victorian style in 1874. Some of the original formal flower-beds have been grassed over to provide a background of smooth lawns for those that remain, and today the planting is entirely of roses. Magnificent trees frame views from the lawns across the park and lake.

House open. Lunches, teas.

**RODMARTON MANOR**, nr Cirencester, Gloucestershire (Mrs Anthony Biddulph)
*Gardens 10 acres*

Designed by Ernest Barnsley in the Cotswold tradition, Rodmarton and its integrated garden are a late flowering of the Arts and Crafts movement. Walls, terraces, strong vistas along stone paths and the firm, solid shapes of topiary provide a structure within which Mrs Biddulph's plant knowledge and gardening skill has free reign. There are many satisfying associations of plant forms and of flower colours, and an instructive use of ground-cover plants to reduce labour spent weeding. 'Rosemary Rose' is underplanted with purple ajuga, 'Iceberg' with purple violas. All seasons are catered for, winter being celebrated by at least a hundred different varieties of snow-drop and masses of hellebores. Plants thriving unexpectedly in the Cotswold climate include *Fremontodendron californicum* and *Trachelospermum asiaticum*. Barnsley's pretty summer-house is decorated with *Clematis orientalis* and the miniature flowers of the rose 'Bloomfield Abundance'.

Teas. Guided tours. Plant sales.

**SEZINCOTE**, Moreton-in-Marsh, Gloucestershire (Mr and Mrs David Peake)
*Gardens 10 acres*

House, orangery and gardens are a unique and delightful fantasy in the Indian style, combining Hindu and Muslim elements. Charles Cockerell, formerly of the East India Company, employed his architect brother to build the house and was advised by Thomas Daniell and Humphry Repton on the gardens. The garden, neglected during the Second World War, was restored by Sir Cyril and Lady Kleinwort advised by Mr Graham Thomas. Their work includes the canals and Irish yews in the South Garden, evocative of Moghul paradise gardens, and all the exceptionally fine planting of the water garden, where many rare plants can be seen. Ornaments include a temple to Surya the sun god, statues of Brahmin bulls and a snake coiled round a column in the snake pond.

*Sezincote: the south garden.*

**SPETCHLEY PARK**, Worcester, Worcestershire, (Major R J Berkeley)
*Gardens 30 acres, park 120 acres*

Many generations of Berkeleys, who have owned Spetchley since 1605, have contributed to the gardens. There are cedar trees dating from the seventeenth century, some of which were planted by John Evelyn, the distinguished diarist and author of *Sylva or a Discourse on Forest Trees*, who was a friend of Sir Robert Berkeley's. Fine trees, the water-lilies on the wide expanse of water known as the Garden Pool, masses of naturalized bulbs

in spring and fine woodland planting all contribute to the visitor's pleasure. The formal gardens near the house are outstanding as an example of Victorian and Edwardian gardening at its best. They were planned and planted by the present owner's grandmother, Rose Berkeley, together with her sister, the famous gardener Ellen Willmott of Warley Place in Essex. Full of rare and unusual plants, the formal structure and exuberant planting recalls summers of a leisurely and elegant era.

Teas on Sundays and bank holidays. Plant sales.

Left: Spetchley Park.

Below: Sudeley Castle: the Queen's Garden.

## SUDELEY CASTLE Winchcombe, Cheltenham, Gloucestershire (the Lady Ashcombe)
*Gardens 8 acres*

The fifteenth century castle was the home of Queen Katherine Parr, the widow of Henry VIII. Her tomb is in the beautiful chapel approached through a walled garden designed by Rosemary Verey. Sudeley was also one of the buildings that Cromwell 'knocked about a bit'. The result is a Banquetting Hall open to the sky, retaining its fireplace and magnificent Gothic windows which look on to the Queen's Garden, a Tudor parterre enclosed by ancient yew hedges and recently planted with old roses, herbs and herbaceous plants to a design by Jane Fearnley-Whittingstall. Elsewhere in the gardens the ruined Tithe Barn houses a collection of species roses from all over the world, an ancient gnarled mulberry tree presides over a spring garden, and there are fine trees, rare shrubs and naturalized bulbs. There are carp in the lily pond, a wide variety of wild fowl on the moat, birds of prey in the falconry and peacocks on the lawns.

Lunches, teas. Guided tours by arrangement. Plant centre specializing in everything for the rose garden.

## WARWICK CASTLE, Warwickshire (Warwick Castle Ltd)
*Gardens 10 acres, park 70 acres*

The castle functioned as a defensive stronghold from 1068 when William the Conqueror built the original fortress until the Civil War when it was defended against the Royalists by the Roundheads. Its commanding strategic position above the River Avon, the mound, walls and towers are an integral part of the gardens and of the landscape made by 'Capability' Brown as his first independent commission. There are two formal areas. Below the Gothic conservatory built in 1786 is a parterre laid out in 1969 by Robert Marnock. Robert Marnock also designed a rose garden of which no trace remained after the Second World War. In the 1980s this has been restored, following Marnock's original drawings, giving a rare chance to see an authentic Victorian rose garden. Trees in the grounds have been planted by Queen Victoria, Prince Albert and Edward VIII when Prince of Wales.

House open. Lunches, teas. Guided tours by arrangement. The 'Warwick Castle' rose is on sale.

## WESTON PARK, Weston-under-Lizard, Shifnal, Shropshire (the Earl of Bradford)
*Gardens 27 acres, park 1,000 acres*

The extensive eighteenth-century pleasure grounds and lake were designed by 'Capability' Brown for Sir Henry Bridgeman, father of the 1st Earl. They were planned as a setting to the hall, and provided walks, carriage drives and vistas to the house, the lake, the Roman bridge by James Paine and Paine's Temple

**Weston Park.**

89

of Diana which housed a tea-room, music-room, vaulted dairy and stone bath. An underground, grotto-like tunnel leads to Pendrill's Cave, which was inhabited by a hermit of that name. There are traces of earlier planting, including some oaks surviving from the medieval deer park and some fine sweet chestnuts which may be the remnants of a double avenue dating from the late seventeenth century when the hall was built.

House open. Lunches, teas.

## North West Cheshire, Lancashire.

**ADLINGTON HALL**, Macclesfield, Cheshire (Mr Charles F Legh)
*Gardens 7 acres, woodland 60 acres*

The home of the Leghs since 1312, the house began as a hunting lodge, and its intimate relationship with the landscape is still evident today – the two oak trees round which it was built being still rooted in the ground. They are the octagonal carved pillars flanking the organ in the great hall. The gardens were landscaped in the mid-eighteenth century by Charles Legh who added the south front with its Ionic portico to the black and white timbered Elizabethan house. The temple to Diana in the wilderness and the shell cottage (the shell decoration added later in about 1950) remain from this period. The yew walk was probably planted in the 1660s, the lime avenue in 1688.

**ARLEY HALL**, Northwich Cheshire (the Hon Michael Flower). See page 46

**BROWSHOLME HALL**, Clitheroe, Lancashire (Mr Christopher Parker)

The landscape surrounding the house, which dates from the early sixteenth century with several later additions and alterations, was the work of Thomas Lister Parker (1779–1858), whose ancestor acquired the site in 1507 and whose descendant lives there today. The terrace with the yew avenue may be earlier than the rest of the landscape, which includes a ha-ha and a large pond with a boathouse. The attractive entrance arch at the front lodge, with its iron gates, was built in 1806 and acts as an eye-catcher for the house.

House open.

**CHOLMONDELEY CASTLE GARDENS**, Malpas, Cheshire (the Marquess and Marchioness of Cholmondeley)
*Gardens 45 acres, park 520 acres*

The landscape was created when the present castle was built in about 1801, and provides a structure of fine trees and water within which, from the 1960s onwards, the present owners have carried out extensive planting of rhododendrons, azaleas and magnolias to suit the acid soil, with the help, at different stages, of Jim Russell and Vernon Russell-Smith. The overall atmosphere is one of tranquil beauty, with much richness in the details. Near the castle there are borders of hybrid musk roses with herbaceous plants and two fine *Pyrus salicifolia* 'Pendula', which lead to a pretty rose garden with arches and lavender. Large, informal groups of shrub roses mark the transition from gardens to park.

Lunches, teas. Plant sales including rhododendrons, azaleas, bedding plants.

**DORFOLD HALL**, Nantwich, Cheshire (Mr R C Roundell)
*Gardens 10 acres, park 200 acres*

The approach is by a straight avenue of magnificent limes set sixty feet (eighteen metres) apart to frame the brick-built Jacobean mansion. The balustraded walls and stone gateway to the cobbled entrance courtyard

Lyme Park: the orangery c. 1815.

are among several outstanding architectural features which give the gardens an air of permanence. On the south side of the house two terraced lawns look out on to the park, their walls planted with hydrangeas, viburnums, shrub roses, peonies and hostas. To the east of the terraces there is a grove of Turkey oak and robinia planted in the early nineteenth century. Beyond it a new woodland, rock and water garden has been made, planted with an interesting collection of rhododendrons, azaleas, magnolias, camellias and shrubs for autumn colour.

House open.

**LYME PARK**, Disley, Stockport, Cheshire (National Trust via Stockport MBC)
*Gardens 16 acres, park, woodland, moorland 1,300 acres*

The gardens at Lyme have been recently restored to the splendour of their Victorian heydey. Typical of the period are the elaborate bedding schemes of annuals in startling colours decorating beds known by their shapes as the panels, the wheel and the cross. Home of the Leghs for six hundred years, the house and gardens also show elements of earlier and later periods, including a lime avenue dating from the 1680s; a sunken Dutch garden (1720s); a c1815 orangery by Wyatt planted with figs and two unidentified 180-year-old camellias; a rose garden (1913); a rhododendron collection; and a herbaceous border planted according to Gertrude Jekyll's colour principles. A connection with the Victorian plant collector Vicary Gibbs is recognized in the restoration of a garden being planted with trees and shrubs introduced or raised by him.

House open. Lunches, teas. Guided tours.

Tatton Park: the 1910 Japanese garden.

**TATTON PARK**, Knutsford, Cheshire (National Trust via Cheshire County Council)
*Gardens 65 acres, park 1,000 acres*

Every gardening style from 1700 onwards can be found in the extensive, immaculately restored and maintained gardens. Developed and extended over four centuries by six generations of the Egerton family, they are full of rare plants, some not found elsewhere in Britain. Wyatt's orangery (1818) and Paxton's fernery (1850s) are both still used for their original purpose. The small beech maze is early, having been well-established by 1795. The arboretum is planted with trees collected from the early 1800s, many originating in Japan. Later developments include a vista to a classical folly (1820); the Italian garden, its elaborate formality typical of the Victorian style of the 1890s; an authentic Japanese garden made by Japanese workmen in 1910, with a thatched tea-house and a Shinto temple brought from Japan; and a typical Edwardian rose garden with a pergola, statuary and beds of polyantha and standard roses edged with pinks. Lady Charlotte's arbour and fountain, named after the wife of the first Baron Egerton, are all that now remain of a flower garden designed by Wyatt in 1814, but the planting is to be restored to Wyatt's plan. Repton made a Red Book for the landscaping of the park.

Lunches, teas. Guided tours. Garden centre.

> *Northumbria* Co Durham, Northumberland

**CHILLINGHAM CASTLE**, Alnwick, Northumberland (Sir Humphrey Wakefield)

The castle and its gardens have recently been restored after fifty years of dereliction. The formal layout and avenues were designed in 1828 by Sir Jeffry de Wyatville for the Earl of Tankerville. The countess was French, and the design was planned to display her French marble urns. Sir Humphrey Wakefield, helped by Miss Isobel Murray, the present gardener, has, since 1982 renovated Wyatville's layout, keeping the box and yew hedges at a greater height than was originally intended, to give the gardens a more enclosed character in keeping with the Tudor period of much of the castle. Lady Tankerville's French urns, sadly vandalized, have been replaced, and fountains have been installed. The wellingtonias and the rockery date from about 1880, and the lake from 1919. The fine trees, roses and unusual herbaceous plants add to the romantic atmosphere of the castle with its medieval curtain wall, ruined monastery, and torture chamber. The restoration project is equally romantic.

Lunches, teas. Guided tours.

**RABY CASTLE**, Staindrop, Darlington, Co Durham (the Lord Barnard)
*Gardens 5 acres, park 250 acres*

**Raby Castle: the lily pond.**

Like the castle, the gardens have seen several phases of development. There are yew hedges which probably date back to the fourteenth century, but the main structure dates from the 1740s when the 2nd Lord Barnard commissioned Thomas Wright, whose Gothic garden buildings and follies were fashionable at that time, to lay out a garden. The walled garden with its hot-air flues, the ha-ha, pond and hedges are his work. In 1786 the 2nd Earl of Darlington built the glass fig house where his 'White Ischia' fig tree still thrives. The herbaceous borders in the east garden were made in the 1920s by the Dowager Lady Barnard, and since 1978 additions have included the heather garden, new planting in the formal garden, the construction of pergolas and a replica of the original Victorian conservatory.

House open. Teas. Guided tours by appointment.

***South East*** **Kent, London, Surrey, East Sussex, West Sussex**

### CHIDDINGSTONE CASTLE,
Edenbridge, Kent (the Trustees of Denys Eyre Bower Bequest)
*Park 33 acres*

The fine Grade II listed landscaped park dating from about 1800 was devastated by the 1987 hurricane. Plans are going ahead for the replacement of lost trees and the surgery needed on those that remain, but as in all gardens that lay in the path of the storm, it is a mammoth and costly undertaking. The grounds contain Georgian Gothic buildings, the water tower, gazebo and orangery being linked by a stone wall.

House open. Teas.

**CHILHAM CASTLE**, Canterbury, Kent
(Viscount Massereene and Ferrard)
*Gardens 25 acres, park 300 acres*

Tradition has it that the terraced gardens were first made by John Tradescant, gardener to the Cecils at Hatfield House, at the time when the Jacobean house was built beside the Norman castle keep. There is a holm oak which dates from this time. The deer park was formed between 1725 and 1735. Much of the garden was destroyed and the ha-ha built to implement a plan by 'Capability' Brown. The gardens were reinstated in two phases, between 1820 and 1850 and in the 1920s and 30s. Today the formal terraces with their long flower borders and yew topiary descend to the informally planted lake garden. There are magnificent views and many fine trees in spite of damage in the 1987 storm.

Lunches, teas.

**FINCHCOCKS**, Goudhurst, Kent (Mr Richard Burnett)
*Gardens 5 acres, park 9 acres*

Built for Edward Bathurst in 1725 and little altered, the Georgian baroque manor house with its fine brickwork is a musical centre of international repute, housing Richard Burnett's remarkable collection of historical keyboard instruments. In the gardens, set in a beautiful Kentish landscape, much replanting in a traditional English style has been done since the Burnetts came in 1970, creating an atmosphere of tranquillity. Unusual plants include maples and dogwoods giving a good display of autumn colour.

House open. Teas.

**FIRLE PLACE**, Lewes, East Sussex (the Viscount Gage)
*Gardens 44 acres, park 171 acres*

During the Second World War, Firle Place was first a girls' school then a military headquarters. Apart from this short period it has been continuously occupied by the Gage family for five hundred years. Alterations to the gardens over the centuries have followed those to the house, the late eighteenth century seeing the construction of the thatched dairy and the incorporation of early fish ponds in the ornamental long pond. In the nineteenth century the formal Italianate terraces, balustrades, fountain and ha-ha were added to form the setting for typically Victorian bedding schemes. Like other gardens in this part of England, Firle suffered from the storm of 1987 which, besides destroying trees and shrubs, reduced the eighteenth-century ice-house to a ruin.

House open. Lunches, teas.

**GODINTON HOUSE**, Godinton Park, Ashford, Kent (Mr Alan Wyndham Green)
*Gardens 12 acres, park 250 acres*

The formal gardens were laid out by Sir Reginald Bloomfield in about 1900 in a style in keeping with the lovely Jacobean house. Completely enclosed by a huge yew hedge, gardens-within-the-garden are subdivided by smaller hedges and paths. Topiary, statuary and cypress trees provide ever-varying shapes and perspectives. The wild garden and shrubbery, almost totally destroyed in the 1987 storm, are being replanted in 1989.

House open.

**GOODNESTONE PARK**, Canterbury, Kent (the Lord and Lady FitzWalter)
*Gardens 7 acres, park 100 acres*

The fine trees in the park (those that still remain after the destruction of the 1987 storm) must have been newly planted when Jane Austen used to visit her sister-in-law's family (who were also the ancestors of the present owners) here. She would have been better able to

Goodnestone Park.

appreciate the three linked wall gardens, with their long vista to the church tower. Today the eighteenth-century walls shelter luxuriant groups of old-fashioned scented roses, clematis, lavender and many unusual herbaceous plants and flowering shrubs. The walled garden is a short walk away from the house, where terraces constructed in the late nineteenth century look out across the park. They have been planted with bold groups of shrub roses. There is also a woodland garden made by the wife of the 20th Lord FitzWalter in the 1920s. A change of soil here means that rhododendrons, camellias and magnolias flourish. Lady FitzWalter has added cornus, eucryphias, blue hydrangeas and the stunning blue Himalayan poppy.

Plant sales.

## GREAT DIXTER, Northiam, East Sussex (the Lloyd family)

This fine twentieth-century garden was planned by Lutyens when he restored the fifteenth-century manor house in 1910 for Nathaniel Lloyd who was himself an important figure in the history of British gardening. Lloyd was a protagonist in the topiary debate, being the author of *Garden Craftsmanship in Yew and Box* on which William Robinson poured

scorn. Ironically, Lloyd shared many of the principles expressed by Robinson in *The Wild Garden* and *The English Flower Garden*, as can be seen at Great Dixter. The topiary garden, sunken garden and other areas integrated by Lutyens' plan with the house and its farm buildings are linked by means of luxuriant but carefully planned planting to orchards, meadow, horsepond and the further landscape. Nathaniel Lloyd's son, Christopher Lloyd, author of gardening classics including *The Well-Tempered Garden* and *Foliage Plants* looks after the gardens and continues to enrich the planting.

House open. Guided tours by arrangement. Plant sales, specially clematis.

## HAMMERWOOD PARK, East Grinstead, West Sussex (Mr David Pinnegar)
*Gardens 8 acres, park 28 acres*

The challenge of fifty years of neglect followed by the devastation of the 1987 storm has been bravely met by the present owner. The house, one of only two Greek revival mansions in England by the architect B H Latrobe, has been restored from a virtual ruin and work has begun on a ten-year plan to restore the gardens and park with the help of various voluntary agencies. Latrobe's brother wrote of the parkland, 'Nature has done a good deal for him. He has low wood and high wood, hills, vales, runs of water, springs, etc, but a little assistance from art is wanting to render this as delicious a Spot as any in the Kingdom.' The eighteenth-century planting of the park with its lake and islands is being restored. There are also a fine rhododendron bank and formal terraces on the south front which date from the ownership between 1864 and 1902 by Oswald Augustus Smith, a relation of Augustus Smith who made the Tresco gardens in the Scilly Isles. Many of the remaining choice trees, shrubs and climbing plants date from this time.

House open. Lunches, teas. Guided tours.

**HEVER CASTLE**, Edenbridge, Kent
(Broadlands Properties Ltd)
*Gardens 30 acres*

The gardens of the moated castle which was
the childhood home of Anne Boleyn owe
their existence to the wealth, energy and
vision of one man. William Waldorf Astor,
an American in love with English history,
bought Hever Castle in 1903. During the next
four years over one thousand men were
employed to create thirty acres of gardens and
landscape, and a thirty-five acre lake. The
castle's Tudor history is celebrated in Anne
Boleyn's orchard, Anne Boleyn's walk (beneath oaks, beeches, limes, maples and cedars),
Anne Boleyn's garden planted with English
herbs, the clipped yew maze and the Chess
garden with its topiary pieces in golden
yew. Elsewhere the remarkable Italian garden,

Hever Castle: pool and Grand Loggia.

made to display classical antiquities collected
by Mr Astor when he was American Minister
in Rome, leads via the Pompeiian wall to the
Grand Loggia looking out over the lake. The
rhododendron walk and spring garden are
followed in flower by the rose garden and the
blue garden.

Lunches, teas. Guided tours. Plant sales.


**THE HIGH BEECHES**, Handcross, West
Sussex (The High Beeches Gardens
Conservation Trust)
*Gardens 33 acres*

Designated by English Heritage as 'outstanding historically', The High Beeches was the

home of that distinguished gardening family, the Loders. Col G H Loder began planting in the oak woodland in 1903, following the principles of William Robinson, the influential author of *The Wild Garden*. Full of rare and beautiful examples of plants suited to the acid soil, particularly rhododendrons, the woodland is watered by natural streams and punctuated by ponds and open glades. The rare trees and shrubs include the national collection of stewartias and many other treasures. There are naturalized primulas, irises and *Peltiphyllum peltatum* following the water courses, meadow plants in long grass and velvety mosses in deep shade. Queen Mary loved this garden and was a frequent visitor. The 1987 storm took a terrible toll, but clearance of fallen trees and shrubs was completed within fifteen months, and replanting is under way. It will continue to be a fine example of early twentieth century naturalistic woodland gardening, a style that was revolutionary in its day, and has had a widespread influence since.

**LEEDS CASTLE**, Maidstone, Kent (Leeds Castle Foundation)
*Gardens 16 acres, park 520 acres*

This most romantic of castles, dating from the ninth century, floats timelessly on its broad mirror of water surrounded by wooded parkland. Russell Page directed improvements to the gardens for Lady Baillie and after her death in 1974 for the Leeds Castle Foundation. He made the Culpeper garden, a walled enclosure of traditional English garden flowers overlooking the great water. This lake formed part of the castle's medieval defences and could be emptied by a sluice to leave a water meadow in times of peace. The recently completed maze and grotto by the architect Vernon Gibberd, the sculptor Simon Verity and designer Diana Reynell is a remarkable example of twentieth-century patronage following a time-honoured tradition. There is also a vineyard, duckery and aviary of jewel-bright exotic birds. The national collections of monarda and nepeta are here.

House open. Lunches, teas. Guided tours. Plant sales.

**LOSELEY PARK**, Guildford, Surrey (Mr James More-Molyneux)
*Gardens 5 acres, park 500 acres*

The same family have lived at Loseley since the house was built in the 1560s, and almost every generation has contributed to the gardens. The moat, an ancient mulberry tree, hedges of yew and box and the walled garden with its three bothies all pre-date the lawns which sweep up to the house linking it to the landscape of the park. Later, Gertrude Jekyll prepared a planting plan for the moat border. Queen Elizabeth I stayed at Loseley three times, James I twice. Today a thriving organic farm helps to support the house and gardens, and Loseley ice cream, yoghurt, cream and vegetables can be bought in the farm shop or sampled in the restaurant in the seventeenth-century tithe barn.

House open. Lunches, teas. Plant sales.

Leeds Castle.

**MICHELHAM PRIORY**, Upper Dicker, Hailsham, East Sussex (Sussex Archaeological Society)
*Gardens 25 acres*

The moated gardens which link the thirteenth-century Augustinian priory to its fourteenth-century gatehouse and sixteenth-century great barn are completely enclosed within the moat which is itself bounded on three sides by the Cuckmere River. During the past ten years the gardens have been extensively planted with a large collection of native trees and many exotic specimens. A large herbaceous border and a border of old roses provide a background of soft colour to the fine stone buildings. Much of the planting is planned to encourage wildlife, and the moat is well stocked with coarse fish. A well-researched physic garden designed by Mrs V Hinze has been set out on a site which the old monastic garden may well have occupied. The plants are grouped according to their uses: herbs for bites, stings, burns and poisons; herbs for the heart, lungs and blood; herbs for depression, insomnia and nightmares; herbs for the head, hair and skin; and so forth.

House open. Lunches, teas. Plant sales.

**MOUNT EPHRAIM**, Hernhill, Faversham, Kent (Mrs M N Dawes)
*Gardens 5 acres, park 5 acres*

The Edwardian layout of 1912 was restored in the 1950s after a period of dereliction. The outstanding feature is the large Japanese rock garden set on a hillside with a series of pools descending to the lake below, stone lanterns and a Japanese stone bridge. Stone balustrading, terraces with a 1986 planting of roses designed by Mary Readman, a topiary garden, orchard walk and herbaceous borders add colour and form elsewhere. Spacious lawns with mature cedars, chestnuts, oaks, purple beech and a sweet chestnut planted to commemorate the Battle of Waterloo, add to the atmosphere of tranquillity.

Teas. Guided tours. Craft centre. Vineyard.

Mount Ephraim: Japanese bridge.

## NEWICK PARK, Newick, East Sussex
(Viscount Brentford)
*Gardens 13 acres, park 200 acres*

Restored by Sir William Joynson-Hicks in the 1920s, the gardens are a fine example of the Victorian picturesque style, with early rock-work on the site of Elizabethan iron-workings, a collection of ferns (some over a hundred years old) and paths winding through the dell and well walk where many of the rare trees and shrubs, specially rhodo-dendrons, were collected by R L Sclater in China. Spring bulbs are followed by flower-ing trees and shrubs, meadow and herbaceous plants, and a good display of autumn colour. Newick Park houses the national collection of candelabra and sikkimensis primulas. There is also a nursery specializing in herbs, cottage garden plants and old roses.

Lunches, teas. Guided tours.

## THE OWL HOUSE GARDENS,
Lamberhurst, Tunbridge Wells, Kent
(Maureen, Marchioness of Dufferin and Ava)
*Gardens 13 acres*

The Owl House has one of those fortunate gardens where both rhododendrons and roses thrive. Lady Dufferin started the garden from virtually nothing in 1952, taking full advant-age of the oak and chestnut woodland slop-ing down to two pools which are probably ancient hammer ponds from which iron was extracted for the local smelting works. The shelter of the woods planted with rare rhodo-dendrons, azaleas and other flowering shrubs, the waterside planting and the sound of bird-song produce an atmosphere of great tran-quillity. Near the fifteenth-century house are informal beds planted for colour and scent, and a meadow where wild orchids flower between tripods supporting climbing roses. A ride cut through a level area of woodland ends in a classical stone temple smothered in wistaria.

**Owl House gardens.**

**PARHAM HOUSE**, Pulborough,
West Sussex (the Trustees of the Parham
Estate)
*Gardens 11 acres*

One of the properties that passed into private
hands as the gift of Henry VIII on his
Dissolution of the Monasteries, the house
was built in 1577, incorporating the smaller
manor house. The fish pond and deer park
are reminders of pre-Tudor origins, but the
pleasure grounds were laid out in the late
eighteenth century by the 12th Lord Zouche.
A broad gravelled path leads through tree-
studded lawns to the four-acre walled garden.
Entered by a wrought-iron gate flanked by a
pair of Istrian stone lions, the walled garden is
divided by broad walks. Planting includes a
blue, gold and white border, two new rose
beds, herbaceous borders and shrubs chosen
for autumn and winter colour as well as for
their flowers. A new arboretum is being
planted alongside the two-and-a-half acre
lake, replacing trees lost in the 1987 storm
and supplementing existing mature trees including holm oak, cut-leaved beech and catalpa,
which are underplanted with massed snowdrops, crocuses and narcissi in many varieties.

House open. Teas. Plant sales.

**PENSHURST PLACE**, Tonbridge, Kent
(Viscount De L'Isle)
*Gardens 13 acres, park 40 acres*

Lord De L'Isle's ancestor, Sir Henry Sidney,
levelled the terraces at Penshurst early in the
reign of Queen Elizabeth I, supporting them
with retaining walls in order to make gardens
which would match the scale and splendour
of the enlarged and extended medieval house.
In the seventeenth-century a further six acres
at a lower level was walled, and this layout,
so beautifully integrated with the house,
remains to this day. As in so many great
gardens, enforced neglect during the Second

Penshurst Place: the Italian garden.

World War was followed by a period of creative restoration. Today the gardens, formally divided as befits their Tudor origins, form a sequence of imaginatively planned 'rooms' each different in scale and conception, providing a succession of interest throughout the seasons, and immaculately maintained. Harsh colours are avoided, and contrasting areas are divided by yew hedges or pleached limes. Among the many delights are a hundred-yard (ninety-metre) border of *Paeonia albiflora*, a knot garden viewed from a mount planted with the prostrate rose 'Rosy Cushion', and, at the centre of a plantation of Kentish cob nuts, a green pavilion of *Vitis coignetiae* surrounded by a pergola supporting roses, clematis and honeysuckle.

House open. Lunches, teas.

## RIVERHILL HOUSE, Sevenoaks, Kent
(Mr John Rogers)
*Gardens 9 acres, park 38 acres*

The pleasure grounds and eighteenth-century wilderness are linked by an ancient track along which King Harold brought the Saxon army to fight at Hastings in 1066. But the importance of the garden dates from 1840 when John Rogers bought the house. A member of the Royal Society and friend of Charles Darwin, he also had connections with Robert Fortune, and several plants collected by Fortune in China came straight to Riverhill and are growing there still. The Italianate terraces were commissioned from John Nasmyth, and the original plans are preserved, as are all John Rogers's, planting records from 1840 to 1860. The 1987 storm was disastrous; three-quarters of the fine trees recorded by Alan Mitchell in a survey in 1986 were lost. But new planting is already under way, and a new shelter belt with a distinguished collection of trees has been planted with grant aid from the Countryside Commission. The new collection was inaugurated with two specimen trees planted by the Duke and Duchess of Kent. Rhododendrons,

azaleas and hydrangeas thrive in the woodland garden.

House open bank holiday weekends. Teas. Plant sales.

## SQUERRYES COURT, Westerham, Kent
(Mr and Mrs John Warde)
*Gardens 30 acres, park 200 acres*

The current restoration of the Anglo-Dutch gardens at Squerryes Court to the layout shown in a print of 1719 is an important event in garden history. The handsomely proportioned, mellow brick house is still in its original form, and the restoration of the parterres, basin and fountain, and the re-establishment of the wilderness will show the gardens as they may have appeared to King William III when he visited Squerryes in c1700. The gardens also include a cenotaph to General Wolfe who was a friend of the Warde family, and a unique seventeenth-century sundial on an eighteenth-century pedestal. Later phases in the history of the garden are represented in the park's eighteenth-century landscape and the Victorian shrubberies.

House open. Teas. Guided tours.

## STANSTED PARK, Rowlands Castle, Hampshire (the Stansted Park Foundation)
*Gardens 40 acres, park 1,635 acres*

The beech avenue at Stansted runs for almost two miles (three kilometres) through the ancient forest of Bere. This and other formal avenues through the park, which is of twelfth-century origin, were planted in the late seventeenth century. They provide an example of the beginnings of the landscape movement, when gardens were opened out to take in distant prospects. The avenues and subsequent landscaping carried out in the eighteenth century by the Earl of Scarbrough caught the attention of Horace Walpole. He wrote 'The very extensive lawns at that seat, richly inclosed by venerable beech woods, and chequered by single beeches of vast size, particularly when you ... survey the landscape that wastes itself in rivers of broken sea, recall exact pictures of Claud Lorrain.' The structure of the park was retained by Lewis Way who replanted it, including the beech avenue, between 1810 and 1830, and built the chapel using parts of older buildings dating back to the twelfth century. The early twentieth century arboretum has fine cedars, pines and tulip trees.

House open. Teas. Plant sales.

## SYON PARK, Brentford, Middlesex (His Grace the Duke of Northumberland)
*Gardens 55 acres, park 130 acres*

It is amazing to find a 'Capability' Brown landscape so close to the centre of London. The park looks towards Kew Gardens across the River Thames, on which a barge carried sad Lady Jane Grey from Syon to the Tower of London to become queen and, a few months later, to lose her head. The landscape was designed for the Earl of Northumberland who commissioned Robert Adam in 1748 to remodel the interior of the sixteenth-century mansion. The 'Great Conservatory' by Dr Charles Fowler was built between 1827 and 1830 and pre-dates Paxton's vast glass palace at Chatsworth which was demolished in 1920.

House open. Lunches, teas. Plant sales.

## WEST DEAN GARDENS, Chichester, West Sussex (the Trustees of the Edward James Foundation)
*Gardens 35 acres, park 200 acres, arboretum 30 acres*

Two main periods of development are represented in the gardens and park at West Dean. The first is shown by the survival of the layout and of many fine trees dating from 1804 when James Wyatt rebuilt the house for

West Dean Gardens: the Edwardian pergola.

the first Baron Selsey. The walled kitchen garden and the palm house were built, and most of the mature beech, limes, horse chestnuts, planes and cedars were planted at this time. Three cedars of Lebanon survive from an earlier planting in 1748. Planting of newly introduced trees and shrubs continued through the mid-nineteenth century, but the second great burst of creativity came when William James bought the estate in 1891. Alterations to and enlargement of the house were carried out by Ernest George and Harold Peto and the gardens as well as the house were extended and embellished to make a fit setting for the lavish country house entertaining of the Edwardian era. Trees planted by visiting royalty, the restored peach house and fig house in the kitchen garden, the three-hundred-foot (ninety-metre) colonnaded pergola, herbaceous borders and the wild garden on which Gertrude Jekyll advised, all recapture the leisurely, hedonistic spirit of this century's first decade.

Plant sales.

## BENINGTON LORDSHIP, Stevenage, Hertfordshire (Mr C H D Bott)
*Gardens 7 acres*

An Edwardian garden for a Georgian house built on the site of a Saxon palace and Norman castle of which the moat, outer bailey and ruined keep survive, Benington Lordship is a fine example of the continuity and adaptability of English domestic life, and has the timeless atmosphere and gentle colouring of an ideal country garden. Started in 1906 on a difficult site exposed to southwest winds with heavy clay soil, today the leisurely Edwardian style of the garden is somehow maintained with just two gardeners where once there were five. There is a rockery, a sunken rose garden, a yew-enclosed Shylock garden, and a productive and ornamental kitchen garden. Of special historic interest are the Norman fish ponds and the neo-Norman folly of about 1830 by Pulham.

Teas. Garden centre.

## BLENHEIM PALACE, Woodstock, Oxfordshire (His Grace the Duke of Marlborough)
*Gardens 90 acres, park 2,000 acres*

One of 'Capability' Brown's finest achievements was the creation, in the 1760s, of a landscape that forms a fit setting for the

Benington Lordship: the gatehouse with snowdrops and aconites.

*Above:*
**Blenheim Palace: the Italian gardens.**

*Below:*
**Broughton Castle.**

grandeur of Blenheim Palace. The Palace, designed by Sir John Vanbrugh, was built for the 1st Duke of Marlborough in recognition of his great victory at the Battle of Blenheim in 1704. Besides Brown's trees, lake and cascade, the elaborate water terraces and formal 'Italian' garden, designed for the 9th Duke by Achille Duchêne between 1910 and 1930, are equally appropriate manifestations of ducal splendour. In the eight-acre kitchen garden with its fourteen-foot (four-metre) walls built in 1705 a bell still hangs that used to summon a regiment of gardeners to their duties.

Palace open. Lunches, teas. Garden centre.

**BROUGHTON CASTLE**, Banbury, Oxfordshire (the Lord Saye and Sele)
*Gardens 2 acres, park 60 acres*

The gardens, partly walled, partly bounded

by the encircling moat, form an intimate foreground to the handsome Tudor mansion grafted on to a medieval manor house. With advice from Lanning Roper, a formal Victorian layout was simplified in 1970, and the planting today is of shrubs, roses and herbaceous perennials. The gatehouse was built by Sir Thomas Wykeham in 1405 and with the castle, the fourteenth-century church and the partly castellated wall which divides the courtyard from lawns running down to the moat, forms a united group of timeless stone buildings in a tranquil setting of mature trees.

House open. Teas. Plant sales.

### CHENIES MANOR, Nr Amersham, Buckinghamshire (Lieutenant-Colonel and Mrs MacLeod-Matthews)
*Gardens 2 acres*

In 1296 King Edward I brought a camel to Chenies; in 1534 King Henry VIII brought Anne Boleyn and the infant Elizabeth; eight years later Kathryn Howard committed adultery there. As Queen, Elizabeth I was a frequent visitor. The unavoidable sense of history in the unspoilt brick manor house where the 'new buildings' date from 1523 and

Chicheley Hall.

1526 is felt also in the gardens. 'Queen Elizabeth's Oak' is about a thousand years old, and a large weeping ash was planted in 1770. The present owners have, since the 1950s, restored the gardens in keeping with the medieval and Tudor history of the house, including a physic garden, topiary and a penitential maze of turf and gravel, the design taken from a painting of c1585 at Woburn Abbey, where the Earls of Bedford lived after they left Chenies. To the north of the house are an orchard and a Victorian kitchen garden.

Teas. Plant sales (culinary herbs).

### CHICHELEY HALL, Newport Pagnell, Buckinghamshire (Mrs John Nutting)
*Gardens 8 acres, park 16 acres*

The beautiful early Georgian house with its exceptionally fine brickwork and stone carving was built for Sir John Chester, Bt.

Chenies Manor.

Docwra's Manor.

The layout of a formal garden remains including a three-sided canal designed in 1700 by George London of the fashionable firm London and Wise, who worked at Hampton Court. There are fine specimen trees in the park to set off the lovely architecture. In 1952 the 2nd Earl Beatty, son of the great naval hero of the First World War, bought the house after a spell of military occupation and use as a school. Since his death his widow, now Mrs John Nutting, has continued to add to the gardens, most recently with a box and pleached lime walk.

House open. Lunches, teas. Guided tours.

## DOCWRA'S MANOR GARDEN,
Shepreth, Royston, Hertfordshire
(Mrs John Raven)
*Gardens 2½ acres, park 2 acres*

Although, since the Ravens bought it in 1954, the garden has evolved rather than being planned, the result is in the tradition of Vita Sackville-West and Lawrence Johnston: a series of gardens within gardens, the layout being dictated by the relationship of the early seventeenth-century house (the brick façade and iron gates were added in the eighteenth century) to the adjoining barns and former farmyard enclosures and by the positions of some fine trees. The overall effect is of cottage-garden profusion within a firm structure, but each area has its own character. The late John Raven was a distinguished botanist and Mrs Raven shared his enthusiasm for wild plants. Throughout the gardens there are rare and exciting plants with the emphasis on species rather than hybrids and on Mediterranean plants which like the dry and sheltered conditions. Treats for the dedicated plantsman to seek out include *Rosa moschata* 'Docwra's Seedling' and *Artemisia arborescens* 'Faith Raven'.

Guided tours. Plant sales.

## KINGSTON HOUSE, Kingston Bagpuize, Oxfordshire (the Lady Tweedsmuir)
*Gardens and ornamental woodland 20 acres, park 40 acres*

The gardens around the house are formal, as befit a house built in about 1670. The terraced lawns are bounded with shrub and herbaceous borders with a view to the park across a ha-ha kept open to the east. The northern boundary of the formal area is the Tudor terrace walk with a brick 'cockpit', all that remains of an earlier manor house. Over the cockpit there is an eighteenth-century brick gazebo. The woodland gardens beyond were planted by Lady Tweedsmuir's aunt, Miss Marlie Raphael between 1945 and 1975. A knowledgeable gardener, she was a friend of Mr Harold Hillier, the nurseryman, and together they chose many rare and interesting plants to make a richly planted garden of natural appearance and of interest at all seasons.

House open. Teas. Plant stall.

## KINGSTONE LISLE PARK, Wantage, Oxfordshire (Mrs Leopold Lonsdale)
*Gardens 10 acres*

The restoration and improvement of the gardens has been carried out over the past forty years to link the house to the fine surrounding landscape. There are ancient clipped yews, fine trees including a cut-leaf beech and a dawyck beech, flowering shrubs, particularly lilacs, philadelphus and roses, and acers and cercidiphyllums for autumn colour. An unusual row of pleached limes with undulating tops is copied from a le Nôtre garden in Belgium. The rose garden with its swagged chains is a smaller scale replica of Queen Mary's Rose Garden in Regent's Park, London.

House open. Plant sales.

## KNEBWORTH HOUSE, Stevenage, Hertfordshire (the Lord Cobbold)
*Gardens 20 acres, park 200 acres*

The gardens at Knebworth have evolved since 1490, changes being wrought, with the architecture of the house, by successive generations of the Lytton family. Sir Edwin Lutyens, who married Lady Emily Lytton in 1897, carried out simplifications to the elaborate Victorian gardens on the south-west front of the house, which had employed fourteen gardeners to set out 36,000 bedding plants each year. From the fantastical turretted and battlemented stucco façade of the house, which Mrs Bulwer-Lytton added to the remains of the Tudor house in 1811–1816, Lutyens' twin avenues of pollarded limes lead through the rose garden to two small gardens. The first is planted today with shrubs and roses following Gertrude Jekyll's recommendations for a golden garden, the second as a blue garden. Beyond, the wilderness, planted with over twenty-seven varieties of hawthorn in 1887 is undergoing restoration. A Lutyens-designed bothy in the walled kitchen garden is planted with *Clematis montana* and 'The Garland', one of Miss Jekyll's favourite roses. In 1980 a drawing by Miss Jekyll for a herb garden for Knebworth came to light, and this has now

been constructed, faithfully following her quincunx plan.

House open. Lunches, teas.

## LITTLECOTE HOUSE, Hungerford, Berkshire (Mr Peter de Savary)
*Gardens 9 acres, park 110 acres*

In 1985 the gardens of the Tudor manor house consisted of lawns, a long herbaceous border, yew hedges, espalier fruit trees and a *Davidia involucrata*. Since then designers Graham Burgess, Susan Muir and S Tett have been involved in an ambitious project to create extensive formal gardens in the Tudor style. The new gardens include a rose parterre planted in a flower pattern with four thousand bedding roses, five knot gardens, two three-hundred-foot (ninety-metre) herbaceous borders in the style of William Robinson, a potager, a medieval garden and an astrological herb garden set out in beds which represent eight themes: astrological, symbolic, bee, tisane, medicinal, cosmetic, dye and culinary

Knebworth House.

herbs. There is also a water garden and a woodland garden.

House open. Lunches, teas. Plant sales.

## LUTON HOO, Luton, Bedfordshire (the Wernher family)
*Gardens 30 acres, park and estate 4,500 acres*

In 1903 Sir Julius Wernher, having successfully pioneered the diamond-mining industry in South Africa, bought Luton Hoo to house his fabulous art collection. He made alterations to the house in the French style, both inside and out, and had two Italianate terraced gardens constructed to the design of Romaine Walker. The terraces still retain their layout with two large *Magnolia soulangeana* and herbaceous borders on the upper terrace and on the lower an elaborate pattern of box-edged rose beds and topiary. Beyond the formal area are four magnificent two-hundred-year old cedars of Lebanon and other fine specimen trees. The secluded rock garden with its two lily ponds was laid out by Sir Julius as a surprise gift to his wife. To the east of the house lies a 'Capability' Brown landscape in full maturity. Commissioned by an earlier owner, the 3rd Earl of Bute, the double lake, undulating grass slopes and wooded hillsides form an archetypal English scene.

House open. Lunches, teas. Guided tours by appointment.

**ROUSHAM PARK**, Steeple Aston, Oxfordshire (Mr C Cottrell-Dormer)
*Gardens 25 acres, park 50 acres*

The only garden designed by William Kent to have survived, Rousham is of the utmost significance in garden history. It was Kent who, as Horace Walpole wrote, 'leaped the fence, and saw that all nature was a garden'. Rousham itself was described by Walpole as 'the most engaging of Kent's works. It is Kentissimo'. He also described it as 'Daphne in little, the sweetest little groves, streams,

Luton Hoo: the rock garden.

glades, porticos, cascades and river imaginable; all the scenes are perfectly classical.' And so it remains today. Sir Charles Cottrell-Dormer, ancestor of the present owner, commissioned Kent's design in 1738, a time when the cross-fertilization of ideas between such men as Kent, Walpole and Alexander Pope

Stonor Park.

was leading up to the flowering of the English landscape movement. The 'natural' contrasts between woodland and open glade, the serpentine courses of paths and watercourses, the careful positioning of buildings and statuary, were all very new at the time, as was the carefully considered relationship of the garden landscape to the wider landscape beyond. The idea was to create an idyllic landscape, and that is what it is. Delightful walled gardens near the house predate Kent's landscape by one hundred years. The box-edged parterre below the round pigeon house is filled with roses.

House open.

**STONOR PARK**, Henley-on-Thames, Oxfordshire (Lord and Lady Camoys)
*Gardens 1 acre, park 230 acres*

The present house with its eighteenth-century front masks buildings going back to the twelfth century, and as long as there has been a building in this benign, south-facing fold of the Chilterns, Stonors have lived here, sometimes in difficult circumstances. Staunch Catholics, they were quietly tenacious of their religion, celebrating Mass in the thirteenth-century chapel without a break when it was dangerous to do so, and sheltering the martyr Edmund Campion. Today the house, the beech-wooded hills and the grazing deer in the park convey a feeling of peaceful permanence. The formal Tudor layout of parts of the garden is still evident, and at the rear of the house eighteenth-century Italianate terraces echo alterations to the interior of the house in the Gothic style.

House open. Teas, lunches by arrangement.

**WOBURN ABBEY**, Woburn, Bedfordshire (the Marquess of Tavistock)
*Gardens and pleasure grounds 43 acres, park and woodland 3,000 acres*

Humphry Repton wrote 'The Improvements I have had the honour to suggest have nowhere been so fully realised as at Woburn Abbey'. He worked there from 1804 until 1810 and illustrated his proposals in the most splendid of his Red Books. Repton's landscape for the magnificent house which was rebuilt by Henry Flitcroft in the mid-eighteenth century is now at its full maturity. Repton altered the approach to the house, enlarged a stream to form a serpentine river and added extensively to the planting in the park. His proposals included 'a dressed flower garden', an American garden, a rustic retreat known as 'The Thornery', a greenhouse and a menagerie. Woburn houses the magnificent art collection of the Dukes of Bedford.

House open. Lunches, teas.

***Wessex*** Avon, Cornwall, Devon, Dorset, Hampshire, Somerset, Wiltshire, Isle of Wight

**ATHELHAMPTON**, Dorchester, Dorset (Lady Cooke)
*Gardens 10 acres, park 10 acres*

Francis Inigo Thomas laid out the Italianate terraced gardens in 1880 to complement the gabled and battlemented fifteenth-century architecture of the stone house. They are a fine example of his work. Four courts lead from the corona, its curved walls punctuated with obelisks in golden Ham stone against a background of dark yew. A central fountain falls into a round pool. The theme of formal water is repeated in the private garden, the Lion's Mouth, and on the sunken lawn with its tranquil topiary below the great terrace, where the two tall garden houses represent joy and summer to the west and sorrow and winter to the east. In the 1970s Sir Robert and Lady Cooke added a canal and an octagonal pond surrounded by pleached limes in the cloister garden which links the white garden

Athelhampton: the Great Court.

to the kitchen garden with its apple and laburnum walk and old varieties of apple trees. Away from the formal gardens, riverside and woodland planting provide a happy contrast.

House open. Teas.

**BARFORD PARK**, Spaxton, Bridgwater, Somerset (Colonel M Stancomb)
*Gardens 5 acres, park 35 acres*

The landscape around this exceptionally pretty brick Queen Anne house was probably laid out in about 1800. The walled flower garden is unusual for the period in that, instead of being discreetly hidden from the house, it is in full view from the windows. Advantage has been taken of this by connecting it to the house with pleached hornbeam hedges to a

Barford Park.

design suggested by Dame Sylvia Crowe in 1957. Fine trees enhance the park and the archery glade, and form the framework of the water and woodland garden, which is planted in a natural style with primulas, gunnera, azaleas and rhododendrons. Candelabra primulas and lilies are particularly fine.

House open. Lunches and teas by appointment.

Barton Manor: the vineyard.

## BARTON MANOR, Whippingham,
East Cowes, Isle of Wight
(Mr and Mrs Anthony Goddard)
*Gardens 10 acres, park 10 acres*

Queen Victoria bought the house in 1845 as a kind of guest annexe to Osborne House and Prince Albert enthusiastically set about obliterating what remained of a house dating back to 'Domesday'. The house and the layout of the gardens are mostly his work, with alterations and additions carried out for Edward VII who kept Barton Manor when he gave Osborne to the nation. Today it is in private ownership and the gardens form a fine setting for the vineyard and winery which the Goddards opened in 1976. Although the hurricane of 1987 destroyed many fine trees, including one planted by Prince Albert on his twenty-seventh birthday, the woodland and water gardens have retained their mature character, and the terraces below the house are an interesting example of Victorian and Edwardian garden style. Unusual plants include a plantation of cork trees and national collections of kniphofias and watsonias.

Lunches, teas. Plant sales including vines, kniphofias, watsonias.

**Palace House, Beaulieu.**

**BEAULIEU ABBEY**, Southampton, Hampshire (Lord Montagu of Beaulieu)
*Gardens 20 acres, park 45 acres*

The gardens at Beaulieu are informally landscaped with trees, shrubs and views to the mill pond. Current projects include the completion of the 1st Lord Montagu's nineteenth-century plans for formal, yew-hedged flower-beds around the house and a walled kitchen garden, and the restoration of earlier features in the landscape. The cloister garth of the ruined Cistercian abbey founded by King John in 1204 is planted with herbs that would have been used by the monks for cooking and medicines.

House open. Lunches, teas. Motor museum.

**BICKLEIGH CASTLE**, Tiverton, Devon (Mr O N Boxall and Mrs F N Boxall)
*Gardens 2 acres, park 8 acres*

In a lovely position on the River Exe, backed by wooded slopes, the gardens are integrated with the fourteenth-century castle gatehouse and its ancillary buildings. The buildings are all of historic and architectural interest and include a barn with a thatched clock turret

**Bickleigh Castle: the moat.**

and a cob-walled, thatched chapel built between 1090 and 1110. Mentioned in the 'Domesday Book' as belonging to the Saxon, Alward, the castle was later the home of the Carew family. Sir George Carew was Vice-Admiral of the *Mary Rose*. The moat is planted with water-lilies and irises, and beyond the beautiful eighteenth-century Italian wrought-iron courtyard gates a large mound rises, planted in the 1930s with every known variety of rhododendron. There is a three-hundred-year-old wistaria and mature trees include two *Gingko biloba* magnolias, a Judas tree and a tulip tree.

House open. Teas.

**BOWOOD HOUSE**, Calne, Wiltshire (the Earl of Shelburne)
*Gardens and park 2,500 acres*

The impact of 'Capability' Brown's landscape, commissioned by the 1st Marquess of Lansdowne who was Prime Minister from 1782 to 1783, is undiminished by the demolition of 'The Big House' in 1955. The remaining double quadrangle, with Robert Adam's classical orangery (now the picture gallery) with its pedimented central portico spanning the south side, is imposing enough. The serpentine lake with its eye-catcher Doric temple on the far bank is one of Brown's finest water compositions and the shady cascade and hermit's cave designed by the Hon Charles Hamilton of Painshill add mystery and a touch of the sublime at the northern end of the lake. The pinetum, begun by the 3rd Marquess of Lansdowne in the 1820s, has many remarkable specimens, and there is an excellent collection of rhododendrons begun in 1854 and added to by every generation since. It is in a separate woodland garden open at the appropriate time of year. On the south front of the house broad, balustraded terraces were added in the Victorian period and are today planted with masses of roses, the parterre beds punctuated with tall clipped yews. The many distinguished visitors to

Bowood House.

Bowood have included Dr Johnson, Lord Macaulay, Maria Edgeworth, King Edward VII and Queen Mary.

House open. Lunches, teas. Guided tours. Garden centre.

**BREAMORE HOUSE**, Fordingbridge, Hampshire (Sir Westrow Hulse)
*Gardens 4 acres, park 12 acres*

The red brick of the handsome 1583 house is set off by green lawns on a raised terrace with a surround of fretted balustrading. The park, with its fine trees, was redesigned by Sir Charles Hulse in 1850. The splendid cedars of Lebanon are of an earlier date, having been planted by Lord Brooke in 1673; and some of the yews may date from the time that the house was built.

Teas.

Bowood House.

**BROADLEAS**, Devizes, Wiltshire (Lady Anne Cowdray and Broadleas Gardens Trust)
*Gardens 8 acres, park 30 acres*

Lady Anne Cowdray's search for a house with a promising garden ended in 1946 when she found Broadleas, a handsome, Regency stone house looking down on to a wilderness on the greensand escarpment. With her knowledge and love of rare and unusual plants she has transformed the jungle into one of the most successful of twentieth-century woodland gardens. The four-acre dell is thickly planted with magnolias, azaleas, rowans and hydrangeas, so that there is something for every season. They give shelter to many rarities. The dell comes as a delightful surprise as it is more or less hidden from the house, which looks across a broad lawn to the parkland landscape beyond. Adjacent to the

**Broadleas.**

house are a sunken rose garden, the roses underplanted with low-growing herbaceous plants; a border of grey-leaved plants; a rock garden; a winter garden carpeted with *Cyclamen coum* and snowdrops; an intimate secret garden for small treasures; and an eight-foot (2.5 metre) wall for tender plants which receive winter protection.

**BRYMPTON d'EVERCY,** Yeovil, Somerset (Mr and Mrs Charles Clive-Ponsonby-Fane). See page 61

**CLAPTON COURT,** Nr Crewkerne, Somerset (Captain Simon Loder)
*Gardens 10 acres*

The woodland and formal gardens on clay and greensand have been reclaimed from dereliction by the present owners since 1979. Captain Loder is a member of the distinguished horticultural dynasty responsible for the creation of Leonardslee, The High Beeches (see entry under **South East**), and The National Trust's Wakehurst Place. Around the house is a series of intimate formal enclosures, laid out in 1949 by the previous

owner, Louis Martineau. They include a rose garden recently redesigned with help from Penelope Hobhouse. The surrounding woodland glades, intersected by a stream and ponds, are full of rare trees, shrubs and waterside plants. The planting is skilfully planned for interest all the year round.

Lunches, teas. Plant centre specializing in rare plants from the gardens. Also fuchsias and pelargoniums.

**COMBE SYDENHAM HALL,**
Monksilver, Taunton, Somerset
(Mr W A C Theed)
*Gardens 2 acres, park 500 acres*

The scene of Sir Francis Drake's courtship of and marriage to Elizabeth Sydenham, the ravaged remains of the Combe Sydenham

**Clapton Court.**

estate are half-way through a comprehensive forty-year restoration plan. This includes the reinstatement of the gardens in the Elizabethan style. The herb garden and garden of old roses are already well established.

House open. Lunches, teas. Plant sales.

## CORSHAM COURT, Corsham, Wiltshire
(the Lord Methuen)
*Gardens 17 acres, park 350 acres*

'Capability' Brown designed not only the landscape but also parts of the house including the magnificent picture gallery, seventy-two feet by twenty-four feet (twenty-two metres by seven metres). However, the history of the manor of Corsham goes back much further, to Saxon times when it was the country Court of Ethelred the Unready, King of Wessex from 987 to 1017. The manor remained a royal possession until sold in 1777 to Mr Paul Methuen who had bought the house in 1745. Brown laid out the two-mile-long (three-kilometre) north walk with its find classical gateway, and replanted the north and south avenues, removing the east avenue to give a clear view of the new park. The thirteen-acre lake proposed by Brown was created by Repton forty years later. A walk through the pleasure gardens with their herbaceous borders, rose beds and ornamental trees leads to Brown's Gothic bath house. Remarkable trees include a *Platanus orientalis* with a canopy circumference of 240 yards (219 metres). Since 1983 Mr Simon Pryce has planned and planted a new arboretum for Lord Methuen.

House open.

## DEANS COURT, Wimborne, Dorset
(Sir Michael and Lady Hanham)
*Gardens 13 acres*

The monastic fish pond, probably of Saxon origin, is fed by the River Wim, and is stocked

Dean's Court.

with mirror carp. The Hanham family, who have lived here since 1548, altered the garden in the eighteenth century from its earlier formal layout, and some of the fine trees date from that time. Others, including a *Taxodium distychum* and a *Liriodendron tulipifera* are earlier, having been brought from Virginia in the seventeenth century. A rare serpentine wall shelters the fruit in the kitchen garden, where everything is organically grown, and where a seed sanctuary of rare old varieties of vegetable is held for the Henry Doubleday Research Association. In the herb garden almost a hundred culinary, medicinal, dye and fragrant plants are grown. The emphasis throughout the garden is on conservation of plants and wildlife.

Teas. Sales area for organically grown herbs and vegetables.

## EASTON GREY, Malmesbury, Wiltshire
(Mrs Diane P Saunders)
*Gardens 12 acres, park 200 acres*

Looking across water meadows to the River

Avon, and backed by fine trees, the Cotswold stone Queen Anne house is surrounded by a formal garden of roses, clematis, flowering shrubs and herbaceous plants. In the large walled garden is a traditional kitchen garden, a rose garden and greenhouses. The informally landscaped areas beyond are full of spring bulbs and fine trees, including an oak planted by King Edward VIII when Prince of Wales. Prime Minister Lord Asquith spent twelve summers at Easton Grey when his sister-in-law, Mrs Graham Smith, lived there.

House open. Lunches, teas.

## EDMONDSHAM HOUSE, Wimborne, Dorset (Mrs Julia Elizabeth Smith)
*Gardens 6 acres, park 30 acres*

Gardening here is carried out by organic methods appropriate to the Tudor and Georgian origins of house and gardens. Chalk cob walls with Victorian brick additions surround the two walled gardens, including a well-run kitchen garden with herbaceous borders. There is a Victorian stable block and dairy, and an unusual grass cockpit, possibly medieval. Spring bulbs are a speciality throughout the garden. Tutorials in organic gardening can be arranged.

Teas for parties booked in advance. Guided tours. Sales area for plants and organic composts.

## EXBURY GARDENS, Exbury, Southampton, Hampshire (Mr E L de Rothschild)
*Gardens 200 acres*

A woodland garden of international importance, Exbury was created in virgin New Forest oak woodland by Lionel de Rothschild, father of the present owner. From 1919 to

**Exbury Gardens: azaleas.**

1935, one hundred and fifty men worked on the project. A unique watering system was devised using twenty-two miles of piping. In the brief period between completion of the gardens and the outbreak of the Second World War, there was a permanent staff of seventy-five. Lionel de Rothschild was a patron of plant- hunting expeditions in the Himalayas, China, Burma and Japan. Rhododendrons and azaleas were his passion and he was an expert hybridizer, creating rhododendrons in new, pure colours that were hardy in the British climate, and the famous Exbury strain of deciduous azaleas. The inevitable war-time neglect took its toll, but Edmund de Rothschild has restored the gardens and carried on his father's work. The planting blends with the natural landscape in Robinsonian style, and there are many plants of interest in the water garden, the iris garden, the winter garden and the camellia walk. But Exbury is first and foremost a collection celebrating wild rhododendron and azalea species alongside the extraordinary variety of hybrids bred from them in this ancient Hampshire forest with its views to the Beaulieu River.

Lunches, teas. Guided tours. Plant sales.

### FORDE ABBEY, Chard, Somerset (Mr and Mrs Mark Roper)
*Gardens 30 acres, park 50 acres*

The golden stone buildings date back to the Cistercian foundation in 1140 with significant additions in the 1520s by Abbot Chard and 1650s when Edmund Prideaux converted the abbey into a private house. His son-in-law Sir Francis Gwyn landscaped the gardens in about 1700, building walls and re-shaping the monks' ponds, linking them with three cascades. Using the framework of the ponds, some fine trees and the natural landscape, the Roper family have, since the beginning of this century, developed the richly varied gardens of today, making use of sheltered walls to grow *Carpenteria, Feijoa, Azara* and other slightly tender plants. The bog garden, rock

Forde Abbey.

garden and arboretum are well stocked with unusual plants.

House open. Lunches, teas. Guided tours on request. Plant centre selling unusual shrubs, etc.

### GAULDEN MANOR, Tolland, Taunton, Somerset (Mr and Mrs J le G Starkie)
*Gardens 3 acres*

The gardens have been developed by the present owners who found a wilderness when they came in 1967. They made a series of small gardens in keeping with the Tudor house which has fine plasterwork dating from the ownership of the Turberville family, whom Thomas Hardy chose to describe as the aristocratic ancestors of Tess in his novel. Parts of the house and the monks' stew pond in the garden show the medieval, monastic origins of the manor. The gardens include the bishop's garden, named for James Turberville, Bishop of Exeter until he refused the Oath of Supremacy to Queen Elizabeth on her accession, a herb garden, secret garden and butterfly garden. Planting includes old roses

Gaulden Manor: the fish pond.

and primulas and other moisture-loving plants in the bog garden.

House open. Teas. Herbs and bog plants for sale.

**HEALE HOUSE**, Woodford, Salisbury, Wiltshire (Major David and Lady Anne Rasch). See page 26

**HOUGHTON LODGE,** Stockbridge, Hampshire (Captain M W Busk)
*Gardens 7 acres, park 6 acres*

The gardens of this delicious Regency Gothic *cottage ornée* are little changed since the house was advertised for sale in *The Times* in 1801 as equipped with a 'handsome approach to the house; terrace, pleasure grounds, kitchen garden'. The house sits comfortably in the pastoral Hampshire landscape, its lawns commanding lovely views over the Test valley. The kitchen garden is surrounded by a fine chalk cob wall, and the beautiful pleasure grounds lead by a serpentine walk through the shrubbery to the grotto. Views of

Houghton Lodge.

the house and from it illustrate the early nineteenth-century 'picturesque' ideal. New planting to repair the damage of the 1987 storm is being researched and planned by David Jacques. Future plans include a greenhouse to demonstrate the hydroponic method of gardening.

Lunches and teas by appointment. Guided tours. Plant sales (fuchsias).

**IFORD MANOR**, Bradford-on-Avon, Wiltshire (Mrs Cartwright-Hignett)
*Gardens 3 acres, pleasure grounds 15 acres*

Harold Peto, the distinguished architect and landscape designer, lived here from 1899 until his death in 1933, and made the gardens, terracing the steep hillside with stone walls. A lover of Italian classical and Renaissance architecture, he built a colonnade, a loggia, an open-fronted casita, an octagonal summerhouse, and cloisters to house his collection of Roman statuary. Skilful planting in the Robinsonian style settles the Italian fantasy happily into the West Country landscape. Peto made his eight gardeners wear bright red

jerseys so that he could keep an eye on them from the house. The present owners are restoring the Japanese garden and future plans include a grotto and the clearing and embellishment of the eighteenth-century woodland walks.

Teas on Sundays. Guided tours.

**LONGLEAT HOUSE**, Warminster, Wiltshire (the Marquess of Bath)
*Gardens 10 acres, arboretum 60 acres, park 900 acres*

The most talented designers of several generations have contributed to Longleat: 'Capability' Brown completely remade the landscape around the magnificent sixteenth-century house, and introduced the chain of lakes below it. Brown's view from Heaven's Gate to the house in its green valley surrounded by wooded hills is one of the glories of English landscape. Repton, whose Red Book is in the library at Longleat, enlarged the lakes and introduced an island. In this

**Longleat House: the Orangery.**

century Russell Page did much to beautify the woodland plantings, removing many conifers alien to Brown's landscape. He planted an avenue of tulip trees and modified and improved the Victorian formal flower gardens around the house.

House open. Lunches, teas. Guided tours by appointment. Garden shop.

## LUCKINGTON COURT, Chippenham, Wiltshire (the Hon Mrs Trevor Horn)
*Gardens 2 acres*

The formal gardens integrate the Queen Anne Cotswold stone house with a beautiful group of ancient buildings, said to have been the property of King Harold. Two fine cedars of Lebanon dominate the gardens which include a good collection of flowering cherries, *Malus* varieties and other flowering shrubs.

## MAPPERTON HOUSE, Beaminster, Dorset (Mr John Montagu)
*Gardens 12 acres*

Listed as Grade II* by English Heritage, the garden has two stone fish ponds and a summer-house which date from the time of Charles II, when the fine Tudor manor house and its terraced garden were enlarged. The Italianate sunken garden with its topiary, carved animals, fountains and formal beds dates from the 1920s, as does the woodland and wild garden planting which links the formal gardens to the landscape beyond. The terraces fall steeply into a lovely sheltered valley surrounded by the beautiful and ancient wooded hills of west Dorset. There are rare and unusual trees and shrubs and in springtime masses of bulbs.

**Mapperton House. (Photograph by Marcus Harrison.)**

## MINTERNE GARDENS, Mintern Magna, Dorchester, Dorset (the Lord Digby)
*Gardens 29 acres, park 400 acres*

Like other fine gardens, that of Minterne began with the planting of essential shelter belts. Admiral Robert Digby acquired the estate from the Churchill family in 1768 and planted the ridges around the house with beech, Scots pines and cedars of Lebanon, setting the framework for a fine later collection of rhododendrons and other trees and shrubs. The water garden was also the admiral's work. A series of cascades descends to the lake below the house with its elegant balustraded bridge, and prospects across the water show the influence of 'Capability' Brown who worked at Sherborne Castle for the admiral's father. Two steeply banked valleys are the home of rhododendrons, magnolias, davidias, acers, and Chusan palms, underplanted with spring bulbs. Beside the water astilbes, rodgersias, gunnera and hemerocallis grow. Five generations of Digbys have contributed to the planting, introducing new trees and shrubs from the expeditions of Wilson, Forrest, Kingdon-Ward and Joseph Rock. The result of this continuity of interest is a garden that appears to have evolved naturally in its corner of the Dorset landscape.

## NUNWELL HOUSE, Brading, Isle of Wight (Colonel and Mrs J A Aylmer)
*Gardens 6 acres*

An ancient mulberry tree still stands at Nunwell, planted by Sir John Oglander who first laid out the gardens in the early seventeenth century. The gardens, always focused upon fine views to the Solent, have evolved through centuries of ownership by the Oglander family. The walled garden dates from the eighteenth century or earlier; the formal garden with its 160-foot (fifty-metre) terrace, pool and fountain was laid out in the nineteenth and early twentieth century, and in 1963 Vernon Russell Smith laid out an arboretum to the west of the house. Since

**Nunwell House: lavender steps.**

1982 the present owners have restored and improved the planting after a period of neglect.

House open. Lunches, teas. Guided tours by arrangement.

## PARNHAM, Beaminster, Dorset (Mr and Mrs John Makepeace)
*Gardens 12 acres, woodland 1½ acres*

The gardens were laid out in 1910, when Hans Sauer restored the interior of the house, which had been 'Gothicized' by John Nash, to the Tudor style of the original building. Sauer's fine balustrading and gazebos, and the series of terraces with their immaculate yew topiary, rills and cascades also pay tribute to his love of France. His work was rescued and restored by the furniture designer/maker John Makepiece and his wife Jennie, who is responsible for most of the planting. The strong architecture of the forecourt is softened by 'Albertine' roses climbing tall stone pillars, and hybrid musk and climbing roses in the borders. The Dutch garden is planted with silver, white and variegated plants; peacocks strut on the flag stones of the iris garden, and there are colourful herbaceous borders in the Italian garden. Beyond the formal gardens is a woodland area with fine trees and shrubs including palms and bamboos. Hidden in the wood are larger-than-life figures of Morecambe and Wise.

Lunches, teas. Guided tours.

## PENCARROW HOUSE, Bodmin, Cornwall (the Molesworth-St Aubyn family)
*Formal and woodland gardens 35 acres, park 35 acres*

Pencarrow's woodland garden is listed Grade II for its fine collections of specimen conifers, rhododendrons and camellias. It was begun in about 1830 by Sir William Molesworth, the radical Victorian politician, who also laid out the formal Italian garden (now much simplified) in front of the Georgian house, and made the massive granite rockery. Sir William was Secretary of State for the Colonies with a particular interest in Australia and New Zealand, a Governor of Kew Gardens and a sponsor of plant collecting expeditions. By 1851 he was able to write 'I have planted in my gardens specimens of all the conifers currently known to man considered possibly capable of surviving in this climate, except

Pencarrow House: Celtic cross.

for ten.' The benign Cornish climate must have been a great asset. Many of the conifers are planted along the mile-long drive which passes an ancient British camp, with rhododendrons and camellias. Others are in the American gardens beyond the lake. Sir William's descendants have replaced occasional casualties and extended the collection. Recently over 550 different rhododendron species and hybrids have been planted.

House open. Lunches, teas. Plant sales include rare conifers, rhododendrons, camellias, geraniums, pelargoniums and fuchsias.

## POWDERHAM CASTLE, Kenton, Exeter, Devon (Lord and Lady Courtenay)
*Gardens 8 acres*

The formal terraced gardens date from the 1840s with the most recent alterations to the castle, which was first built for Sir Philip Courtenay in about 1390. The elaborate Victorian beds have been simplified to a rectangular layout of lawns and borders, punctuated by an urn, sundial and yew topiary dolphins. The rose garden is laid out to a formal pattern. Woodland established in the eighteenth century forms the background to the castle, and from the terraces there are fine views to the east. To the west and south an informal landscape of trees and shrubs sets off the lake. An extensive planting programme is continuing, with the emphasis on scented roses, both old and modern.

House open. Teas. Plant sales, specializing in lavender.

## PRIDEAUX PLACE, Padstow, Cornwall (Mr Peter Prideaux-Brune)
*Gardens 11.5 acres, park 11.5 acres*

Edmund Prideaux laid out the gardens in the eighteenth century, the style influenced, as were his alterations to the Elizabethan manor, by his travels in Italy on the Grand Tour. His

Prideaux Place.

drawings show a formal garden with hedged walks, and a sunken flower garden, which is being restored. The present owner's great-grandfather used to take his guests to see the sunken garden's elaborate planting on the way to church on Sundays. The gardeners

Rotherfield Park. (Photograph by George Wright.)

were hiding behind hedges, and after church the returning party would find the garden completely replanted. Edmund Prideaux also built a classical temple, a grotto and a stone arbour to display his collection of Roman antiquities. His son Humphrey landscaped the grounds and made a walk to a high point with fine views across the Camel estuary. There is a ninth-century Celtic cross in the garden.

Teas. Plant sales.

**ROTHERFIELD PARK** Alton, Hampshire (Lieutenant-Colonel Sir James Scott)
*Gardens 10 acres, park 200 acres*

The garden is on a hill above the golden stone house with its romantic Victorian towers, turrets and colonnade under which visitors may have tea. There is a tranquil rose garden planted in the style of Gertrude Jekyll and a walk between yew hedges with contrasting buttresses of golden yew leading through iron gates to the walled garden. Here there are herbaceous borders, espalier fruit trees, fan-trained apples on the walls and, in the greenhouse, fan-trained apricots. Beyond the gardens a lime avenue and avenues radiating through woodland from *rond points* of beech and yew remain from an early eighteenth-century planting, and picturesque glades and parkland trees date from the early nineteenth century. Among the trees which were damaged but survived the 1987 hurricane are very old sweet chestnuts (*Castanea sativa*), and a fine old oak.

House open. Teas.

## SHELDON MANOR, Chippenham, Wiltshire (Major Martin Gibbs)
*Gardens 12 acres, woodland 6½ acres*

The manor dates from 1282 and, with its chapel, raised apple house and other handsome outbuildings, is the survivor of a vanished medieval village. Its timeless atmosphere is also felt in the gardens, although most of the planting dates from 1952 when the Gibbs family returned to find it a bramble-ridden wilderness. It is a classic example of romantically luxuriant planting within a strong framework of linked rectangular enclosures. The garden owes much of its beauty to the colour and scent of old-fashioned roses. They clothe the buttressed walls, ramble with clematis through ancient orchard trees and thrive in areas of rough grass. Rarities among them include 'Cooper's Burmese Rose', 'Comtesse du Cayla', 'Louis XIV', *R. Anemonoides* 'Ramona', 'La Mortola' and the unidentified rambling apricot-coral Sheldon Rose. Besides the roses there are many rare and interesting trees and shrubs, including cockspur thorns, a dozen sorbus varieties, a fine white Judas tree and three very ancient hollow yew trees within which Muscovy ducks nest.

House open. Lunches, teas. Guided tours.

Sheldon Manor.

Sherborne Castle.

## SHERBORNE CASTLE, Sherborne, Dorset (Mr Simon Wingfield Digby)
*Gardens 30 acres*

Landscaped by 'Capability' Brown between 1756 and 1777, the grounds of Sherborne Castle vindicate his theory that fine architec-

Smedmore House.

ture is best set off by uninterrupted lawns sweeping up to the walls and windows of the house. Framed by mature trees including a fine *Gingko biloba*, the lawns slope down to the fifty-acre lake, and from the opposite bank the ruins of a twelfth-century castle look back towards the turretted 'new' castle, the work of Sir Walter Raleigh and later the Digby family. 'Raleigh's Seat' commands a view of both castles. On a terrace in the garden 'Pope's Seat' recalls the poet's interest in Sherborne and its landscape.

House open. Lunches, teas.

## SMEDMORE HOUSE, Kimmeridge, Wareham, Dorset (Mr Philip Mansel)
*Gardens 1.5 acres*

In 1620 'A Survey of Dorset' recorded 'Smedmore, where Sir William Clavile des-cended of antient Gentrie, built a little newe house and beautified it with pleasant gardens'. His descendants live there today, and the layout of the gardens is little changed. Dramatic views of the coast contrast with intimate walled gardens, which shelter unusual climbing plants including *Clianthus puniceus* and a white wistaria. *Buddleia × Weyeriana* was bred here in 1914 by Major William van der Weyer who also planted many of the hydrangeas which, with fuchsias and tender shrubs and climbers, are a speciality. The herbaceous border was laid out by the historian Sir Arthur Bryant who leased the house in the 1950s. An usual feature is a tiger's grave and headstone dated 1885.

House open. Plants sold from the nursery in the largest of the walled gardens.

**STANWAY HOUSE**, Stanway, Cheltenham, Gloucestershire (the Lord Neidpath)
*Gardens 4 acres, park 100 acres*

The history of the gardens of this handsome and romantic Jacobean squire's house built of golden stone is well documented. A Kip drawing of 1713 shows a walled parterred garden to the south of the house, of which one wall still remains, pierced by six 'spectacles' which enable those in the garden to see out without being seen. A delightful painting by William Taylor in 1848 shows the formal canal and cascade which were probably constructed in about 1720 and, alas, filled in during the 1840s. Traces of the layout remain, and the stone pyramid built at the head of the cascade in 1750 by 'Robert Tracy, Gentleman' (a translation of the Latin inscription) as a memorial to his father 'John Tracy, Gentleman' is intact. Other elements of the baroque landscape garden which have survived are the avenues of oak and chestnut, and a former elm

avenue now replanted with lime. Above the canal site a circular box hedge encloses a dog graveyard dating from about 1900. It is hoped to restore the water garden and parterre.

House open.

**WILTON HOUSE**, Wilton, Salisbury, Wiltshire (the Trustees of the Wilton House Trust)
*Gardens 35 acres, park 250 acres*

Henry, 9th Earl of Pembroke, created the classical landscape at Wilton to replace an elaborate formal garden. A friend of Lord Burlington and William Kent, in 1737 he designed, with Roger Morris, the irresistibly beautiful Palladian bridge which spans the River Nadder. The classical stone pavilion on the hill across the river was designed by Sir William Chambers. The simple landscape of river and fine trees includes cedars of Lebanon which date from 1636. The fountain in the forecourt commemorates the life of the 16th

Wilton House: the forecourt gardens.

Earl, and the garden around it, designed by David Vicary, was laid out in 1971 by the 17th Earl who lives at Wilton with his family. The fountain is bordered with flowering shrubs and surrounded by pleached limes.

House open. Lunches, teas. Plant sales.

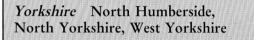

*Yorkshire* North Humberside,
North Yorkshire, West Yorkshire

### BRAMHAM PARK, Wetherby, West Yorkshire (Mr George Lane Fox)
*Gardens and pleasure grounds 166 acres, park 600 acres*

The gardens and pleasure grounds are a unique example of the early eighteenth-century style of le Nôtre's Versailles. Laid out when the Palladian house was built for Robert Benson, 1st Lord Bingley, long, broad, tree-lined vistas radiate through the woodland, terminating with classical buildings: a temple by James Paine later consecrated as a chapel, a large stone urn, an octagonal Gothic temple, an obelisk and three more temples. Broad stretches of formal water reflect trees and sky, and a current project is the completion of cascades designed for Robert Benson by John Wood of Bath but never carried out.

House open.

Bramham Park: the rose garden.

Burton Constable Hall.

### BURTON CONSTABLE HALL,
Sproatley, Hull, Humberside
(Mr J R Chichester-Constable)
*Gardens 4 acres, park 10 acres*

'Capability' Brown's landscape, carried out in the 1770s, can be compared with his plans which are displayed in the fine red-brick Elizabethan house. There are twenty acres of lakes and a handsome, arched and balustraded stone bridge. Recently new clumps of trees have been planted to replace the originals, which are reaching the end of their life. The design of the gardens around the house is simple, to set off the architecture of the house and the eighteenth-century orangery by Thomas Atkinson of York. There are lawns, ancient yew trees, crumbling statuary, spring bulbs and herbaceous borders in summer.

House open. Lunches, teas.

### CASTLE HOWARD, York (the Hon Simon Howard)
*Gardens 250 acres, park 10,000 acres*

An early and sublime example of the idealized landscape of the eighteenth century, the grounds were planned by Vanbrugh as a fit setting for the magnificent house that he designed for Charles Howard, 3rd Earl of Carlisle, and laid out between 1700 and 1750. The architecture of the house, of Vanbrugh's

**Castle Howard.**

Temple of the Four Winds and of Hawksmoor's Mausoleum is in mutual harmony with woods, water and open space. The 7th Earl commissioned William Nesfield to add the cascade, basin and waterfall to the south lake. From 1975 onwards a fine collection of ornamental trees and shrubs, especially rhododendrons (over seven hundred varieties) has been made in Ray Wood. The eleven-acre walled garden is subdivided to form a series of rose gardens, with one of the most distinguished and best displayed collections of old roses in Britain.

House open. Lunches, teas. Guided tours by appointment. Garden centre.

**CONSTABLE BURTON HALL**, Leyburn, North Yorkshire (Mr M C A Wyvill)
*Gardens 7 acres, park 40 acres*

The garden is laid out to complement the fine Palladian house designed by John Carr and started in 1768. The house is set in an eighteenth-century landscaped park with fine trees, two lime avenues and a Georgian bridge. A ha-ha and ice-house remain from this period. There are herbaceous borders, a water garden and rock garden and pleasant walks through informal shrubberies.

**HAREWOOD HOUSE**, Harewood, Leeds, West Yorkshire (the Earl of Harewood)
*Gardens 30 acres, park 60 acres*

The imposing terrace with its statuary and fountains was designed by Sir Charles Barry when he altered the house for the 3rd Earl in the 1840s. The box parterre on the terrace has been replanted to its original design and the custom of summer bedding to patterns which vary year to year, has been revived. The terrace is backed by 150 yards (137 metres) of herbaceous border, planned to provide colour from June until autumn. Barry's terrace looks out over 'Capability' Brown's landscape: one of his finest, with views across the lake to undulating parkland. An informal sunken woodland garden comes as a surprise at one end of the lake, where a bridge above a cascade gives a view to a rocky dell of rhododendrons, waterside plants and an oriental pavilion. On the far side of the lake there are two rose gardens.

House open. Lunches, teas. Guided tours. Plant sales.

**NEWBY HALL**, Skelton-on-Ure, Ripon, North Yorkshire (Mr Robin Compton). See page 39

**NORTON CONYERS**, Ripon, North Yorkshire (Sir James Graham)
*Gardens 2 acres, park 120 acres*

Charles I, one of several royal visitors to the Graham family at Norton Conyers, played on the bowling green which still survives. The Jacobean front of the house, with its

**Norton Conyers: the orangery (1774).**

curly gables, conceals an earlier building. In the seventeenth century Graham cousins owned Levens Hall and Nunnington, where James II's French gardener, M Beaumont, laid out formal gardens. There is no record of Beaumont ever visiting Norton Conyers, but his influence may have percolated there, and the fine lead urns and statues attributed to Van Nost may have come from Nunnington. The two-acre walled garden is entered through a beautiful wrought-iron gate, and has as its centre-piece a handsome orangery built in 1774, when Sir Bellingham Graham made alterations to the house and laid out the park with its fashionable serpentine approach to the house. The walled garden is planted with old-fashioned and unusual hardy plants, and there is a bed of eighteenth-century plants.

House open. Teas for booked groups. Guided tours for booked groups. Nursery selling hardy plants.

**RIPLEY CASTLE**, Nr Harrogate, North Yorkshire. (Sir Thomas Ingilby)
*Gardens and pleasure grounds 12 acres, park 150 acres*

Home of the Ingilbys for over 660 years, the castle's gardens, pleasure grounds and park bear witness to the extravagant enthusiasm of Sir William Amcotts Ingilby who rebuilt the estate village in the French style. From 1817–18 he constructed formal walled gardens of four acres, two sixty-foot (eighteen-metre) hot-houses, (one remains), a majestic stone palm house and garden room, twenty-six acres of lake to a 'Capability' Brown plan, and eight acres of pleasure grounds planted with trees and shrubs. Most of this remains. There are 394 feet (120 metres) of herbaceous border, fine climbing plants including blue wistaria and old-fashioned roses, and a collection of rare old varieties of apple and pear trees.

House open. Lunches, teas. Guided tours by arrangement. Plant sales.

Ripley Castle: garden room (1817–18).

## STOCKELD PARK, Wetherby, West Yorkshire (Mr and Mrs P G F Grant)
*Gardens 4 acres*

Fine trees, park and woodland surround the Palladian house designed by the eighteenth-century architect James Paine and built for the Middleton family on the edge of the Vale of York. The gardens include a herb garden, rose garden and wilderness.

House open. Teas at weekends.

## SUTTON PARK, Sutton-on-the-Forest, North Yorkshire (Mrs Nancie M D Sheffield)
*Gardens 3 acres, park 50 acres*

When Mrs Sheffield and her husband bought the house in 1962 they acquired a jungle of laurel and other overgrown, neglected evergreens, a legacy, no doubt of Victorian planting. The assets were two brick-walled terraces on the south side of the house overlooking the park, shelter from mature trees and a fine cedar of Lebanon in the park which they brought into the garden as they extended it. The top terrace is now paved with mellow York flag stones full of self-seeded alpine phlox and sisyrinchium. Wire gazebos at either end are covered in roses and clematis and beds under the house windows are planted for scent with nicotiana, heliotrope, regale lilies, apple mint and night-scented stock. The second terrace has old roses and tall herbaceous plants in blue, yellow, white and grey, densely planted to outwit weeds. A third terrace is quietly green with a formal stretch of water and leads through an informal glade to the temple walk planted with

Stockeld Park.

white cherries and masses of spring bulbs. There is a fully restored Georgian ice-house in the grounds.

House open. Lunches, teas.

## THORP PERROW ARBORETUM,
Bedale, North Yorkshire (Sir John Ropner)
*Arboretum 70 acres*

The collection of trees made by Sir Leonard Ropner, the present owner's father, is of European, and possibly of world importance. He began planting in 1927 and continued almost until his death at the age of eighty-two in 1977. The collection includes several trees which are the largest of their kind in Britain, among them two limes, *Tilia insularis* 'Nakai' and *Tilia tuan* 'Szysz', and many rarities including *Sorbus keissleri* and *Pyrus serrulata*. They are arranged in such a way as to form a fine woodland landscape, with areas planned

specifically for autumn colour, areas planted with daffodils by the ton and a wealth of wild flowers including primroses, cowslips, bluebells, forget-me-nots, campions and fox-gloves. Insect and bird life flourish.

*Scotland* Borders, Dumfries and Galloway, Fife, Grampian, Highlands, Lothian, Strathclyde, Tayside

## ARBIGLAND GARDENS, Kirkbean,
Dumfries (Captain and Mrs J B Blackett)
*Gardens 2 acres, park 15 acres*

'This gem of a garden . . .' (James Truscott in *Private Gardens of Scotland*) was first laid out in 1740 for William Craik by his gardener John Paul, whose son John Paul Jones became famous as the father of the American navy. Admiral Jones worked in the gardens at Arbigland as a boy. The walled garden, the sunken garden and the lake date from this time. The present owner's great-great uncle

Arbigland Gardens.

Ardtornish: Loch Aline.

made the Japanese garden and his grandmother, a skilfull and dedicated gardener, made many improvements from 1919 onwards. The beauty of the garden with its formal areas, woodland and water above a sandy bay on the Solway Firth owes much to the benign climate which allows such plants as *Embothrium coccineum*, *Eucryphia glutinosa* and *Pittosporum tenuifolium* 'Kohuhu' to thrive.

Teas. Guided tours by request.

## ARDTORNISH, Argyll (Mrs John Raven)
*Gardens 25 acres*

This woodland garden in an idyllic position on the shore of Loch Aline has been developed over the past hundred years. An early head gardener between 1916 and 1923 was Mr Besant who later had charge of the Glasgow Parks Department and was awarded the VMH, the Royal Horticultural Society's highest award. He carried out much of the early planting with a team of eight gardeners which had increased to twelve when Owen and Emmeline Hugh Smith came to Ardtornish in 1930. Today their daughter, Faith Raven, runs the gardens with one part-time assistant. She and her late husband John Raven introduced many rare plants, taking full advantage of habitats provided by the acid soil, the moist climate, outcrops of rock and several burns running through the grounds. Besides species rhododendrons there are semi-tender plants such as embothriums, eucryphias and *Hoheria lyallii*. The primula garden at the foot of a steep slope is also planted with peony species and spiraeas. Acers are a speciality and, with liquidamber, birch and beech, provide spectacular autumn colour.

Plant sales.

Blairquhan: the glass-house (1820).

## BLAIRQUHAN, Straiton Maybole, Ayrshire (Mr James Hunter Blair)
*Gardens 10 acres, park 500 acres*

The c1810 landscape of the five-hundred acre park is intact. Sir David Hunter Blair, 3rd Baronet, who built the castle, was an amateur landscape architect and laid out the park. The three-mile (five-kilometre) approach is entered by a bridge and lodge designed by the architect William Burn and passes through the river gorge with waterfalls at two points to a lime avenue planted some hundred years earlier. In the walled gardens is an 1820 glasshouse. The main wall is pierced by flues for heating. In about 1860 Sir Edward Hunter Blair added the pinetum which includes one of the original *Sequoia gigantea* introduced from America. There are many rare trees and shrubs, specially rhododendrons and azaleas.

House open. Lunches, teas. Guided tours.

## CAWDOR CASTLE, Nairn (the Earl Cawdor)
*Gardens 5 acres, park 773 acres*

The castle has been the home of the Thanes of Cawdor, with their colourful and doom-laden history, since the fourteenth century. Today the forbidding atmosphere of the fortress is disarmed by a setting of lawns, fine

Cawdor Castle.

trees, hedges, fruit, flowers, shrubs and herbs. Begun in 1720, the gardens have been altered and enhanced by each generation, and the 1990s will see the addition of a herb garden, knot garden, maze, orchard and paradise garden.

House open. Lunches, teas. Guided tours (specialist).

## CRARAE GLEN GARDENS, Inveraray, Argyll (Crarae Gardens Charitable Trust)
*Gardens 45 acres*

Roy Lancaster has said that Crarae Glen resembles a Himalayan ravine more closely than any other British garden. Lady Campbell started the garden in the early 1900s, probably encouraged by her nephew Reginald Farrer, the famous plant collector. Subsequent generations have added to the beauty of the steep, rocky banks of the Crarae burn and its surroundings by planting what has now become a very distinguished collection of rare trees and shrubs arranged with great sensitivity to the landscape. Sir George Campbell who planted between 1925 and 1967 had two golden rules: 'Never plant too close' and 'Try to ensure that the plants look natural in their setting'. By observing these rules he succeeded in making a beautiful and romantic place.

Refreshments at the visitor centre by arrangement. Guided tours.

## DUNROBIN CASTLE, Golspie, Sutherland (the Sutherland Trust)
*Gardens 5 acres*

The gardens of this archetypal Scottish baronial castle are today much as they were when laid out in 1850 by Sir Charles Barry for the 2nd Duke of Sutherland. Terraces fall away from the turretted house towards the sea in the grand, formal French style, their focal point being a large parterre with a central stone basin and fountain, the parterre designed in the pattern of a Scottish targe (shield). The summer-house which houses the museum and overlooks the gardens was built in 1732 and extended in 1878.

House open. Teas.

## EARLSHALL CASTLE, Leuchars, St Andrews, Fife (Lady Earlshall)
*Gardens 3 acres, park 50 acres*

Sir Robert Lorimer restored the derelict 1546 castle in the 1890s with great sensitivity and designed gardens entirely appropriate to the sixteenth-century building. Below the bedroom where Mary Queen of Scots used to stay, he set out the topiary garden, of clipped yews forming four Scottish saltires. Enclosures within the gardens are divided by holly and

Earlshall Castle.

yew hedges and a yew walk leads to an arbour with a curved seat designed by Lorimer. Near the arbour a terrace is planted with roses, and elsewhere there are colourful herbaceous borders. From the gatehouse an avenue of pleached limes continues into woodlands where visitors can follow a nature trail.

House open. Lunches, teas.

## GLAMIS CASTLE, Glamis, Angus (Mary, Countess of Strathmore and Kinghorne)
*Gardens 2 acres*

The romantic, turretted castle was the childhood home of Queen Elizabeth the Queen Mother, whose ancestors had lived there since 1372, and was the birthplace of Princess Margaret, Countess of Snowdon. The Italian garden, designed in 1907 by Cecilia, wife of the 14th Earl, is enclosed by yew hedges. A fan-shaped parterre is spread below the terrace, and pleached beech alleys form diagonal vistas between formal beds and box-edged parterres infilled with gravel. There are beech bowers, two gazebos and a fountain. The wrought-iron entrance gates were made

Glamis Castle: pleached beech walk.

in 1980 by local blacksmith George Sturrock to commemorate the Queen Mother's eightieth birthday. On the lawns in front of the castle there is an intriguing baroque stone sundial.

House open. Lunches, teas. Guided tours of house only.

**THE HIRSEL**, Coldstream, Berwickshire
(Lord Home of The Hirsel)
*Park and woodland 1,198 acres*

Former Prime Minister Sir Alec Douglas-Home opens the grounds of his family home to visitors all the year round, and has installed an interpretative museum and a craft centre in the old farm steading beside the lake. Thousands of bulbs and many shrubs and roses have been planted since 1960. The lake was made in the late 1700s, but much of the tree-planting is earlier: there is a sycamore outside the walled garden that is said to have been planted to commemorate the Battle of Flodden in 1513, and the remains of a four-

hundred-year-old Spanish chestnut stand on the banks of the River Leet. Early in the year snowdrops and aconites carpet the ground under fine trees, and at all times the riverside and lakeside walks reveal richly varied bird life. In late May and early June Dundock Wood is ablaze with rhododendrons and azaleas, many of them planted in 1881 in peat carted from sixteen miles (twenty-six kilometres) away. The estate is managed for conservation of the woods and their wildlife.

Lunches, teas.

The Hirsel.

## HOPETOUN HOUSE, South Queensferry, Edinburgh (Hopetoun House Preservation Trust)
*Gardens and park 100 acres*

A virtually unaltered example of early eighteenth-century architecture and land-scaping, Hopetoun was built by Sir William Bruce of Kinross on the site of the castle of Abercorn, and extended by William Adam in the 1720s. John Mackay wrote of it in the eighteenth century 'This fine Palace and Garden lies in the middle of a spacious Park well stocked with deer ... and under the Earl's great Terrace [which overlooks the Forth] is a Bed of Oysters from whence his kitchen is supplied all the Year round in the greatest quantities'. The broad vistas through woodland, the wilderness and the bastioned terrace walk with viewpoints to ruined castles, Stirling town and the Forth were probably planned by Bruce. There is a nature trail through the park.

House open. Lunches, teas. Guided tours. Plant centre.

## MANDERSTON, Duns, Berwickshire (Mr Adrian Palmer)
*Gardens 56 acres, park 150 acres*

A beautifully preserved monument to Edwardian opulence, Manderston House and its garden terraces were planned with no expense spared by the architect John Kinross for Sir James Miller and his wife, the daughter of Lord Scarsdale of Kedleston Hall. Neo-Georgian in style, the house presides over descending, balustraded terraces linked by broad flights of ornamental steps. The wider setting is of romantic eighteenth-century wooded parkland with a narrow serpentine lake. The top terrace is planted with grey and purple foliage plants, fuchsias and hydrangeas. On the main terrace stone-edged fountain pools and statuary are surrounded by parterres of massed floribunda roses and hostas, punctuated by clipped yew and holly.

Manderston.

To the north a walk leads to elaborate iron-work gates in high stone walls. This is the entrance to the formal walled gardens with an elaborate stone fountain, parterre beds which incorporate four marble seats in their pattern, and a stone pergola covered in roses. A trel-lised gazebo, a rockery, a sunken garden and the Lily Court displaying marble statues and lead water tanks are further formal features. Of the glasshouses, one range is still in use, containing a fernery with tufa rocks. Build-ings include a boathouse and a marble dairy.

House open. Lunches, teas. Guided tours. Plant sales.

## MELLERSTAIN HOUSE, Gordon, Berwickshire (the Earl of Haddington)
*Gardens 3 acres, park 150 acres*

Mellerstain's formal gardens are a rare ex-ample of Sir Reginald Blomfield's work. Designed in 1909, they are well-maintained with little alteration to the planting. Blomfield wrote 'Lord and Lady Binning were enthusi-astic on the matter of garden design, and with their help I laid out an important garden here with terraces, a crypto-porticus, parterres and water-pieces'. This was superimposed on an axial scheme by William Adam who built two wings of the fine house, his son Robert later completing the work with the central core. Adam's main vista leads to a canal and cascade. There is a thatched cottage of about 1825. The landscape of the park and woodland is outstanding, with extensive views from the garden terrace to the lake and the Cheviot Hills beyond. The woodlands date from agricultural improvements carried out in c1710 by Lady Grizel Baillie.

House open. Lunches, teas.

## MERTOUN GARDENS, St Boswells, Melrose, Roxburghshire (His Grace the Duke of Sutherland)
*Gardens 20 acres*

The house, designed by Sir William Bruce, was built in 1703–1705 high above the River Tweed. Many of the fine specimen trees probably date from that time. The extensive lawns in front of the house are bounded on one side by the tree-covered banks of the Tweed and to the other by borders of shrub roses, azaleas and herbaceous plants and an

arboretum established over the last twenty-five years. Garden walks cross and recross the Maidenhall Burn as it flows to the Tweed, and near one of the bridges is a circular dovecote built in 1567. The walled garden contains three acres of fruit trees, vegetables and flowers, all immaculately maintained.

## SCONE PALACE, Perth (the Earl of Mansfield)
*Gardens 2 acres*

Scone was the capital of the Picts until 836, the scene of Macbeth's death and the site of the coronation of Scottish kings including Robert the Bruce. The layout of the gardens by John Louden for the 3rd Earl of Mansfield dates from 1803, when the house was extended in the Gothic style. The pinetum, planted by the 4th Earl in 1848 and extended by the 8th Earl in 1984 is an outstanding collection of rare conifers. The original Douglas fir is here, grown from seed sent from America in 1826 by David Douglas who was born at Scone and was a gardener there. Walks through

Torosay Castle: the Japanese garden.

Scone Palace.

the woodland garden lead through rhododendrons, azaleas and other shrubs introduced by David Douglas to the Monks' Playgreen and Friar's Den of the former abbey.

House open. Lunches, teas. Guided tours on request.

## TOROSAY CASTLE, Isle of Mull, Argyll
(Mr Christopher James)
*Gardens 12 acres, park 50 acres*

The Victorian Scottish baronial house overlooks Loch Linnhe. The descending Italianate terraces are a fine example of the architect Sir Robert Lorimer's work. The fountain terrace, flanked by two stone gazebos, looks down on to the lion terrace, and all the terraces have fine herbaceous borders. The statue walk was made to display Walter Murray Guthrie's collection of eighteenth-century Italian statuary, nineteen charming figures of men and women by Antonio Bonazza. Beyond the formal gardens and surrounded by impressive trees are the water garden, eucalyptus walk, rock garden and, at the lochside, a tranquilly austere Japanese garden. The plants which flourish here, many rare, demonstrate the beneficial influence of the Gulf Stream.

House open. Lunches, teas. Guided tours on request.

## TRAQUAIR HOUSE, Innerleithen, Peeblesshire (Mr Peter Maxwell Stuart)
*Gardens 5 acres*

The garden architecture of the oldest inhabited house in Scotland was built at the end of the seventeenth century by James Smith for the 4th Earl. He built the double terrace with its twin gazebos and the iron gates which screen the tree-sided courtyard. The wooded landscape was established by 1750 and has been replanted as necessary over the centuries. More recently a half-acre maze was planted in 1980. The management policy is to encourage wildlife in the grounds and increase the large number of wild flowers.

House open. Lunches, teas. Plant sales.

## *Wales* Clwyd, Dyfed, Gwent, Gwynedd, Glamorgan

## BODRHYDDAN, Rhuddlan, Clwyd
(Colonel, the Lord Langford)
*Gardens 5 acres, park 200 acres*

The box-edged parterre on the seventeenth-century south front of the brick-built house is a rare surviving design by William Nesfield, made in 1875 for the present owner's grandfather, Conwy Grenville Hercules Rowley-Conwy. There is a central stone fountain and lily pond, and an orangery is currently being built. Clipped yew walks lead to lawns shaded by ancient yews and oaks. On the house walls are *Rosa banksia lutea*, *Wistaria sinensis* and *Magnolia grandiflora*, all over one hundred years old. An exceptionally large standard specimen of 'La France', the first hybrid tea rose (1867) was planted here before 1911 and flowers prolifically. In the woodland Pleasaunce a 1612 pavilion by Inigo Jones houses St Mary's Well, revered since pagan times, and said to have been used for clandestine marriages.

House open. Teas.

**BRYN BRAS CASTLE**, Llanrug, Caernarfon, North Wales (Mr and Mrs N Gray-Parry)
*Gardens 3 acres, park 29 acres*

The Victorian layout of the gardens, begun in 1839 and completed in 1887, remains intact, and is in keeping with the romantically pictur-esque Regency castle with its turrets, towers and castellations. The gardens lead by a gentle transition from the formality of lawns, walled garden and knot garden through ornamental woodland and water to a hill walk with spectacular views to Mount Snowdon and the sea. A description of 1887 is still accurate: 'Surrounding the castle are about ten acres of Ornamental Grounds, noted for their rural and picturesque appearance, and through which runs a small stream, forming four ponds of various sizes (all well stocked with Trout), rivulets and cascades, shady and tim-bered walks, rosary and tennis lawn.' In the 1920s the castellated observation tower in the woods, the summer-house (now the tea-room), the arched walls of the knot garden and the gladiator statues were added. Much restoration work has been carried out by the present owners, and is continuing.

House open. Teas.

**PICTON CASTLE**, Haverfordwest, Pembrokeshire, Dyfed (the Picton Castle Trust)
*Gardens 30 acres, park 400 acres*

The castle has been the home of the Philipps family since the fifteenth century. During the past thirty-five years the present generation has created a woodland garden from an overgrown jungle, planting rhododendrons, azaleas, camellias, magnolias, cherries and many other plants.

Lunches, teas.

# PART IV
# LISTINGS

## Components

### Arboreta

Arbigland, Dumfries
Arbury Hall, Warwickshire
Ardtornish, Argyllshire
Arley Hall, Cheshire
Batsford Arboretum, Gloucestershire
Blairquhan, Ayrshire
Blenheim Palace, Oxfordshire
Bodrhyddan Hall, Clwyd
Bowood House Wiltshire
Broadleas, Wiltshire
Brympton d'Evercy, Somerset
Bryn Bras castle, Gwynedd
Castle Howard, Yorkshire
Chatsworth House, Derbyshire
Chillingham Castle, Northumberland
Cholmondeley Castle, Cheshire
Corsham Court, Wiltshire
Crarae Glen, Argyllshire
Eastnor Castle, Herefordshire
Elsham Hall, South Humberside
Elton Hall, Cambridgeshire
Euston Hall, Norfolk
Forde Abbey, Somerset
Goodnestone Park, Kent
Helmingham Hall, Suffolk
Hergest Croft, Herefordshire
Hodnet Hall, Shropshire
Holker Hall, Cumbria
Kingstone Lisle Park, Oxfordshire
Longleat House, Wiltshire
Luton Hoo, Bedfordshire
Manderston, Berwickshire
Mannington Hall, Norfolk
Mertoun, Roxburghshire
Minterne Gardens, Dorset
Muncaster Castle, Cumbria
Newby Hall, Yorkshire
Nunwell House, Isle of Wight
Parham House, West Sussex
Pencarrow, Cornwall
Ripley Castle, Yorkshire
Riverhill House, Kent
Rockingham Castle, Leicestershire
Rotherfield Park, Hampshire
Sezincote, Gloucestershire
Stansted Park, Hampshire
Stanway House, Gloucestershire
Sutton Park, Yorkshire
Tatton Park, Cheshire
Thorp Perrow Arboretum, Yorkshire
West Dean Gardens, West Sussex
Whatton House, Leicestershire

### Bog Gardens

Ardtornish, Argyllshire
Arley Hall, Cheshire
Bodrhyddan Hall, Clwyd
Bowood House, Wiltshire
Bryn Bras Castle, Gwynedd
Chillingham Castle, Northumberland

Constable Burton Hall, Yorkshire
Crarae Glen, Argyllshire
Dorfold Hall, Cheshire
Exbury Gardens, Hampshire
Forde Abbey, Somerset
Gaulden Manor, Somerset
Harewood House, Yorkshire
Haughley Park, Suffolk
Heale House, Wiltshire
Hergest Croft, Herefordshire
Hodnet Hall, Shropshire
Mannington Hall, Norfolk
Mapperton House, Dorset
Moccas Court, Hereford
Newby Hall, Yorkshire
Newick Park, East Sussex
The Owl House, Kent
Pencarrow, Cornwall (under development)
Sezincote, Gloucestershire
Stanton Harcourt, Oxfordshire
Whatton House, Leicestershire

### Herb Gardens

Arley Hall, Cheshire
Barnsley House, Gloucestershire
Beaulieu Abbey, Hampshire
Bramham Park, Yorkshire
Broadleas, Wiltshire
Chenies Manor, Buckinghamshire
Combe Sydenham, Somerset
Dalemain, Cumbria
Deans Court, Dorset
Doddington Hall, Lincolnshire
Earlshall Castle, Fife
Elton Hall, Cambridgeshire
Gaulden Manor, Somerset
Goodnestone Park, Kent
Grimsthorpe Castle, Lincolnshire
Haddon Hall, Derbyshire
Helmingham Hall, Suffolk
Hever Castle, Kent
Holdenby House, Northamptonshire
Houghton Lodge, Hampshire
Kentwell Hall, Suffolk
Knebworth House, Hertfordshire
Leeds Castle, Kent (part of cottage garden)
Levens Hall, Cumbria
Littlecote House, Wiltshire
Mannington Hall, Norfolk
Michelham Priory, East Sussex
Norton Conyers, Yorkshire
Painswick Rococo Gardens, Gloucestershire
(to be restored)
Parham House, West Sussex
Parnham, Dorset
Picton Castle, Dyfed
The Priory, Lavenham, Suffolk
Ripley Castle, Yorkshire
Rockingham Castle, Leicestershire
Smedmore House, Dorset
Stanway House, Gloucestershire

Stockeld Park, Yorkshire
Traquair House, Peeblesshire
Whatton House, Leicestershire

### Herbaceous Borders

Arbigland, Dumfries
Arbury Hall, Warwickshire
Arley Hall, Cheshire
Barford Park, Somerset
Barton Manor, Isle of Wight
Belvoir Castle, Lincolnshire
Benington Lordship, Hertfordshire
Berkeley Castle, Gloucestershire
Blairquhan, Ayrshire
Bowood House, Wiltshire
Bramdean House, Hampshire
Bramham Park, Yorkshire
Breamore House, Hampshire
Broadleas, Wiltshire
Broughton Castle, Oxfordshire
Bryn Bras Castle, Gwynedd
Burton Constable Hall, North Humberside
Castle Howard, Yorkshire
Cawdor Castle, Nairn
Chatsworth House, Derbyshire
Chenies Manor, Buckinghamshire
Chicheley Hall, Buckinghamshire
Chilham Castle, Kent
Chillingham Castle, Northumberland
Cholmondeley Castle, Cheshire
Clapton Court, Somerset
Combe Sydenham, Somerset
Constable Burton Hall, Yorkshire
Corsham Court, Wiltshire
Dalemain, Cumbria
Docwra's Manor, Hertfordshire
Doddington Hall, Lincolnshire
Dunrobin Castle, Sutherland
Earlshall Castle, Fife
Eastnor Castle, Herefordshire
Eccleshall Castle, Staffordshire
Edmondsham House, Dorset
Elton Hall, Cambridgeshire
Euston Hall, Norfolk
Finchcocks, Kent
Firle Place, East Sussex
Forde Abbey, Somerset
Glamis Castle, Angus
Godinton Park, Kent
Goodnestone Park, Kent
Great Dixter, East Sussex
Grimsthorpe Castle, Lincolnshire
Haddon Hall, Derbyshire
Harewood House, Yorkshire
Helmingham Hall, Suffolk
Hergest Croft, Herefordshire
The Hirsel, Berwickshire
Hodnet Hall, Shropshire
Holdenby House, Northamptonshire
Holker Hall, Cumbria
Houghton Lodge, Hampshire
How Caple Court, Herefordshire
Hutton-in-the-Forest, Cumbria

Kingston House, Oxfordshire
Kingstone Lisle Park, Oxfordshire
Knebworth House, Hertfordshire
Lamport Hall, Northamptonshire
Layer Marney Tower, Essex
Leeds Castle, Kent
Levens Hall, Cumbria
Littlecote House, Wiltshire
Longleat House, Wiltshire
Loseley Park, Surrey
Luton Hoo, Bedfordshire
Lyme Park, Cheshire
Manderston, Berwickshire
Mannington Hall, Norfolk
Mapperton House, Dorset
Mellerstain House, Berwickshire
Mertoun, Roxburghshire
Michelham Priory, East Sussex
Misarden Park, Gloucestershire
Mount Ephraim, Kent
Newby Hall, Yorkshire
Norton Conyers, Yorkshire
Nunwell House, Isle of Wight
Otley Hall, Suffolk
The Owl House, Kent
Painswick Rococo Gardens, Gloucestershire
Parham House, West Sussex
Parnham, Dorset
Penshurst Place, Kent
Powderham Castle, Devon
Prideaux Place, Cornwall
Raby Castle, Durham
Ragley Hall, Warwickshire
Ripley Castle, Yorkshire
Rockingham Castle, Leicestershire
Rodmarton Manor, Gloucestershire
Rotherfield Park, Hampshire
Rousham, Oxfordshire
Smedmore House, Dorset
Somerleyton Hall, Suffolk
Spains Hall, Essex
Spetchley Park, Worcestershire
Squerryes Court, Kent
Stanton Harcourt, Oxfordshire
Stanway House, Gloucestershire
Stockeld Park, Yorkshire
Stonor Park, Oxfordshire
Sutton Park, Yorkshire
Syon Park, Middlesex
Tatton Park, Cheshire
Torosay Castle, Argyllshire
Traquair House, Peeblesshire
West Dean Gardens, West Sussex
Whatton House, Leicestershire
Wilton House, Wiltshire

## Japanese or Chinese Gardens

Arbigland, Dumfries
Heale House, Wiltshire
Iford Manor, Wiltshire
Manderston, Berwickshire
Mount Ephraim, Kent
Muncaster Castle, Cumbria
Tatton Park, Cheshire
Torosay Castle, Argyllshire
Whatton House, Leicestershire

## Kitchen Gardens

Adlington Hall, Cheshire
Ardtornish, Argyllshire
Arley Hall, Cheshire
Barnsley House, Gloucestershire
Belvoir Castle, Lincolnshire
Benington Lordship, Hertfordshire
Berkeley Castle, Gloucestershire
Blairquhan, Ayrshire

Blenheim Palace, Oxfordshire
Bowood House, Wiltshire
Bramdean House, Hampshire
Broadleas, Wiltshire
Chenies Manor, Buckinghamshire
Chicheley Hall, Buckinghamshire
Chilham Castle, Kent
Cholmondeley Castle, Cheshire
Corsham Court, Wiltshire
Deans Court, Dorset
Doddington Hall, Lincolnshire
Earlshall Castle, Fife
Easton Grey House, Wiltshire
Edmondsham House, Dorset
Firle Place, East Sussex
Forde Abbey, Somerset
Gaulden Manor, Somerset
Godinton Park, Kent
Goodnestone Park, Kent
Harewood House, Yorkshire
Haughley Park, Suffolk
Heale House, Wiltshire
Helmingham Hall, Suffolk
Hodnet Hall, Shropshire
Holdenby House, Northamptonshire
Grimsthorpe Castle, Lincolnshire
Hergest Croft, Herefordshire
Houghton Lodge, Hampshire
Iford Manor, Wiltshire
Kentwell Hall, Suffolk
Kingstone Lisle Park, Oxfordshire
Littlecote House, Wiltshire
Loseley Park, Surrey
Manderston, Berwickshire
Mapperton House, Dorset
Melbourne Hall, Derbyshire
Mertoun, Roxburghshire
Michelham Priory, East Sussex
Misarden Park, Gloucestershire
Norton Conyers, Yorkshire
Painswick Rococo Gardens, Gloucestershire
  (to be restored)
Picton Castle, Dyfed
The Priory, Lavenham, Suffolk
Rainthorpe Hall, Norfolk
Ripley Castle, Yorkshire
Rodmarton Manor, Gloucestershire
Rotherfield Park, Hampshire
Rousham, Oxfordshire
Spains Hall, Essex
Spetchley Park, Worcestershire
Stanway House, Gloucestershire
Stonor Park, Oxfordshire
Sutton Park, Yorkshire
Weston Park, Shropshire
Whatton House, Leicestershire

## Knot Gardens

Barnsley House, Gloucestershire
Bryn Bras Castle, Gwynedd
Combe Sydenham, Somerset
Dalemain, Cumbria
Doddington Hall, Lincolnshire
Elton Hall, Cambridgeshire
Grimsthorpe Castle, Lincolnshire
Helmingham Hall, Suffolk
Holme Pierrepont Hall, Nottinghamshire
Houghton Lodge, Hampshire
Lamport Hall, Northamptonshire
Littlecote House, Wiltshire
Mannington Hall, Norfolk
Penshurst Place, Kent
The Priory, Lavenham, Suffolk (planned)
Rainthorpe Hall, Norfolk

## Landscaped Parks

Arbigland, Dumfries

Arbury Hall, Warwickshire
Arley Hall, Cheshire
Barford Park, Somerset
Benington Lordship, Hertfordshire
Berkeley Castle, Gloucestershire
Blairquhan, Ayrshire
Blenheim Palace, Oxfordshire. Brown.
Bodrhyddan Hall, Clwyd
Bowood House, Wiltshire. Brown, Repton.
Breamore House, Hampshire
Broughton Castle, Oxfordshire
Brympton d'Evercy, Somerset
Burton Constable Hall, North Humberside.
  Brown.
Castle Howard, Yorkshire
Chatsworth House, Derbyshire. Brown.
Chilham Castle, Kent. Brown.
Chillington Hall, Staffordshire. Brown.
Chillingham Castle, Northumberland
Constable Burton Hall, Yorkshire
Corby Castle, Cumbria
Corsham Court, Wiltshire. Brown, Repton.
Dalemain, Cumbria
Doddington Hall, Lincolnshire
Dorfold Hall, Cheshire
Edmondsham House, Dorset
Elsham Park, South Humberside
Elton Hall, Cambridgeshire
Euston Hall, Norfolk. Kent, Brown.
Finchcocks, Kent
Firle Place, East Sussex
Forde Abbey, Somerset
Godinton Park, Kent
Goodnestone Park, Kent
Grimsthorpe Castle, Lincolnshire. Brown.
Hammerwood Park, West Sussex
Harewood House, Yorkshire. Brown,
  Repton.
Haughley Park, Suffolk
Heale House, Wiltshire
Helmingham Hall, Suffolk
Hergest Croft, Herefordshire
The Hirsel, Berwickshire
Hodnet Hall, Shropshire
Holker Hall, Cumbria
Hopetoun House, Lothian
Houghton Lodge, Hampshire
Hutton-in-the-Forest, Cumbria
Kentwell Hall, Suffolk. Repton.
Kingston House, Oxfordshire
Kingstone Lisle Park, Oxfordshire
Lamport Hall, Northamptonshire
Leeds Castle, Kent
Levens Hall, Cumbria
Longleat House, Wiltshire. Brown, Repton.
Luton Hoo, Bedfordshire. Brown.
Lyme Park, Cheshire
Manderston, Berwickshire
Mannington Hall, Norfolk
Mellerstain House, Berwickshire
Mertoun, Roxburghshire
Minterne Gardens, Dorset
Muncaster Castle, Cumbria
Moccas Court, Herefordshire. Brown,
  Repton.
Newby Hall, Yorkshire
Nunwell House, Isle of Wight
Powderham Castle, Devon
Raby Castle, Durham
Ragley Hall, Warwickshire
Ripley Castle, Yorkshire. Brown.
Rockingham Castle, Leicestershire
Rotherfield Park, Hampshire
Rousham, Oxfordshire. Kent.
Scone Palace, Perth
Sherborne Castle, Dorset
Spains Hall, Essex
Spetchley Park, Worcestershire
Squerryes Court, Kent
Somerleyton Hall, Suffolk
Stansted Park, Hampshire

Stanway House, Gloucestershire
Sutton Park, Yorkshire
Syon Park, Middlesex. Brown.
Tatton Park, Cheshire. Repton.
Torosay Castle, Argyllshire
Traquair House, Peeblesshire
Warwick Castle, Warwickshire. Brown.
West Dean Gardens, West Sussex
Weston Park, Shropshire. Brown.
Whatton House, Leicestershire
Woburn Abbey, Bedfordshire. Repton.

## Mazes

Blenheim Palace, Oxfordshire (under construction)
Breamore House, Hampshire (2, outside garden)
Chatsworth House, Derbyshire
Chenies Manor, Buckinghamshire
Doddington Hall, Lincolnshire
Hever Castle, Kent
Kentwell Hall, Suffolk (brick paved)
Leeds Castle, Kent
Longleat House, Wiltshire
Somerleyton Hall, Suffolk
Tatton Park, Cheshire
Traquair House, Peeblesshire

## Orchards

Ardtornish, Argyllshire
Benington Lordship, Hertfordshire
Blenheim Palace, Oxfordshire
Bramdean House, Hampshire
Bramham Park, Yorkshire
Brympton d'Evercy, Somerset
Chatsworth House, Derbyshire
Chenies Manor, Buckinghamshire
Corsham Court, Wiltshire
Deans Court, Dorset
Docwra's Manor, Hertfordshire
Doddington Hall, Lincolnshire
Elton Hall, Cambridgeshire
Finchcocks, Kent
Earlshall Castle, Fife
Easton Grey House, Wiltshire
Gaulden Manor, Somerset
Great Dixter, East Sussex
Grimsthorpe Castle, Lincolnshire
Heale House, Wiltshire
Hergest Croft, Herefordshire
Hever Castle, Kent
Helmingham Hall, Suffolk
Hutton-in-the-Forest, Cumbria
Iford Manor, Wiltshire
Kingston House, Oxfordshire
Levens Hall, Cumbria
Mapperton House, Dorset
Michelham Priory, East Sussex
Mount Ephraim, Kent
Newby Hall, Yorkshire
The Owl House, Kent
Painswick Rococo Gardens, Gloucestershire
Parham House, West Sussex
Penshurst Place, Kent
The Priory, Lavenham, Suffolk (planned)
Rainthorpe Hall, Norfolk
Rockingham Castle, Leicestershire
Rotherfield Park, Hampshire
Sheldon Manor, Wiltshire
Spains Hall, Essex
Stanway House, Gloucestershire
Stonor Park, Oxfordshire
Traquair House, Peeblesshire

## Parterres

Arbigland, Dumfries
Blairquhan, Ayrshire
Bodrhyddan Hall, Clwyd
Bowood House, Wiltshire
Bramham Park, Yorkshire
Castle Howard, Yorkshire
Chillingham Castle, Northumberland
Doddington Hall, Lincolnshire
Dunrobin Castle, Sutherland (3)
Elton Hall, Cambridgeshire
Godinton Park, Kent
Grimsthorpe Castle, Lincolnshire
Harewood House, Yorkshire
Helmingham Hall, Suffolk
Holme Pierrepont Hall, Nottinghamshire
Hopetoun House, Lothian
Levens Hall, Cumbria
Littlecote House, Wiltshire
Longleat House, Wiltshire
Manderston, Berwickshire
Mannington Hall, Norfolk
Melbourne Hall, Derbyshire
Mellerstain House, Berwickshire
Nunwell House, Isle of Wight
The Owl House, Kent
Penshurst Place, Kent
Rodmarton Manor, Gloucestershire
Rousham, Oxfordshire
Squerryes Court, Kent
Stanway House, Gloucestershire (to be restored)
Tatton Park, Cheshire
Warwick Castle, Warwickshire

## Pineta

Blairquhan, Ayrshire
Bowood House, Wiltshire
Bryn Bras Castle, Gwynedd
Cawdor Castle, Nairn
Chatsworth House, Derbyshire
Crarae Glen, Argyllshire
Eastnor Castle, Herefordshire
Exbury Gardens, Hampshire (being developed)
Hergest Croft, Herefordshire
Mertoun, Roxburghshire
Pencarrow, Cornwall
Scone Palace, Perth
Tatton Park, Cheshire

## Rock Gardens

Ardtornish, Argyllshire
Arley Hall, Cheshire
Benington Lordship, Hertfordshire
Bryn Bras Castle, Gwynedd
Chatsworth House, Derbyshire
Chilham Castle, Kent
Chillingham Castle, Northumberland
Cholmondeley Castle, Cheshire
Clapton Court, Somerset
Constable Burton Hall, Yorkshire
Deans Court, Dorset
Docwra's Manor, Hertfordshire
Dorfold Hall, Cheshire
Exbury Gardens, Hampshire
Forde Abbey, Somerset
Harewood House, Yorkshire
Hergest Croft, Herefordshire
Hever Castle, Kent
Goodnestone Park, Kent
Iford Manor, Wiltshire
Lamport Hall, Northamptonshire
Luton Hoo, Bedfordshire
Manderston, Berwickshire
Mount Ephraim, Kent
Newby Hall, Yorkshire

Newick Park, East Sussex
Pencarrow, Cornwall
Prideaux Place, Cornwall
Rainthorpe Hall, Norfolk
Rockingham Castle, Leicestershire
Spetchley Park, Worcestershire
Squerryes Court, Kent
Sutton Park, Yorkshire
Syon Park, Middlesex
Tatton Park, Cheshire
Torosay Castle, Argyllshire
Warwick Castle, Warwickshire
Whatton House, Leicestershire

## Rose Gardens

Arbigland, Dumfries
Arbury Hall, Warwickshire
Arley Hall, Cheshire
Belvoir Castle, Lincolnshire
Benington Lordship, Hertfordshire
Bickleigh Castle, Devon
Blairquhan, Ayrshire
Blenheim Palace, Oxfordshire
Bowood House, Wiltshire
Bramham Park, Yorkshire
Broadleas, Wiltshire
Bryn Bras Castle, Gwynedd
Castle Howard, Yorkshire
Cawdor Castle, Nairn
Chatsworth House, Derbyshire
Chilham Castle, Kent
Chillingham Castle, Northumberland
Cholmondeley Castle, Cheshire
Clapton Court, Somerset
Combe Sydenham, Somerset
Corsham Court, Wiltshire
Doddington Hall, Lincolnshire
Dorfold Hall, Cheshire
Earlshall Castle, Fife
Easton Grey House, Wiltshire
Eccleshall Castle, Staffordshire
Elton Hall, Cambridgeshire
Euston Hall, Norfolk
Exbury Gardens, Hampshire
Gaulden Manor, Somerset
Godinton Park, Kent
Goodnestone Park, Kent
Great Dixter, East Sussex
Grimsthorpe Castle, Lincolnshire
Haddon Hall, Derbyshire
Harewood House, Yorkshire
Helmingham Hall, Suffolk
Hergest Croft, Herefordshire
Hever Castle, Kent
Hodnet Hall, Shropshire
Holker Hall, Cumbria
Holme Pierrepont Hall, Nottinghamshire
How Caple Court, Herefordshire
Kingstone Lisle Park, Oxfordshire
Knebworth House, Hertfordshire
Lamport Hall, Northamptonshire
Layer Marney Tower, Essex
Levens Hall, Cumbria
Littlecote House, Wiltshire
Luton Hoo, Bedfordshire
Manderston, Berwickshire
Mannington Hall, Norfolk
Misarden Park, Gloucestershire
Mount Ephraim, Kent
Newby Hall, Yorkshire
Nunwell House, Isle of Wight
The Owl House, Kent
Parnham, Dorset
Penshurst Place, Kent
Powderham Castle, Devon
Raby Castle, Durham
Ragley Hall, Warwickshire
Rockingham Castle, Leicestershire
Rodmarton Manor, Gloucestershire

Rotherfield Park, Hampshire
St Osyth's Priory, Essex
Spains Hall, Essex
Spetchley Park, Worcestershire
Stanton Harcourt, Oxfordshire
Stockeld Park, Yorkshire
Stonor park, Oxfordshire
Sudeley Castle, Gloucestershire
Sutton Park, Yorkshire
Syon Park, Middlesex
Tatton Park, Cheshire
Traquair House, Peeblesshire
Warwick Castle, Warwickshire
Whatton House, Leicestershire
Wilton House, Wiltshire

## Walled Gardens

Adlington Hall, Cheshire
Arbigland, Dumfries
Arbury Hall, Warwickshire
Ardtornish, Argyllshire
Arley Hall, Cheshire
Athelhampton, Dorset
Barford Park, Somerset
Barton Manor, Isle of Wight
Benington Lordship, Hertfordshire
Berkeley Castle, Gloucestershire
Blairquhan, Ayrshire
Blenheim Palace, Oxfordshire
Bramdean House, Hampshire
Bramham Park, Yorkshire
Breamore House, Hampshire
Broadleas, Wiltshire
Broughton Castle, Oxfordshire
Brympton d'Evercy, Somerset
Bryn Bras Castle, Gwynedd
Castle Howard, Yorkshire
Cawdor Castle, Nairn
Chenies Manor, Buckinghamshire
Chicheley Hall, Buckinghamshire
Combe Sydenham, Somerset
Corsham Court, Wiltshire
Dalemain, Cumbria
Deans Court, Dorset
Docwra's Manor, Hertfordshire
Doddington Hall, Lincolnshire
Dorfold Hall, Cheshire
Dunrobin Castle, Sutherland
Earlshall Castle, Fife
Easton Grey House, Wiltshire
Eccleshall Castle, Staffordshire
Edmondsham House, Dorset
Elsham Hall, South Humberside
Finchcocks, Kent
Gaulden Manor, Somerset
Godinton Park, Kent
Goodnestone Park, Kent
Great Dixter, East Sussex
Grimsthorpe Castle, Lincolnshire
Haddon Hall, Derbyshire
Harewood House, Yorkshire
Haughley Park, Suffolk
Heale House, Wiltshire
Helmingham Hall, Suffolk
Hever Castle, Kent
Holme Pierrepont Hall, Nottinghamshire
Hopetoun House, Lothian
Houghton Lodge, Hampshire
Hutton-in-the Forest, Cumbria
Iford Manor, Wiltshire
Kentwell Hall, Suffolk
Levens Hall, Cumbria
Littlecote House, Wiltshire
Longleat House, Wiltshire
Loseley Park, Surrey
Manderston, Berwickshire
Mannington Hall, Norfolk
Mertoun, Roxburghshire
Misarden Park, Gloucestershire

Newick Park, East Sussex
Norton Conyers, Yorkshire
The Owl House, Kent
Painswick Rococo Gardens, Gloucestershire
Parnham, Dorset
Pencarrow, Cornwall
Penshurst Place, Kent
Picton Castle, Dyfed
Powderham Castle, Devon
Raby Castle, Durham
Ripley Castle, Yorkshire
Rockingham Castle, Leicestershire
Rodmarton Manor, Gloucestershire
Rotherfield Park, Hampshire
Rousham, Oxfordshire
Smedmore House, Dorset
Somerleyton Hall, Suffolk
Spains Hall, Essex
Spetchley Park, Worcestershire
Stansted Park, Hampshire
Stanway House, Gloucestershire
Stonor Park, Oxfordshire
Sudeley Castle, Gloucestershire
Tatton Park, Cheshire
Torosay Castle, Argyllshire
West Dean Gardens, West Sussex
Weston Park, Shropshire
Whatton House, Leicestershire

## Terraces

Arbigland, Dumfries
Arley Hall, Cheshire
Athelhampton, Dorset
Barford Park, Somerset
Barnsley House, Gloucestershire
Barton Manor, Isle of Wight
Belvoir Castle, Lincolnshire
Benington Lordship, Hertfordshire
Berkeley Castle, Gloucestershire
Blairquhan, Ayrshire
Blenheim Palace, Oxfordshire
Bowood House, Wiltshire
Breamore House, Hampshire
Broughton Castle, Oxfordshire
Browsholme Hall, Lancashire
Brympton d'Evercy, Somerset
Castle Howard, Yorkshire
Cholmondeley Castle, Cheshire
Clapton Court, Somerset
Dalemain, Cumbria
Doddington Hall, Lincolnshire
Dorfold Hall, Cheshire
Dunrobin Castle, Sutherland
Eastnor Castle, Herefordshire
Easton Grey House, Wiltshire
Elsham Hall, South Humberside
Elton Hall, Cambridgeshire
Euston Hall, Norfolk
Firle Place, East Sussex
Finchcocks, Kent
Godinton Park, Kent
Goodnestone Park, Kent
Great Dixter, East Sussex
Haddon Hall, Derbyshire
Hammerwood Park, West Sussex
Harewood House, Yorkshire
Heale House, Wiltshire
Hergest Croft, Herefordshire
Hodnet Hall, Shropshire
Holdenby House, Northamptonshire
Holker Hall, Cumbria
Hopetoun House, Lothian
Houghton Lodge, Hampshire
How Caple Court, Herefordshire
Hutton-in-the-Forest, Cumbria
Iford Manor, Wiltshire
Kingston House, Oxfordshire
Layer Marney Tower, Essex
Loseley Park, Surrey

Luton Hoo, Bedfordshire
Manderston, Berwickshire
Melbourne Hall, Derbyshire
Mellerstain House, Berwickshire
Misarden Park, Gloucestershire
Moccas Court, Herefordshire
Mount Ephraim, Kent
Muncaster Castle, Cumbria
Newby Hall, Yorkshire
Nunwell House, Isle of Wight
The Owl House, Kent
Painswick Rococo Gardens, Gloucestershire
Parnham, Dorset
Penshurst Place, Kent
Powderham Castle, Devon
Prideaux Place, Cornwall
The Priory, Lavenham, Suffolk
Raby Castle, Durham
Ragley Hall, Warwickshire
Rainthorpe Hall, Norfolk
Riverhill House, Kent
Rockingham Castle, Leicestershire
Rodmarton Manor, Gloucestershire
Rotherfield Park, Hampshire
Sheldon Manor, Wiltshire
Spetchley Park, Worcestershire
Stanway House, Gloucestershire
Stonor Park, Oxfordshire
Sudeley Castle, Gloucestershire
Sutton Park, Yorkshire
Tatton Park, Cheshire
Torosay Castle, Argyllshire
Traquair House, Peeblesshire
Warwick Castle, Warwickshire
Weston Park, Shropshire

## Woodland Gardens

Arbigland, Dumfries
Arbury Hall, Warwickshire
Ardtornish, Argyllshire
Arley Hall, Cheshire
Athelhampton, Dorset
Barford Park, Somerset
Barton Manor, Isle of Wight
Beaulieu Abbey, Hampshire
Belvoir Castle, Lincolnshire
Berkeley Castle, Gloucestershire
Blairquhan, Ayrshire
Blenheim Palace, Oxfordshire
Bodrhyddan Hall, Clwyd
Bowood House, Wiltshire
Bramham Park, Yorkshire
Broadleas, Wiltshire
Bryn Bras Castle, Gwynedd
Castle Howard, Yorkshire
Chatsworth House, Derbyshire
Chicheley Hall, Buckinghamshire
Cholmondeley Castle, Cheshire
Clapton Court, Somerset
Corsham Court, Wiltshire
Crarae Glen, Argyllshire
Dalemain, Cumbria
Dorfold Hall, Cheshire
Eastnor Castle, Herefordshire
Exbury Gardens, Hampshire
Forde Abbey, Somerset
Godinton Park, Kent
Goodnestone Park, Kent
Grimsthorpe Castle, Lincolnshire
Hammerwood Park, West Sussex
Harewood House, Yorkshire
Haughley Park, Suffolk
Heale House, Wiltshire
Hergest Croft, Herefordshire
The High Beeches, West Sussex
The Hirsel, Berwickshire
Hodnet Hall, Shropshire
Holdenby House, Northamptonshire
Holker Hall, Cumbria

Hopetoun House, Lothian
How Caple Court, Herefordshire
Hutton-in-the-Forest, Cumbria
Iford Manor, Wiltshire
Kingston House, Oxfordshire
Leeds Castle, Kent
Littlecote House, Wiltshire
Longleat House, Wiltshire
Luton Hoo, Bedfordshire
Manderston, Berwickshire
Mannington Hall, Norfolk
Mapperton House, Dorset
Melbourne Hall, Derbyshire
Minterne Gardens, Dorset
Misarden Park, Gloucestershire
Mount Ephraim, Kent
Muncaster Castle, Cumbria
Newby Hall, Yorkshire
Newick Park, East Sussex
Nunwell House, Isle of Wight
The Owl House, Kent
Painswick Rococo Gardens, Gloucestershire
Parnham, Dorset
Pencarrow, Cornwall
Picton Castle, Dyfed
Powderham Castle, Devon
Riverhill House, Kent
Rockingham Castle, Leicestershire
Spetchley Park, Worcestershire
Squerryes Court, Kent
Sutton Park, Yorkshire
Syon Park, Middlesex
Tatton Park, Cheshire
Thorp Perrow Arboretum, Yorkshire
Torosay Castle, Argyllshire
Traquair House, Peeblesshire
Weston Park, Shropshire
Whatton House, Leicestershire

## Wildernesses

Adlington Hall, Cheshire
Ardtornish, Argyllshire
Arley Hall, Cheshire
Athelhampton, Dorset
Belvoir Castle, Lincolnshire
Bramham Park, Yorkshire
Bryn Bras Castle, Gwynedd
Cawdor Castle, Nairn
Chillingham Castle, Northumberland
Combe Sydenham, Somerset
Constable Burton Hall, Yorkshire
Corby Castle, Cumbria
Corsham Court, Wiltshire
Crarae Glen, Argyllshire
Deans Court, Dorset
Docwra's Manor, Hertfordshire

Doddington Hall, Lincolnshire
Dorfold Hall, Cheshire
Eccleshall Castle, Staffordshire
Elsham Hall, South Humberside
Finchcocks, Kent
Godinton Park, Kent
Hammerwood Park, West Sussex
Helmingham Hall, Suffolk
Hopetoun House, Lothian
How Caple Court, Herefordshire
Hutton-in-the-Forest, Cumbria
Knebworth House, Hertfordshire
Lamport Hall, Northamptonshire
Levens Hall, Cumbria
Mannington Hall, Norfolk
Mapperton House, Dorset
Mellerstain House, Berwickshire
Michelham Priory, East Sussex
Muncaster Castle, Cumbria
Norton Conyers, Yorkshire
Otley Hall, Suffolk
Painswick Rococo Gardens, Gloucestershire
Parnham, Dorset
Powderham Castle, Devon
Prideaux Place, Cornwall
Riverhill House, Kent
Stanton Harcourt, Oxfordshire
Stockeld Park, Yorkshire
Syon Park, Middlesex
Traquair House, Peeblesshire
Warwick Castle, Warwickshire
West Dean Gardens, West Sussex
Whatton House, Leicestershire

## Other Themes

Arley Hall, Cheshire. Scented garden
Athelhampton, Dorset. White garden
Barnsley House, Gloucestershire. Laburnum tunnel
Barton Manor, Isle of Wight. Scented secret garden, vineyard
Belvoir Castle, Lincolnshire. Spring gardens
Bryn Bras Castle, Gwynedd. Rowan grove
Chatsworth House, Derbyshire. Azalea dell, conservatory garden
Chenies Manor, Buckinghamshire. White garden, sunken garden
Chillingham Castle, Northumberland. Lady Katharine's borders
Clapton Court, Somerset. Yellow border, spring garden
Dorfold Hall, Cheshire. Spring garden
Earlshall Castle, Fife. Secret garden
Eccleshall Castle, Staffordshire. Lime walk, woodland walk

Elsham Hall, South Humberside. Butterfly garden
Euston Hall, Norfolk. White garden
Exbury Gardens, Hampshire. Iris garden, winter garden, camellia walk
Gaulden Manor, Somerset. White garden, secret garden, bishop's garden, duck garden, scent garden, butterfly garden
Goodnestone Park, Kent. White garden
Haddon Hall, Derbyshire. Delphinium border
Heale House, Wiltshire. Snowdrop walk
Hever Castle, Kent. Italian garden, Anne Boleyn's garden
The High Beeches, West Sussex. Wild-flower meadows
Holdenby House, Northamptonshire. Elizabethan garden, fragrant border, silver border
Holker Hall, Cumbria. Autumn walks
Hopetoun House, Lothian. Spring garden
Knebworth House, Hertfordshire. Blue garden, gold garden, dogs' cemetery
Levens Hall, Cumbria. Topiary garden, bowling green, beech circles and *allées*
Littlecote House, Wiltshire. Medieval garden
Lyme Park, Cheshire. Dutch garden, Vicary Gibbs garden
Mannington Hall, Norfolk. Heritage rose garden
Mapperton House, Dorset. Spring garden
Moccas Court, Herefordshire. Sundial garden
Newby Hall, Yorkshire. Autumn garden, white garden, Wilson's corner
Norton Conyers, Yorkshire. Gold and silver borders, bed of 18th-century plants, bowling green
Painswick Rococo Gardens, Gloucestershire. Snowdrop grove
Parnham, Dorset. Iris garden
Pencarrow, Cornwall. American garden, Italian garden
Penshurst Place, Kent. White garden, spring garden
Raby Castle, Durham. Heather garden
Rodmarton Manor, Gloucestershire. White garden
Somerleyton Hall, Suffolk. Lady Somerleyton's garden
Stanway House, Gloucestershire. Grasswork
Sutton Park, Yorkshire. White garden, iris garden
Tatton Park, Cheshire. Italian garden, Lady Charlotte's fountain and arbour, fernery

# Buildings and Structures

## Arbours

Arley Hall, Cheshire
Barnsley House, Gloucestershire
Benington Lordship, Hertfordshire
Blairquhan, Ayrshire
Castle Howard, Yorkshire
Corsham Court, Wiltshire
Earlshall Castle, Fife

Glamis Castle, Angus (2 pleached beech bowers)
Hammerwood Park, West Sussex
Heale House, Wiltshire
Hergest Croft, Herefordshire
Holker Hall, Cumbria
Iford Manor, Wiltshire
Lamport Hall, Northamptonshire
Mannington Hall, Norfolk
Melbourne Hall, Derbyshire

Nunwell House, Isle of Wight
The Owl House, Kent
Painswick Rococo Gardens, Gloucestershire (to be restored)
Pencarrow, Cornwall
Rousham, Oxfordshire
Somerleyton Hall, Suffolk
Sudeley Castle, Gloucestershire
Tatton Park, Cheshire

## Bothies

Blairquhan, Ayrshire
Bowood House, Wiltshire
Castle Howard, Yorkshire
Easton Grey House, Wiltshire
Elsham Hall, South Humberside
Godinton Park, Kent
Harewood House, Yorkshire
Hergest Croft, Herefordshire
Holdenby House, Northamptonshire
Levens Hall, Cumbria
Littlecote House, Wiltshire
Loseley Park, Surrey
Powderham Castle, Devon
Ripley Castle, Yorkshire
Rotherfield Park, Hampshire
Somerleyton Hall, Suffolk
Stansted Park, Hampshire
Tatton Park, Cheshire
Traquair House, Peeblesshire
Whatton House, Leicestershire

## Bridges

Adlington Hall, Cheshire
Arbigland, Dumfries
Arbury Hall, Warwickshire
Ardtornish, Argyllshire
Athelhampton, Dorset
Benington Lordship, Hertfordshire
Bickleigh Castle, Devon
Blairquhan, Ayrshire
Blenheim Palace, Oxfordshire
Bowood House, Wiltshire
Bryn Bras Castle, Gwynedd
Burton Constable Hall, North Humberside
Castle Howard, Yorkshire
Cawdor Castle, Nairn
Chiddingstone Castle, Kent
Chilham Castle, Kent
Chillingham Castle, Northumberland
Chillington Hall, Staffordshire
Cholmondeley Castle, Cheshire
Constable Burton Hall, Yorkshire
Corsham Court, Wiltshire
Deans Court, Dorset
Doddington Hall, Lincolnshire
Easton Grey House, Wiltshire
Eccleshall Castle, Staffordshire
Euston Hall, Norfolk
Exbury Gardens, Hampshire
Haddon Hall, Derbyshire
Harewood House, Yorkshire
Heale House, Wiltshire
Helmingham Hall, Suffolk
Hever Castle, Kent
The Hirsel, Berwickshire
Hodnet Hall, Shropshire
How Caple Court, Herefordshire
Iford Manor, Wiltshire
Kentwell Hall, Suffolk
Levens Hall, Cumbria
Littlecote House, Wiltshire
Longleat House, Wiltshire
Loseley Park, Surrey
Manderston, Berwickshire
Mannington Hall, Norfolk
Melbourne Hall, Derbyshire
Minterne Gardens, Dorset
Moccas Court, Herefordshire
Mount Ephraim, Kent
Newick Park, Sussex
The Owl House, Kent
Powderham Castle, Devon
Prideaux Place, Cornwall
Rainthorpe Hall, Norfolk
Ripley Castle, Yorkshire (2)
Riverhill House, Kent
Rotherfield Park, Hampshire

Rousham, Oxfordshire
Scone Palace, Perthshire
Sezincote, Gloucestershire
Spetchley Park, Worcestershire
Stanton Harcourt, Oxfordshire
Syon Park, Middlesex
Tatton Park, Cheshire
Torosay Castle, Argyllshire
Traquair House, Peeblesshire
Warwick Castle, Warwickshire
Weston Park, Shropshire
Wilton House, Wiltshire

## Conservatories

Bowood House, Wiltshire
Chatsworth House, Derbyshire
Elton Hall, Cambridgeshire
Hergest Croft, Herefordshire
Iford Manor, Wiltshire
Mapperton House, Dorset
Raby Castle, Durham
Rousham, Oxfordshire
Somerleyton Hall, Suffolk
Spains Hall, Essex
Spetchley Park, Worcestershire
Syon Park, Middlesex
Tatton Park, Cheshire
Warwick Castle, Warwickshire
Weston Park, Shropshire

## Dovecotes

Arbigland, Dumfries
Athelhampton, Dorset
Berkeley Castle, Gloucestershire
Brympton d'Evercy, Somerset
Bryn Bras Castle, Gwynedd
Chicheley Hall, Buckinghamshire
Corby Castle, Cumbria
Corsham Court, Wiltshire
Earlshall Castle, Fife
Elsham Hall, South Humberside
Finchcocks, Kent
Firle Place, East Sussex
Harewood House, Yorkshire
Heale House, Wiltshire
The Hirsel, Berwickshire
Hodnet Hall, Shropshire
Holker Hall, Cumbria
Houghton Lodge, Hampshire
Hutton-in-the-Forest, Cumbria
Kentwell Hall, Suffolk
Longleat House, Wiltshire
Loseley Park, Surrey
Manderston House, Berwickshire
Mapperton House, Dorset
Melbourne Hall, Derbyshire
Mertoun, Roxburghshire (1567)
Michelham Priory, East Sussex
Painswick Rococo Gardens, Gloucestershire
Prideaux Place, Cornwall
Rousham, Oxfordshire
Somerleyton Hall, Suffolk
Spains Hall, Essex
Squerryes Court, Kent
Stanton Harcourt, Oxfordshire
Woburn Abbey, Bedfordshire

## Follies

Arbigland, Dumfries
Arbury Hall, Warwickshire
Benington Lordship, Hertfordshire
Bowood House, Wiltshire. Chapel
Bramham Park, Yorkshire
Bryn Bras Castle, Gwynedd

Castle Howard, Yorkshire
Chillington Hall, Staffordshire
Combe Sydenham, Somerset
Corsham Court, Wiltshire
Firle Place, East Sussex
Hodnet Hall, Shropshire
Hopetoun House, Lothian
Houghton Lodge, Hampshire
How Caple Court, Herefordshire
Iford Manor, Wiltshire (several)
Manderston, Berwickshire
Mannington Hall, Norfolk
Painswick Rococo Gardens, Gloucestershire
Powderham Castle, Devon
Rotherfield Park, Hampshire
Rousham, Oxfordshire
Sheldon Manor, Wiltshire
Sherborne Castle, Dorset
Tatton Park, Cheshire
Traquair House, Peeblesshire
Weston Park, Shropshire
Whatton House, Leicestershire
Woburn Abbey, Bedfordshire

## Gazebos

Athelhampton, Dorset
Batsford Arboretum, Gloucestershire
Bowood House, Wiltshire
Dalemain, Cumbria
Easton Grey House, Wiltshire
Euston Hall, Norfolk
Glamis Castle, Angus (2)
Godinton Park, Kent
Harewood House, Yorkshire
Holme Pierrepont Hall, Nottinghamshire
Hopetoun House, Lothian
How Caple Court, Herefordshire
Kentwell Hall, Suffolk
Iford Manor Wiltshire
Kingston House, Oxfordshire
Layer Marney Tower, Essex
Longleat House, Wiltshire
Luton Hoo, Bedfordshire
Painswick Rococo Gardens, Gloucestershire
Parnham, Dorset
Penshurst Place, Kent
Raby Castle, Durham
Ripley Castle, Yorkshire
Squerryes Court, Kent
Stanton Harcourt, Oxfordshire
Sutton Park, Yorkshire
Torosay Castle, Argyllshire
Traquair House, Peeblesshire
West Dean Gardens, West Sussex

## Glass-Houses

Ardtornish, Argyllshire
Arley Hall, Cheshire
Barnsley House, Gloucestershire
Benington Lordship, Hertfordshire
Blairquhan, Ayrshire
Blenheim Palace, Oxfordshire
Bowood House, Wiltshire
Breamore House, Hampshire
Bryn Bras Castle, Gwynedd
Chatsworth House, Derbyshire
Cholmondeley Castle, Cheshire
Clapton Court, Somerset
Combe Sydenham, Somerset
Docwra's Manor, Hertfordshire
Easton Grey House, Wiltshire
Edmondsham House, Dorset
Elsham Hall, South Humberside
Exbury Gardens, Hampshire
Forde Abbey, Somerset
Godinton Park, Kent

Grimsthorpe Castle, Lincolnshire
Hammerwood Park, West Sussex
Harewood House, Yorkshire
Haughley Park, Suffolk
Hergest Croft, Herefordshire
Hever Castle, Kent
Holdenby House, Northamptonshire
Houghton Lodge, Hampshire
Kentwell Hall, Suffolk
Kingstone Lisle Park, Oxfordshire
Layer Marney Tower, Essex
Leeds Castle, Kent (13)
Littlecote House, Wiltshire
Manderston, Berwickshire
Melbourne Hall, Derbyshire
Mertoun, Roxburghshire
Michelham Priory, East Sussex
The Owl House, Kent
Parham House, West Sussex
Powderham Castle, Devon
Rainthorpe Hall, Norfolk
Ripley Castle, Yorkshire
Rodmarton Manor, Gloucestershire
Rotherfield Park, Hampshire
Somerleyton Hall, Suffolk
Spains Hall, Essex
Stansted Park, Hampshire
Stonor Park, Oxfordshire
Sutton Park, Yorkshire
Tatton Park, Cheshire
West Dean Gardens, West Sussex
Whatton House, Leicestershire

## Grottoes

Blenheim Palace, Oxfordshire
Bowood House, Wiltshire
Bramham Park, Yorkshire
Chatsworth House, Derbyshire
Chiddingstone Castle, Kent (caves)
Chillingham Castle, Northumberland
Hever Castle, Kent
Houghton Lodge, Hampshire
Leeds Castle, Kent
Manderston, Berwickshire
Mapperton House, Dorset
Melbourne Hall, Derbyshire
Nunwell House, Isle of Wight
Pencarrow, Cornwall
Prideaux Place, Cornwall
Rockingham Castle, Leicestershire
Sezincote, Gloucestershire
Weston Park, Shropshire
Whatton House, Leicestershire
Woburn Abbey, Bedfordshire

## Ha-Has

Arley Hall, Cheshire
Barford Park, Somerset
Belvoir Castle, Lincolnshire
Benington Lordship, Hertfordshire
Blairquhan, Ayrshire
Blenheim Palace, Oxfordshire
Bodrhyddan Hall, Clwyd
Bowood House, Wiltshire
Bramham Park, Yorkshire
Breamore House, Hampshire
Broadleas, Wiltshire
Burton Constable Hall, North Humberside
Browsholme Hall, Lancashire
Brympton d'Evercy, Somerset
Castle Howard, Yorkshire
Chatsworth House, Derbyshire
Chenies Manor, Buckinghamshire
Chicheley Hall, Buckinghamshire
Chiddingstone Castle, Kent
Chilham Castle, Kent
Chillingham Castle, Northumberland

Chillington Hall, Staffordshire
Clapton Court, Somerset
Constable Burton Hall, Yorkshire
Corsham Court, Wiltshire
Dalemain, Cumbria
Ditchingham Hall, Suffolk
Dorfold Hall, Cheshire
Easton Grey House, Wiltshire
Elsham Hall, South Humberside
Elton Hall, Cambridgeshire
Finchcocks, Kent
Forde Abbey, Somerset
Grimsthorpe Castle, Lincolnshire
Hammerwood Park, West Sussex
Haughley Park, Suffolk
Hergest Croft, Herefordshire
The Hirsel, Berwickshire
Holdenby House, Northamptonshire
Hopetoun House, Lothian
Kingston House, Oxfordshire
Knebworth House, Hertfordshire
Levens Hall, Cumbria (earliest: 1690)
Littlecote House, Wiltshire
Longleat House, Wiltshire
Luton Hoo, Bedfordshire
Manderston, Berwickshire
Mapperton House, Dorset
Mertoun, Roxburghshire
Moccas Court, Herefordshire
Mount Ephraim, Kent
Newick Park, East Sussex
Norton Conyers, Yorkshire
Nunwell House, Isle of Wight
Parham House, West Sussex
Parnham, Dorset
Raby Castle, Durham
Rainthorpe Hall, Norfolk
Ripley Castle, Yorkshire
Rodmarton Manor, Gloucestershire
Rotherfield Park, Hampshire
Rousham, Oxfordshire
Sherborne Castle, Dorset
Somerleyton Hall, Suffolk
Spetchley Park, Worcestershire
Squerryes Court, Kent
Stansted Park, Hampshire
Stockeld Park, Yorkshire
Syon Park, Middlesex
Tatton Park, Cheshire
Weston Park, Shropshire
Woburn Abbey Bedfordshire

## Ice-Houses

Arbury Hall, Warwickshire
Belvoir Castle, Lincolnshire
Blairquhan, Ayrshire
Blenheim Palace, Oxfordshire
Bodrhyddan Hall, Clwyd
Bowood House, Wiltshire
Bramham Park, Yorkshire
Chatsworth House, Derbyshire
Chillington Hall, Staffordshire
Constable Burton Hall, Yorkshire
Corsham Court, Wiltshire
Dorfold Hall, Cheshire
Eastnor Castle, Herefordshire
Easton Grey House, Wiltshire (remains)
Eccleshall Castle, Staffordshire
Firle Place, East Sussex (ruins)
Hodnet Hall, Shropshire
Holdenby House, Northamptonshire
Hopetoun House, Lothian
Kingstone Lisle Park, Oxfordshire
Leeds Castle, Kent
Levens Hall, Cumbria
Littlecote House, Wiltshire
Manderston, Berwickshire
Melbourne Hall, Derbyshire
Mertoun, Roxburghshire

Moccas Court, Herefordshire
Newick Park, East Sussex
Parnham, Dorset
Pencarrow, Cornwall
Picton Castle, Dyfed
Ragley Hall, Warwickshire
Ripley Castle, Yorkshire
Rotherfield Park, Hampshire
Scone Palace, Perth
Sherborne Castle, Dorset
Squerryes Court, Kent
Sutton Park, Yorkshire
Syon Park, Middlesex
Tatton Park, Cheshire
Warwick Castle, Warwickshire
Whatton House, Leicestershire (bogey hole)
Woburn Abbey, Bedfordshire (remains)

## Mounts

Benington Lordship, Hertfordshire
Bickleigh Castle, Devon
Otley Hall, Suffolk
Penshurst Place, Kent
The Priory, Lavenham, Suffolk
Rockingham Castle, Leicestershire
Warwick Castle, Warwickshire

## Orangeries

Blenheim Palace, Oxfordshire
Bodrhyddan Hall, Clwyd (under
   construction)
Bowood House, Wiltshire
Burton Constable Hall, North
   Humberside
Chatsworth House, Derbyshire
Elsham Hall, South Humberside
Hutton-in-the Forest, Cumbria
Longleat House, Wiltshire
Lyme Park, Cheshire
Mapperton House, Dorset
Norton Conyers, Yorkshire
Ripley Castle, Yorkshire
Sezincote, Gloucestershire
Sherborne Castle, Dorset
Somerleyton Hall, Suffolk
Squerryes Court, Kent
Sutton Park, Yorkshire
Tatton Park, Cheshire
West Dean Gardens, West Sussex

## Pergolas

Athelhampton, Dorset
Blairquhan, Ayrshire
Bowood House, Wiltshire
Castle Howard, Yorkshire
Forde Abbey, Somerset
Heale House, Wiltshire
Hergest Croft, Herefordshire
Hever Castle, Kent
Holker Hall, Cumbria
How Caple Court, Herefordshire
Manderston, Berwickshire
Mannington Hall, Norfolk
Mapperton House, Dorset
Newby Hall, Yorkshire
The Owl House, Kent
Penshurst Place, Kent
Raby Castle, Durham
Rockingham Castle, Leicestershire
Rodmarton Manor, Gloucestershire
Rousham, Oxfordshire
Somerleyton Hall, Suffolk
Stonor Park, Oxfordshire
Sutton Park, Yorkshire
Syon Park, Middlesex

147

Tatton Park, Cheshire
West Dean Gardens, West Sussex
Whatton House, Leicestershire

## Ruins

Ardtornish, Argyllshire
Beaulieu Abbey, Hampshire
Benington Lordship, Hertfordshire
Chenies Manor, Buckinghamshire
Chillingham Castle, Northumberland
Corsham Court, Wiltshire
Eccleshall Castle, Staffordshire
Hodnet Hall, Shropshire
How Caple Court, Herefordshire
Lamport Hall, Northamptonshire
Leeds Castle, Kent
Mannington Hall, Norfolk
Powderham Castle, Devon
Prideaux Place, Cornwall
Rockingham Castle, Leicestershire
St Osyth's Priory, Essex
Squerryes Court, Kent
Sudeley Castle, Gloucestershire.
  Banquetting hall, tithe barn

## Statuary

Arbigland, Dumfries
Arbury Hall, Warwickshire
Arley Hall, Cheshire
Athelhampton, Dorset
Barnsley House, Gloucestershire
Barton Manor, Isle of Wight
Batsford Arboretum, Gloucestershire
Belvoir Castle, Lincolnshire
Benington Lordship, Hertfordshire
Bowood House, Wiltshire
Bramham Park, Yorkshire
Blenheim Palace, Oxfordshire
Bryn Bras Castle, Gwynedd
Burton Constable Hall, North Humberside
Castle Howard, Yorkshire
Chatsworth House, Derbyshire
Chicheley Hall, Buckinghamshire
Chillingham Castle, Northumberland
Cholmondeley Castle, Cheshire
Corby Castle, Cumbria
Doddington Hall, Lincolnshire
Dorfold Hall, Cheshire
Easton Grey House, Wiltshire
Elsham Hall, South Humberside
Elton Hall, Cambridgeshire
Forde Abbey, Somerset
Gaulden Manor, Somerset
Godinton Park, Kent
Grimsthorpe Castle, Lincolnshire
Helmingham Hall, Suffolk
Hergest Croft, Herefordshire
Hever Castle, Kent
Hodnet Hall, Shropshire
Holker Hall, Cumbria
How Caple Court, Herefordshire
Iford Manor, Wiltshire
Knebworth House, Hertfordshire
Lamport Hall, Northamptonshire
Layer Marney Tower, Essex
Littlecote House, Wiltshire
Longleat House, Wiltshire
Manderston, Berwickshire
Mannington Hall, Norfolk
Mapperton House, Dorset
Melbourne Hall, Derbyshire
Newby Hall, Yorkshire
Norton Conyers, Yorkshire
Nunwell House, Isle of Wight
The Owl House, Kent
Painswick Rococo Gardens, Gloucestershire
Parham House, West Sussex
Parnham House, Dorset

Penshurst Place, Kent
Powderham Castle, Devon
Prideaux Place, Cornwall
The Priory, Lavenham, Suffolk
Riverhill House, Kent
Rockingham Castle, Leicestershire
Rousham, Oxfordshire
Sheldon Manor, Wiltshire
Somerleyton Hall, Suffolk
Sudeley Castle, Gloucestershire
Sutton Park, Yorkshire
Tatton Park, Cheshire
Torosay Castle, Argyllshire. Statue walk
Traquair House, Peeblesshire
Weston Park, Shropshire
Whatton House, Leicestershire
Woburn Abbey, Bedfordshire

## Summer-Houses

Adlington Hall, Cheshire
Arbigland, Dumfries
Arley Hall, Cheshire
Athelhampton, Dorset
Barford Park, Somerset
Barnsley House, Gloucestershire
Batsford Arboretum, Gloucestershire
Belvoir Castle, Lincolnshire
Bodrhyddan Hall, Clwyd
Bramdean House, Hampshire (2, including
  an apple house)
Bramham Park, Yorkshire
Breamore House, Hampshire
Broadleas, Wiltshire
Bryn Bras Castle, Gwynedd
Chatsworth House, Derbyshire
Chicheley Hall, Buckinghamshire
Chillingham Castle, Northumberland
Clapton Court, Somerset
Dalemain, Cumbria
Dunrobin Castle, Sutherland
Earlshall Castle, Fife
Eastnor Castle, Herefordshire
Easton Grey House, Wiltshire
Finchcocks, Kent
Firle Place, East Sussex (thatched dairy)
Hammerwood Park, West Sussex
Heale House, Wiltshire
Helmingham Hall, Suffolk
Hodnet Hall, Shropshire
How Caple Court, Herefordshire
Hutton-in-the-Forest, Cumbria
Kingstone Lisle Park, Oxfordshire
Lamport Hall, Northamptonshire
Leeds Castle, Kent
Longleat House, Wiltshire
Loseley Park, Surrey
Manderston, Berwickshire
Mapperton House, Dorset
Melbourne Hall, Derbyshire
Otley Hall, Suffolk
The Owl House, Kent
Parham House, West Sussex
Pencarrow, Cornwall
Powderham Castle, Devon
Raby Castle, Durham
Rainthorpe Hall, Norfolk
Ripley Castle, Yorkshire
Rodmarton Manor, Gloucestershire
Rotherfield Park, Hampshire
Spains Hall, Essex
Spetchley Park, Worcestershire
Stonor Park, Oxfordshire
Tatton Park, Cheshire
Traquair House, Peeblesshire
West Dean Gardens, West Sussex

## Temples

Adlington Hall, Cheshire

Barnsley House, Gloucestershire
Blenheim Palace, Oxfordshire
Bowood House, Wiltshire
Bramham Park, Yorkshire
Brympton d'Evercy, Somerset
Castle Howard, Yorkshire
Chatsworth House, Derbyshire
Chillington Hall, Staffordshire
Cholmondeley Castle, Cheshire
Corby Castle, Cumbria
Docwra's Manor, Hertfordshire
Doddington Hall, Lincolnshire
Elton Hall, Cambridgeshire
Euston Hall, Norfolk
Mannington Hall, Norfolk
Prideaux Place, Cornwall
Rousham, Oxfordshire
Sezincote, Gloucestershire
Spains Hall, Essex
Spetchley Park, Worcestershire
Sutton Park, Yorkshire
Tatton Park, Cheshire
Weston Park, Shropshire
Woburn Abbey, Bedfordshire

## Other buildings

Adlington Hall, Cheshire. Shell cottage
Bowood House, Wiltshire. Boathouse,
  *cottage ornée*
Browsholme Hall, Lancashire. Entrance
  arch, boathouse
Brympton d'Evercy, Somerset. Parish
  church, priest house, clock tower
Castle Howard, Yorkshire. Mausoleum,
  pyramid
Chiddingstone Castle, Kent. Hermit's
  hollow tree
Chillingham Castle, Northumberland.
  Medieval church, monastery ruins, torture
  chamber, jousting wall
Corsham Court, Wiltshire. Gothic bath
  house
Eastnor Castle, Herefordshire. Obelisk
Easton Grey House, Wiltshire. Parish
  church in grounds
Elsham Hall, South Humberside. Windmill
Gaulden Manor, Somerset. Old barns
Haughley Park, Suffolk. Seventeenth-
  century barn
Heale House, Wiltshire. Japanese tea-house
Hever Castle, Kent. Loggia
Hodnet Hall, Shropshire. Tithe barn
HoldenbyHouse, Northamptonshire.
  Elizabethan arches
Houghton Lodge, Hampshire. Chalk cob
  walls
How Caple Court, Herefordshire.
  Seventeenth-century barns, church, old
  stables
Iford Manor, Wiltshire. Cloister, casita
Kingston House, Oxfordshire. Cockpit
Knebworth House, Hertfordshire.
  Mausoleum, memorials in dogs' cemetery
Levens Hall, Cumbria. Smoke-house
Mellerstain House, Berwickshire. Thatched
  cottage and garden
Mount Ephraim, Kent. 2 pavilions
Muncaster Castle, Cumbria. Castle,
  octagonal dairy
Pencarrow, Cornwall. Ancient British
  encampment, cockpit
Powderham Castle, Devon. Granary
Prideaux Place, Cornwall. Dairy and bake-
  house under restoration
Raby Castle, Durham. *Cottage ornée*
Ripley Castle, Yorkshire. Palm house
Sheldon Manor, Wiltshire. Chapel, apple
  house on staddle stones

Sherborne Castle, Dorset. Raleigh's seat, Pope's seat
Somerleyton Hall, Suffolk. Peach cases, aviary, loggia
Spetchley Park, Worcestershire. Root house

Stanton Harcourt, Oxfordshire. Medieval kitchen
Stockeld Park, Yorkshire. Chapel, stable block
Sudeley Castle, Gloucestershire. Chapel, tithe barn ruins

Tatton Park, Cheshire. Glass fernery with rock-work
Torosay Castle, Argyllshire. Castle, colonnade, rotunda
Weston Park, Shropshire. Tunnel

# Plants

## Avenues

Arbigland, Dumfries. Wellingtonia
Arbury Hall, Warwickshire. Lime
Ardtornish, Argyllshire. *Betula pubescens*
Athelhampton, Dorset. Pleached limes
Beaulieu Abbey, Hampshire. Horse chestnut
Benington Lordship, Hertfordshire. Oak
Blairquhan, Ayrshire. Lime, etc
Blenheim Palace, Oxfordshire. Lime
Bramham Park, Yorkshire. Beech
Breamore House, Hampshire. Lime
Brympton d'Evercy, Somerset. London planes, limes
Castle Howard, Yorkshire. Lime
Chatsworth House, Derbyshire. Tulip trees
Chicheley Hall, Buckinghamshire. Lime
Chilham Castle, Kent. Lime
Chillingham Castle, Northumberland, Lime, mixed hardwoods
Chillington Hall, Staffordshire
Constable Burton Hall, Yorkshire. Lime (2)
Corsham Court, Wiltshire. Lime
Doddington Hall, Lincolnshire
Dorfold Hall, Cheshire. Lime
Dunrobin Castle, Sutherland. *Sorbus intermedia*
Easton Grey House, Wiltshire. Hornbeam, yew
Elsham Hall, South Humberside. *Populus robusta*, Turkey oak
Elton Hall, Cambridgeshire. Lime
Euston Hall, Norfolk. Lime
Finchcocks, Kent. Lime
Forde Abbey, Somerset. Lime
Godinton Park, Kent. Cherries and sorbus
Goodnestone Park, Kent. Lime
Grimsthorpe Castle, Lincolnshire. Oak
Haughley Park, Suffolk. Lime
Heale House, Wiltshire. Black poplar, beech and maple
Helmingham Hall, Suffolk. Oak
Hergest Croft, Herefordshire. Conifers
Hever Castle, Kent. Chestnut (storm damaged)
Hodnet Hall, Shropshire. Lime, beech
Holdenby Hall, Northamptonshire. Cherry, Siberian crab
Hopetoun House, Lothian. Lime
Kentwell Hall, Suffolk. Lime
Kingston House, Oxfordshire. Beech, *Prunus avium* 'Flora Plena'
Knebworth House, Hertfordshire. Horse chestnut and lime, pollarded lime
Lamport Hall, Northants. Lime
Levens Hall, Cumbria. Oak
Littlecote House, Wiltshire. Lime
Longleat House, Wiltshire. *Tilia platyphyllos* 'rubra', Liriodendron
Lyme Park, Cheshire. Lime, sycamore
Manderston, Berwickshire. Lime

Mannington Hall, Norfolk. Lime
Melbourne Hall, Derbyshire. Yew tunnel
Newby Hall, Yorkshire. Lime
Painswick Rococo Gardens, Gloucestershire. Yew, beech
Pencarrow, Cornwall. Monkey puzzle, specimen conifers, rhododendron and camellia
Penshurst Place, Kent. Lime
Powderham Castle, Devon. Oaks, limes and cedars
Rainthorpe Hall, Norfolk. Oak, Scots pine
Rockingham Castle, Leicestershire. Lime
Rotherfield Park, Hampshire. Lime, beech in wood
Rousham, Oxfordshire. Lime
St Osyth's Priory, Essex. Chestnut
Sheldon Manor, Wiltshire. Lime
Somerleyton Hall, Suffolk. Lime
Sudeley Castle, Gloucestershire. Lime
Stansted Park, Hampshire. Beech
Stanway House, Gloucestershire. Lime, oak, chestnut
Syon Park, Middlesex
Tatton Park, Cheshire
Traquair House, Peeblesshire. Sycamore, plane
Warwick Castle, Warwickshire. Cedar of Lebanon
Whatton House, Leicestershire

## Formal Bedding

Arbigland, Dumfries
Arbury Hall, Warwickshire
Barford Park, Somerset
Barton Manor, Isle of Wight
Beaulieu Abbey, Hampshire
Berkeley Castle, Gloucestershire
Bodrhyddan Hall, Clwyd
Bramham Park, Yorkshire
Castle Howard, Yorkshire
Cawdor Castle, Nairn
Chicheley Hall, Buckinghamshire
Combe Sydenham, Somerset
Doddington Hall, Lincolnshire
Dunrobin Castle, Sutherland
Easton Grey House, Wiltshire
Edmondsham House, Dorset
Elsham Hall, South Humberside
Finchcocks, Kent
Forde Abbey, Somerset
Godinton Park, Kent
Grimsthorpe Castle, Lincolnshire
Harewood House, Yorkshire
Helmingham Hall, Suffolk
Hergest Croft, Herefordshire
Hever Castle, Kent
Holdenby House, Northamptonshire
Holker Hall, Cumbria

Houghton Lodge, Hampshire
Hutton-in-the-Forest, Cumbria
Kingstone Lisle Park, Oxfordshire
Lamport Hall, Northamptonshire
Levens Hall, Cumbria
Littlecote House, Wiltshire
Lyme Park, Cheshire
Manderston, Berwickshire
Mannington Hall, Norfolk
Mapperton House, Dorset
Melbourne Hall, Derbyshire
Otley Hall, Suffolk
The Owl House, Kent
Rockingham Castle, Leicestershire
Somerleyton Hall, Suffolk
Stonor Park, Oxfordshire
Sudeley Castle, Gloucestershire
Sutton Park, Yorkshire
Tatton Park, Cheshire

## Fine Trees

Adlington Hall, Cheshire
Arbigland, Dumfries
Arbury Hall, Warwickshire
Ardtornish, Argyllshire
Arley Hall, Cheshire
Barford Park, Somerset
Barton Manor, Isle of Wight
Batsford Arboretum, Gloucestershire
Beaulieu Abbey, Hampshire
Belvoir Castle, Lincolnshire
Benington Lordship, Hertfordshire
Berkeley Castle, Gloucestershire
Bickleigh Castle, Devon
Blairquhan, Ayrshire (largest cut-leaved beech in Britain)
Blenheim Palace, Oxfordshire
Bodrhyddan Hall, Clwyd
Bowood House, Wiltshire
Bramdean House, Hampshire
Bramham Park, Yorkshire
Breamore House, Hampshire
Broadleas, Wiltshire
Broughton Castle, Oxfordshire
Brympton d'Evercy, Somerset
Bryn Bras Castle, Gwynedd
Burton Constable Hall, North Humberside
Castle Howard, Yorkshire
Cawdor Castle, Nairn
Chatsworth House, Derbyshire
Chicheley Hall, Buckinghamshire
Chilham Castle, Kent
Chillingham Castle, Northumberland
Chillington Hall, Staffordshire
Cholmondeley Castle, Cheshire
Clapton Court, Somerset
Combe Sydenham, Somerset
Constable Burton Hall, Yorkshire
Corby Castle, Cumbria

Corsham Court, Wiltshire
Dalemain, Cumbria
Deans Court, Dorset
Doddington Hall, Lincolnshire
Dorfold Hall, Cheshire
Dunrobin Castle, Sutherland
Earlshall Castle, Fife
Eastnor Castle, Herefordshire
Easton Grey House, Wiltshire
Eccleshall Castle, Staffordshire
Edmondsham House, Dorset
Elsham Hall, South Humberside
Elton Hall, Cambridgeshire
Euston Hall, Norfolk
Finchcocks, Kent
Forde Abbey, Somerset
Gaulden Manor, Somerset
Godinton Park, Kent
Goodnestone Park, Kent
Grimsthorpe Castle, Lincolnshire
Harewood House, Yorkshire
Haughley Park, Suffolk
Heale House, Wiltshire
Helmingham Hall, Suffolk
Hergest Croft, Herefordshire
Hever Castle, Kent
The High Beeches, Sussex
The Hirsel, Berwickshire
Hodnet Hall, Shropshire
Holdenby House, Northamptonshire
Holker Hall, Cumbria
Holme Pierrepont Hall, Nottinghamshire
Hopetoun House, Lothian
Houghton Lodge, Hampshire
How Caple Court, Herefordshire
Hutton-in-the-Forest, Cumbria
Kentwell Hall, Suffolk
Kingston House, Oxfordshire
Kingstone Lisle Park, Oxfordshire
Knebworth House, Hertfordshire
Lamport Hall, Northamptonshire
Layer Marney Tower, Essex
Leeds Castle, Kent
Levens Hall, Cumbria
Littlecote House, Wiltshire
Longleat House, Wiltshire
Loseley Park, Surrey
Luton Hoo, Bedfordshire
Manderston, Berwickshire
Mannington Hall, Norfolk
Mapperton House, Dorset
Mellerstain House, Berwickshire
Michelham Priory, East Sussex
Minterne Gardens, Dorset
Misarden Park, Gloucestershire
Melbourne Hall, Derbyshire
Moccas Court, Herefordshire
Mount Ephraim, Kent
Muncaster Castle, Cumbria
Newby Hall, Yorkshire
Newick Park, East Sussex
Norton Conyers, Yorkshire
Nunwell House, Isle of Wight
Painswick Rococo Gardens, Gloucestershire
Parham House, West Sussex
Parnham, Dorset
Pencarrow, Cornwall
Picton Castle, Dyfed
Powderham Castle, Devon
Raby Castle, Durham
Ragley Hall, Warwickshire
Rainthorpe Hall, Norfolk
Ripley Castle, Yorkshire
Riverhill House, Kent
Rockingham Castle, Leicestershire
Rotherfield Park, Hampshire
Rousham, Oxfordshire
Scone Palace, Perth
Sheldon Manor, Wiltshire
Sherborne Castle, Dorset
Smedmore House, Dorset

Somerleyton Hall, Suffolk
Spetchley Park, Worcestershire
Squerryes Court, Kent
Stansted Park, Hampshire
Stanway House, Gloucestershire
Stockeld Park, Yorkshire
Stonor Park, Oxfordshire
Sudeley Castle, Gloucestershire
Sutton Park, Yorkshire
Synon Park, Middlesex
Tatton Park, Cheshire
Thorp Perrow Arboretum, Yorkshire
Torosay Castle, Argyllshire
Traquair House, Peeblesshire
Warwick Castle, Warwickshire
West Dean Gardens, West Sussex
Weston Park, Shropshire
Whatton House, Leicestershire
Wilton House, Wiltshire
Woburn Abbey, Bedfordshire

## Mature Hedges

Adlington Hall, Cheshire. Yew
Athelhampton, Dorset. Yew
Arbury Hall, Warwickshire
Arley Hall, Cheshire. Yew
Barford Park, Somerset. Yew, hornbeam
Barton Manor, Isle of Wight. Bay
Beaulieu Abbey, Hampshire. Yew
Belvoir Castle, Lincolnshire. Yew, hornbeam
Benington Lordship, Hertfordshire. Yew
Berkeley Castle, Gloucestershire. Box
Bowood House, Wiltshire
Bramdean House, Hampshire. Box, yew
Bramham Park, Yorkshire. Beech
Breamore House, Hampshire. Yew
Broughton Castle, Oxfordshire. Oak
Bryn Bras Castle, Gwynedd
Castle Howard, Yorkshire. Yew
Cawdor Castle, Nairn. Yew
Chicheley Hall, Buckinghamshire
Chilham Castle, Kent. Yew
Chillingham Castle, Northumberland. Yew, box
Cholmondeley Castle, Cheshire. Yew, thuia
Clapton Court, Somerset. Yew, hornbeam, laurel
Corsham Court, Wiltshire. Yew
Dunrobin Castle, Sutherland
Earlshall Castle, Fife. Yew, holly
Easton Grey House, Wiltshire
Edmondsham House, Dorset. Beech
Euston Hall, Norfolk. Yew
Finchcocks, Kent. Yew
Forde Abbey, Somerset. Yew
Gaulden Manor, Somerset. Beech
Glamis Castle, Angus. Box, yew
Godinton Park, Kent. Yew
Goodnestone Park, Kent. Yew
Great Dixter, East Sussex
Grimsthorpe Castle, Lincolnshire. Yew
Haddon Hall, Derbyshire. Beech
Haughley Park, Suffolk. Holly, yew, thuia, osmarea
Heale House, Wiltshire. Yew
Hergest Croft, Herefordshire. Yew
Holker Hall, Cumbria. Beech, hornbeam with yew
Hopetoun House, Lothian. Beech, yew
Houghton Lodge, Hampshire. Yew
How Caple Court, Herefordshire. Yew
Kentwell Hall, Suffolk. Yew
Kingston House, Oxfordshire. Beech, yew, box
Knebworth House, Hertfordshire. Yew
Layer Marney Tower, Essex. Yew
Levens Hall, Cumbria. Beech, yew, box

Littlecote House, Wiltshire. Yew
Longleat House, Wiltshire. Beech, box, yew
Loseley Park, Surrey. Yew
Luton Hoo, Bedfordshire
Manderston, Berwickshire. Beech
Mannington Hall, Norfolk
Mapperton House, Dorset. Beech
Mellerstain House, Berwickshire
Michelham Priory, East Sussex
Misarden Park, Gloucestershire. Yew
Mount Ephraim, Kent. Yew, holly
Newby Hall, Yorkshire. Yew, copper beech
Norton Conyers, Yorkshire
Nunwell House, Isle of Wight. Lonicera
Parnham, Dorset. Yew
Penshurst Place, Kent. Yew
Picton Castle, Dyfed. Escallonia
Raby Castle, Durham. Yew
Rainthorpe Hall, Norfolk. Yew, holly, box
Rockingham Castle, Leicestershire. Yew
Rotherfield Park, Hampshire. Yew (golden buttresses), laurel
Rousham, Oxfordshire. Yew
Sheldon Manor, Wiltshire. Yew, hornbeam
Somerleyton Hall, Suffolk
Spetchley Park, Worcestershire
Squerryes Court, Kent. Yew
Stansted Park, Hampshire
Stanton Harcourt, Oxfordshire. Beech
Sudeley Castle, Gloucestershire. Yew
Sutton Park, Yorkshire. Beech
Tatton Park, Cheshire
Torosay Castle, Argyllshire. Yew, escallonia
Traquair House, Peeblesshire. Beech
Warwick Castle, Warwickshire. Yew, box
West Dean Gardens, West Sussex. Yew
Whatton House, Leicestershire. Laurel
Wilton House, Wiltshire. Yew

## Naturalized Bulbs

Arbigland, Dumfries
Arbury Hall, Warwickshire
Ardtornish, Argyllshire
Athelhampton, Dorset
Barford Park, Somerset
Barnsley House, Gloucestershire
Barton Manor, Isle of Wight
Beaulieu Abbey, Hampshire
Belvoir Castle, Lincolnshire
Benington Lordship, Hertfordshire
Bickleigh Castle, Devon
Blairquhan, Ayrshire
Blenheim Palace, Oxfordshire
Bowood House, Wiltshire
Bramdean House, Hampshire
Bramham Park, Yorkshire
Breamore House, Hampshire
Broadleas, Wiltshire
Brympton d'Evercy, Somerset
Bryn Bras Castle, Gwynedd
Burton Constable Hall, North Humberside
Castle Howard, Yorkshire
Cawdor Castle, Nairn
Chatsworth House, Derbyshire
Chicheley Hall, Buckinghamshire
Chiddingstone Castle, Kent
Chillingham Castle, Northumberland
Chillington Hall, Staffordshire
Cholmondeley Castle, Cheshire
Clapton Court, Somerset
Constable Burton Hall, Yorkshire
Corsham Court, Wiltshire
Deans Court, Dorset
Doddington Hall, Lincolnshire
Dorfold Hall, Cheshire
Dunrobin Castle, Sutherland
Earlshall Castle, Fife
Eastnor Castle, Herefordshire
Easton Grey House, Wiltshire

Eccleshall Castle, Staffordshire
Edmondsham House, Dorset
Elsham Hall, South Humberside
Elton Hall, Cambridgeshire
Finchcocks, Kent
Firle Place, East Sussex
Forde Abbey, Somerset
Godinton Park, Kent
Goodnestone Park, Kent
Great Dixter, East Sussex
Grimsthorpe Castle, Lincolnshire
Haddon Hall, Derbyshire
Harewood House, Yorkshire
Haughley Park, Suffolk
Heale House, Wiltshire
Helmingham Hall, Suffolk
Hergest Croft, Herefordshire
Hever Castle, Kent
The High Beeches, West Sussex
The Hirsel, Berwickshire
Hodnet Hall, Shropshire
Holdenby House, Northamptonshire
Holker Hall, Cumbria
Holme Pierrepont Hall, Nottinghamshire
Hopetoun House, Lothian
Houghton Lodge, Hampshire
How Caple Court, Herefordshire
Hutton-in-the-Forest, Cumbria
Iford Manor, Wiltshire
Kentwell Hall, Suffolk
Kingston House, Oxfordshire
Layer Marney Tower, Essex
Leeds Castle, Kent
Littlecote House, Wiltshire
Longleat House, Wiltshire
Luton Hoo, Bedfordshire
Mannington Hall, Norfolk
Mapperton House, Dorset
Misarden Park, Gloucestershire
Melbourne Hall, Derbyshire
Mount Ephraim, Kent
Newby Hall, Yorkshire
Newick Park, East Sussex
Nunwell House, Isle of Wight
Otley Hall, Suffolk
The Owl House, Kent
Painswick Rococo Gardens, Gloucestershire
Parham House, West Sussex
Parnham, Dorset
Penshurst Place, Kent
Powderham Castle, Devon
The Priory, Lavenham, Suffolk
Ragley Hall, Warwickshire
Rainthorpe Hall, Norfolk
Riverhill House, Kent
Rockingham Castle, Leicestershire
Rousham, Oxfordshire
Scone Palace, Perth
Sheldon Manor, Wiltshire
Spetchley Park, Worcestershire
Squerryes Court, Kent
Stanton Harcourt, Oxfordshire
Stockeld Park, Yorkshire
Sudeley Castle, Gloucestershire
Sutton Park, Yorkshire
Syon Park, Middlesex
Tatton Park, Cheshire
Thorp Perrow Arboretum, Yorkshire
Torosay Castle, Argyllshire
Traquair House, Peeblesshire
Warwick Castle, Warwickshire
Whatton House, Leicestershire
Wilton House, Wiltshire

## Nutteries

Edmondsham House, Dorset
Elsham Hall, South Humberside
Forde Abbey, Somerset
Heale House, Wiltshire

Hergest Croft, Herefordshire
Otley Hall, Suffolk (2)
The Owl House, Kent
Penshurst Place, Kent
The Priory, Lavenham, Suffolk
Rainthorpe Hall, Norfolk
Stanton Harcourt, Oxfordshire

## Pleaching

Arley Hall, Cheshire
Athelhampton, Dorset. Lime
Barnsley House, Gloucestershire. Lime
Benington Lordship, Hertfordshire. Lime
Barford Park, Somerset. Hornbeam
Castle Howard, Yorkshire. Hornbeam
Chatsworth House, Derbyshire. Lime
Clapton Court, Somerset. Lime
Doddington Hall, Lincolnshire. Hornbeam
Earlshall Castle, Fife.
Hergest Croft, Herefordshire. Apples, pears
Helmingham Hall, Suffolk. Pear, peach,
   apple, cherry
Houghton Lodge, Hampshire. Espalier fruit
   trees
Kentwell Hall, Suffolk. Lime, apples, pears
Kingstone Lisle Park, Oxfordshire
Lyme Park, Cheshire. Lime
Mannington Hall, Norfolk. Lime
The Owl House, Kent. Apples
Parnham, Dorset. Lime
Penshurst Place, Kent. Lime
Sheldon Manor, Wiltshire. Hornbeam
Wilton House, Wiltshire. Lime

## Rare or Unusual Bulbs

Barnsley House, Gloucestershire
Bramdean House, Hampshire
Broadleas, Wiltshire
Cawdor Castle, Nairn
Clapton Court, Somerset
Docwra's Manor, Hertfordshire
Helmingham Hall, Suffolk
Hergest Croft, Herefordshire
Holker Hall, Cumbria
Houghton Lodge, Hampshire
Kingston House, Oxfordshire
Newby Hall, Yorkshire
Spetchley Park, Worcestershire

## Rare or Unusual Herbaceous Plants

Arbigland, Dumfries
Arley Hall, Cheshire
Barnsley House, Gloucestershire
Benington Lordship, Hertfordshire
Bramdean House, Hampshire
Broadleas, Wiltshire
Brympton d'Evercy, Somerset
Castle Howard, Yorkshire
Cawdor Castle, Nairn
Chillingham Castle, Northumberland
Clapton Court, Somerset
Dalemain, Cumbria
Docwra's Manor, Hertfordshire
Elton Hall, Cambridgeshire
Forde Abbey, Somerset
Goodnestone Park, Kent
Great Dixter, East Sussex
Heale House, Wiltshire
Helmingham Hall, Suffolk
Hergest Croft, Herefordshire
Holdenby House, Northamptonshire
Holker Hall, Cumbria
How Caple Court, Herefordshire

Hutton-in-the-Forest, Cumbria
Knebworth House, Hertfordshire
Leeds Castle, Kent
Levens Hall, Cumbria
Luton Hoo, Bedfordshire
Mount Ephraim, Kent
Newby Hall, Yorkshire
Norton Conyers, Yorkshire
Parnham, Dorset
Raby Castle, Durham
Ripley Castle, Yorkshire
Rodmarton Manor, Gloucestershire
Rotherfield Park, Hampshire
Sheldon Manor, Wiltshire
Smedmore House, Dorset
Somerleyton Hall, Suffolk
Spetchley Park, Worcestershire
Stonor Park, Oxfordshire
Whatton House, Leicestershire

## Rare or Unusual Shrubs

Arbigland, Dumfries
Ardtornish, Argyllshire
Arley Hall, Cheshire
Barnsley House, Gloucestershire
Batsford Arboretum, Gloucestershire
Blairquhan, Ayrshire. Azaleas, etc
Blenheim Palace, Oxfordshire
Bramdean House, Hampshire
Broadleas House, Wiltshire
Brympton d'Evercy, Somerset
Castle Howard, Yorkshire
Cawdor Castle, Nairn
Cholmondeley Castle, Cheshire
Clapton Court, Somerset
Constable Burton Hall, Yorkshire
Corsham Court, Wiltshire
Crarae Glen, Argyllshire
Dalemain, Cumbria
Docwra's Manor, Hertfordshire
Dorfold Hall, Cheshire
Easton Grey House, Wiltshire
Exbury Gardens, Hampshire
Finchcocks, Kent
Forde Abbey, Somerset
Goodnestone Park, Kent
Harewood House, Yorkshire
Heale House, Wiltshire
Helmingham Hall, Suffolk
Hergest Croft, Herefordshire
The High Beeches, West Sussex
Hodnet Hall, Shropshire
Holdenby House, Northamptonshire
Holker Hall, Cumbria
How Caple Court, Herefordshire
Kingston House, Oxfordshire
Longleat House, Wiltshire
Mannington Hall, Norfolk. Species roses
Mapperton House, Dorset
Minterne Gardens, Dorset
Muncaster Castle, Cumbria
Newby Hall, Yorkshire
Newick Park, East Sussex
Painswick Rococo Gardens, Gloucestershire
Parnham, Dorset
Pencarrow, Cornwall
Riverhill House, Kent
Sheldon Manor, Wiltshire
Smedmore House, Dorset
Somerleyton Hall, Suffolk
Spetchley Park, Worcestershire
Tatton Park, Cheshire
Torosay Castle, Argyllshire
Whatton House, Leicestershire

## Rare or Unusual Trees

Arbigland, Dumfries

Arbury Hall, Warwickshire
Ardtornish, Argyllshire
Athelhampton, Dorset
Batsford Arboretum, Gloucestershire
Belvoir Castle, Lincolnshire. Chusan palms
Blairquhan, Ayrshire
Blenheim Palace, Oxfordshire
Bramdean House, Hampshire
Broadleas, Wiltshire
Brympton d'Evercy, Somerset
Castle Howard, Yorkshire
Cawdor Castle, Nairn
Chenies Manor, Buckinghamshire (very
   ancient specimen oak)
Cholmondeley Castle, Cheshire
Clapton Court, Somerset
Corsham Court, Wiltshire
Crarae Glen, Argyllshire
Dalemain, Cumbria
Deans Court, Dorset
Dorfold Hall, Cheshire
Eastnor Castle, Herefordshire
Easton Grey House, Wiltshire
Eccleshall Castle, Staffordshire
Edmondsham House, Dorset
Elton Hall, Cambridgeshire
Exbury Gardens, Hampshire
Finchcocks, Kent
Forde Abbey, Somerset
Goodnestone Park, Kent
Harewood House, Yorkshire
Haughley Park, Suffolk
Heale House, Wiltshire
Hergest Croft, Herefordshire
Hever Castle, Kent
The High Beeches, West Sussex
Hodnet Hall, Shropshire
Holker Hall, Cumbria
How Caple Court, Herefordshire
Kingston House, Oxfordshire
Kingstone Lisle Park, Oxfordshire
Layer Marney Hall, Essex. Loquat
Longleat House, Wiltshire
Luton Hoo, Bedfordshire
Mannington Hall, Norfolk
Mapperton House, Dorset
Mellerstain House, Berwickshire
Michelham Priory, East Sussex
Minterne Gardens, Dorset
Mount Ephraim, Kent
Muncaster Castle, Cumbria
Newby Hall, Yorkshire
Newick Park, East Sussex
Nunwell House, Isle of Wight
Parnham, Dorset
Pencarrow, Cornwall
Ripley Castle, Yorkshire
Riverhill House, Kent
Rockingham Castle, Leicestershire
Sheldon Manor, Wiltshire
Sherborne Castle, Dorset
Smedmore House, Dorset
Somerleyton Hall, Suffolk
Spetchley Park, Worcestershire
Stanway House, Gloucestershire
Stonor Park, Oxfordshire
Syon Park, Middlesex
Tatton Park, Cheshire
Thorp Perrow Arboretum, Yorkshire
Torosay Castle, Argyllshire
West Dean Gardens, West Sussex
Whatton House, Leicestershire

## Rhododendrons

Adlington Hall, Cheshire
Arbigland, Dumfries
Arbury Hall, Warwickshire
Arley Hall, Cheshire
Barton Manor, Isle of Wight

Beaulieu Abbey, Hampshire
Belvoir Castle, Lincolnshire
Bickleigh Castle, Devon
Blairquhan, Ayrshire
Blenheim Palace, Oxfordshire
Bodrhyddan Hall, Clwyd
Bowood House, Wiltshire
Bramham Park, Yorkshire
Broadleas, Wiltshire
Bryn Bras Castle, Gwynedd
Castle Howard, Yorkshire
Cawdor Castle, Nairn
Chatsworth House, Derbyshire
Chillingham Castle, Northumberland
Chillington Hall, Staffordshire
Cholmondeley Castle, Cheshire
Clapton Court, Somerset
Corby Castle, Cumbria
Crarae Glen, Argyllshire
Doddington Hall, Lincolnshire
Dorfold Hall, Cheshire
Dunrobin Castle, Sutherland
Exbury Gardens, Hampshire
Forde Abbey, Somerset
Goodnestone Park, Kent
Hammerwood Park, West Sussex
Harewood House, Yorkshire
Haughley Park, Suffolk
Hergest Croft, Herefordshire
Hever Castle, Kent
The High Beeches, West Sussex
The Hirsel, Berwickshire
Hodnet Hall, Shropshire
Holdenby House, Northamptonshire
Holker Hall, Cumbria
Hopetoun House, Lothian
Hutton-in-the-Forest, Cumbria
Leeds Castle, Kent
Longleat House, Wiltshire
Luton Hoo, Bedfordshire
Lyme Park, Cheshire
Manderston, Berwickshire
Mannington Hall, Norfolk
Mellerstain House, Berwickshire
Minterne Gardens, Dorset
Moccas Court, Herefordshire
Mount Ephraim, Kent
Muncaster Castle, Cumbria
Newby Hall, Yorkshire
Newick Park, East Sussex
The Owl House, Kent
Parnham, Dorset
Pencarrow, Cornwall
Picton Castle, Dyfed
Powderham Castle, Devon
Ragley Hall, Warwickshire
Rainthorpe Hall, Norfolk
Ripley Castle, Yorkshire
Riverhill House, Kent
Rotherfield Park, Hampshire
St Osyth's Priory, Essex
Scone Palace, Perth
Somerleyton Hall, Suffolk
Spetchley Park, Worcestershire
Squerryes Court, Kent
Stockeld Park, Yorkshire
Syon Park, Middlesex
Tatton Park, Cheshire
Torosay Castle, Argyllshire
Traquair House, Peeblesshire
Warwick Castle, Warwickshire
Weston Park, Shropshire
Whatton House, Leicestershire
Woburn Abbey, Bedfordshire

## Roses

Arbigland, Dumfries
Arbury Hall, Warwickshire
Arley Hall, Cheshire

Barnsley House, Gloucestershire
Barton Manor, Isle of Wight
Belvoir Castle, Lincolnshire
Benington Lordship, Hertfordshire
Berkeley Castle, Gloucestershire
Bickleigh Castle, Devon
Blairquhan, Ayrshire
Blenheim Palace, Oxfordshire
Bowood House, Wiltshire
Bramdean House, Hampshire
Bramham Park, Yorkshire
Broadleas, Wiltshire
Broughton Castle, Oxfordshire
Brympton d'Evercy, Somerset
Bryn Bras Castle, Gwynedd
Castle Howard, Yorkshire
Cawdor Castle, Nairn
Chatsworth House, Derbyshire
Chicheley Hall, Buckinghamshire
Chilham Castle, Kent
Chillingham Castle, Northumberland
Cholmondeley Castle, Cheshire
Clapton Court, Somerset
Combe Sydenham, Somerset
Corsham Court, Wiltshire
Dalemain, Cumbria
Docwra's Manor, Hertfordshire
Doddington Hall, Lincolnshire
Dorfold Hall, Cheshire
Dunrobin Castle, Sutherland
Earlshall Castle, Fife
Eastnor Castle, Herefordshire
Easton Grey House, Wiltshire
Eccleshall Castle, Staffordshire
Elsham Hall, South Humberside
Elton Hall, Cambridgeshire
Euston Hall, Norfolk
Exbury Gardens, Hampshire
Gaulden Manor, Somerset
Godinton Park, Kent
Goodnestone Park, Kent
Great Dixter, East Sussex
Grimsthorpe Castle, Lincolnshire
Haddon Hall, Derbyshire
Hammerwood Park, West Sussex
Harewood House, Yorkshire
Heale House, Wiltshire
Helmingham Hall, Suffolk
Hergest Croft, Herefordshire
Hever Castle, Kent
The Hirsel, Berwickshire
Hodnet Hall, Shropshire
Holdenby House, Northamptonshire
Holker Hall, Cumbria
Holme Pierrepont Hall, Nottinghamshire
Houghton Lodge, Hampshire
How Caple Court, Herefordshire
Hutton-in-the-Forest, Cumbria
Iford Manor, Wiltshire
Kingston House, Oxfordshire
Kingstone Lisle Park, Oxfordshire
Knebworth House, Hertfordshire
Layer Marney Tower, Essex
Levens Hall, Cumbria
Littlecote House, Wiltshire
Longleat House, Wiltshire
Loseley Park, Surrey
Luton Hoo, Bedfordshire
Manderston, Berwickshire
Mannington Hall, Norfolk
Melbourne Hall, Derbyshire
Mellerstain House, Berwickshire
Michelham Priory, East Sussex
Misarden Park, Gloucestershire
Mount Ephraim, Kent
Newby Hall, Yorkshire
Norton Conyers, Yorkshire
Nunwell House, Isle of Wight
The Owl House, Kent
Painswick Rococo Gardens, Gloucestershire
Parham House, West Sussex

Parnham, Dorset
Powderham Castle, Devon
Raby Castle, Durham
Ragley Hall, Warwickshire
Rainthorpe Hall, Norfolk
Ripley Castle, Yorkshire
Rockingham Castle, Leicestershire
Rodmarton Manor, Gloucestershire
Rotherfield Park, Hampshire
Rousham, Oxfordshire
St Osyth's Priory, Essex
Sheldon Manor, Wiltshire
Somerleyton Hall, Suffolk
Spetcheley Park, Worcestershire
Stanton Harcourt, Oxfordshire
Stockeld Park, Yorkshire
Stonor Park, Oxfordshire
Sudeley Castle, Gloucestershire
Sutton Park, Yorkshire
Syon Park, Middlesex
Tatton Park, Cheshire
Torosay Castle, Argyllshire
Traquair House, Peeblesshire
Warwick Castle, Warwickshire
West Dean Gardens, West Sussex

Whatton House, Leicestershire
Wilton House, Wiltshire

## Topiary

Arley Hall, Cheshire
Athelhampton, Dorset
Barnsley House, Gloucestershire
Bickleigh Castle, Devon
Bodrhyddan Hall, Clwyd
Bramdean House, Hampshire
Breamore House, Hampshire
Brympton d'Evercy, Somerset
Chenies Manor, Buckinghamshire
Chilham Castle, Kent
Doddington Hall, Lincolnshire
Earlshall Castle, Fife
Elton Hall, Cambridgeshire
Godinton Park, Kent
Great Dixter, East Sussex
Grimsthorpe Castle, Lincolnshire
Haddon Hall, Derbyshire
Heale House, Wiltshire
Helmingham Hall, Suffolk
Hergest Croft, Herefordshire

Hever Castle, Kent
Holme Pierrpont Hall, Nottinghamshire
Hopetoun House, Lothian
Houghton Lodge, Hampshire
Levens Hall, Cumbria
Longleat House, Wiltshire
Luton Hoo, Bedfordshire
Manderston, Berwickshire
Mapperton House, Dorset
Misarden Park, Gloucestershire
Mount Ephraim, Kent
Parnham, Dorset
Powderham Castle, Devon
Rockingham Castle, Leicestershire
Rodmarton Manor, Gloucestershire
Rotherfield Park, Hampshire
St Osyth's Priory, Essex
Sheldon Manor, Wiltshire
Somerleyton Hall, Suffolk
Squerryes Court, Kent
Stanton Harcourt, Oxfordshire
Sudeley Castle, Gloucestershire
Sutton Park, Yorkshire
Tatton Park, Cheshire
Warwick Castle, Warwickshire

# Livestock

Adlington Hall, Cheshire. Doves
Arbigland, Dumfries. Deer, peacocks
Barford Park, Somerset. Peacocks, waterfowl
Barton Manor, Isle of Wight. Waterfowl
Belvoir Castle, Lincolnshire. Peacocks
Berkeley Castle, Gloucestershire. Deer, free-flying butterfly house
Bickleigh Castle, Devon. Waterfowl
Blairquhan, Ayrshire. Waterfowl
Blenheim Palace, Oxfordshire. Waterfowl
Bodrhyddan Hall, Clwyd. Horses and foals
Bowood House, Wiltshire. Deer, waterfowl
Bramham Park, Yorkshire. Deer, peacocks, horses, poultry, ducks, geese
Brympton d'Evercy, Somerset. Ducks
Bryn Bras Castle, Gwynedd. Peacocks, wild birds and animals
Burton Constable Hall, North Humberside. Peacocks, waterfowl
Castle Howard, Yorkshire. Deer, peacocks waterfowl
Cawdor Castle, Nairn. White ducks, Highland cattle, Soay sheep
Chicheley Hall, Buckinghamshire. Waterfowl
Chilham Castle, Kent. Peacocks, waterfowl
Chillingham Castle, Northumberland. Deer
Cholmondeley Castle, Cheshire. Rare breeds of farm animals
Combe Sydenham, Somerset. Deer, peacocks, waterfowl
Corsham Court, Wiltshire. Peacocks, waterfowl
Dalemain, Cumbria. Deer
Deans Court, Dorset. Peacocks
Docwra's Manor, Hertfordshire. Rare newts
Earlshall, Fife. Highland cattle
Eastnor Castle, Herefordshire. Deer, waterfowl

Elsham Hall, South Humberside. Deer, domestic animals, peacocks, waterfowl, bird garden
Exbury Gardens, Hampshire. Peacocks, waterfowl, ornamental pheasants
Forde Abbey, Somerset. Waterfowl
Gaulden Manor, Somerset
Harewood House, Yorkshire. Waterfowl
Haughley Park, Suffolk. Sheep
Heale House, Wiltshire. Jacob sheep, doves
Helmingham Hall, Suffolk. Deer, Highland cattle
Hever Castle, Kent. Waterfowl
Hodnet Hall, Shropshire. Waterfowl, black swans
Holdenby House, Northamptonshire. Rare breeds of cattle and sheep, birds of prey, ornamental pheasants, monkeys, 'Cuddle Farm' of small animals
Holker Hall, Cumbria. Deer, geese
Holme Pierrepont Hall, Nottinghamshire. Jacob sheep
Hopetoun House, Lothian. Red and fallow deer, St Kilda sheep
Houghton Lodge, Hampshire. Waterfowl, wild swans, geese, donkeys
Hutton-in-the-Forest, Cumbria. Guinea fowl
Kentwell Hall, Suffolk. Peacocks, waterfowl, rare farm breeds
Kingstone Lisle Park, Oxfordshire
Knebworth House, Hertfordshire. Deer, sheep
Layer Marney Tower, Essex. Deer, waterfowl, Dexter cattle
Leeds Castle, Kent. Peacocks, waterfowl, mixed aviary collection
Levens Hall, Cumbria. Bagot goats
Littlecote House, Wiltshire. Peacocks, rare farm breeds

Longleat House, Wiltshire. Deer, peacocks, waterfowl
Loseley Park, Surrey. Waterfowl, cockatoos, rare farm breeds
Manderston, Berwickshire. Waterfowl, swans
Mannington Hall, Norfolk. Waterfowl, pheasants, sheep
Mapperton House, Dorset. Wild deer
Melbourne Hall, Derbyshire. White peacocks, ornamental pheasants
Mellerstain House, Berwickshire. Waterfowl
Mertoun, Roxburghshire. Golden and silver pheasants
Michelham Priory, East Sussex. Waterfowl
Muncaster Castle, Cumbria. Peacocks, waterfowl, owls
Newick Park, East Sussex. Peacocks
Otley Hall, Suffolk. Ducks, black swans
The Owl House, Kent. Waterfowl
Painswick Rococo Gardens, Gloucestershire. Wildlife
Parham House, West Sussex. Deer
Parnham, Dorset. Wild deer, waterfowl
Pencarrow, Cornwall. Peacocks, pets' corner
Powderham Castle, Devon. Deer, peacocks, waterfowl, horses, sheep, cattle
Raby Castle, Durham. Deer, waterfowl, Longhorn cattle
Ragley Hall, Warwickshire. Peacocks, waterfowl
Ripley Castle, Yorkshire. Deer, waterfowl
Riverhill House, Kent. Ornamental pheasants
Rousham, Oxfordshire. Bantams, Longhorn cattle
St Osyth's Priory, Essex. Deer, peacocks
Sheldon Manor, Wiltshire. Llama, silky bantams, white Muscovy ducks
Sherborne Castle, Dorset. Waterfowl

Spetchley Park, Worcestershire. Deer, peacocks
Squerryes Court, Kent. Waterfowl
Stanton Harcourt, Oxfordshire. Jacob sheep, Jersey cows, British White cows
Stonor Park, Oxfordshire. Deer
Sudeley Castle, Gloucestershire. Falconry, peacocks, waterfowl

Sutton Park, Yorkshire. Bantams, Jacob sheep
Syon Park, Middlesex. Peacocks, waterfowl, cattle
Tatton Park, Cheshire. Deer, waterfowl
Torosay Castle, Argyllshire. Waterfowl
Traquair House, Peeblesshire

Warwick Castle, Warwickshire. Muntjac deer, peacocks, waterfowl, swans
Weston Park, Shropshire. Deer, waterfowl
Whatton House, Leicestershire. Silver pheasants
Woburn Abbey, Bedfordshire, Deer, waterfowl

# Water Features

## Canals

Athelhampton, Dorset
Bramham Park, Yorkshire
Chatsworth House, Derbyshire
Chicheley Hall, Buckinghamshire
Corsham Court, Wiltshire
Forde Abbey, Somerset
Gaulden Manor, Somerset
How Caple Court, Herefordshire (to be restored)
Littlecote House, Wiltshire
Otley Hall, Suffolk
Powderham Castle, Devon
Sheldon Manor, Wiltshire (swimming pool)
Stanway House, Gloucestershire (to be restored)
Sutton Park, Yorkshire
Syon Park, Middlesex

## Cascades

Arbigland, Dumfries
Barford Park, Somerset
Blenheim Palace, Oxfordshire
Bowood House, Wiltshire
Bramham Park, Yorkshire
Bryn Bras Castle, Gwynedd
Castle Howard, Yorkshire
Chatsworth House, Derbyshire
Chiddingstone Castle, Kent
Corby Castle, Cumbria
Crarae Glen, Argyllshire (natural)
Elsham Hall, South Humberside
Exbury Gardens, Hampshire
Forde Abbey, Somerset
Harewood House, Yorkshire
Hergest Croft, Herefordshire
Hever Castle, Kent
Hodnet Hall, Shropshire (several)
Holker Hall, Cumbria
How Caple Court, Herefordshire (to be restored)
Leeds Castle, Kent
Longleat House, Wiltshire
Lyme Park, Cheshire
Mellerstain House, Berwickshire
Minterne Gardens, Dorset
Newby Hall, Yorkshire
Painswick Rococo Gardens, Gloucestershire
Parnham, Dorset
Pencarrow, Cornwall
Rousham, Oxfordshire
Stanway House, Gloucestershire (to be restored)

## Fish Ponds

Adlington Hall, Cheshire

Arbigland, Dumfries
Athelhampton, Dorset
Barford Park, Somerset
Barnsley House, Gloucestershire
Benington Lordship, Hertfordshire
Berkeley Castle, Gloucestershire
Bickleigh Castle, Devon
Blairquhan, Ayrshire
Blenheim Palace, Oxfordshire
Bramdean House, Hampshire
Bramham Park, Yorkshire
Breamore House, Hampshire
Browsholme Hall, Lancashire
Brympton d'Evercy, Somerset
Burton Constable Hall, North Humberside
Castle Howard, Yorkshire
Chatsworth House, Derbyshire
Chicheley Hall, Buckinghamshire
Chilham Castle, Kent
Chillingham Castle, Northumberland
Cholmondeley Castle, Cheshire
Combe Sydenham, Somerset
Corsham Court, Wiltshire
Deans Court, Dorset
Easton Grey House, Wiltshire
Euston Hall, Norfolk
Exbury Gardens, Hampshire
Forde Abbey, Somerset
Gaulden Manor, Somerset
Goodnestone Park, Kent
Great Dixter, East Sussex
Harewood House, Yorkshire
Haughley Park, Suffolk
Heale House, Wiltshire
Hergest Croft, Herefordshire
Hodnet Hall, Shropshire (several)
Holdenby House, Northamptonshire (Elizabethan)
Hopetoun House, Lothian
Iford Manor, Wiltshire
Kentwell Hall, Suffolk
Leeds Castle, Kent
Littlecote House, Wiltshire
Longleat House, Wiltshire
Lyme Park, Cheshire
Mannington Hall, Norfolk
Mapperton House, Dorset
Melbourne Hall, Derbyshire
Mellerstain House, Berwickshire
Mertoun, Roxburghshire
Mount Ephraim, Kent
Newick Park, East Sussex. Elizabethan hammer ponds
Otley Hall, Suffolk
The Owl House, Kent
Painswick Rococo Gardens, Gloucestershire
Parnham, Dorset
Penshurst Place, Kent
Rockingham Castle, Leicestershire
Rotherfield Park, Hampshire
Rousham, Oxfordshire

Somerleyton Hall, Suffolk (12)
Stanton Harcourt, Oxfordshire. Medieval stew ponds
Stanway House, Gloucestershire
Stonor Park, Oxfordshire
Sudeley Castle, Gloucestershire
Tatton Park, Cheshire
Traquair House, Peeblesshire
Whatton House, Leicestershire
Woburn Abbey, Bedfordshire

## Fountains

Arbigland, Dumfries
Athelhampton, Dorset
Barnsley House, Gloucestershire
Barton Manor, Isle of Wight
Blenheim Palace, Oxfordshire
Bodrhyddan Hall, Clwyd
Bowood House, Wiltshire
Bramham Park, Yorkshire
Castle Howard, Yorkshire
Chatsworth House, Derbyshire
Chillingham Castle, Northumberland
Combe Sydenham, Somerset
Corsham Court, Wiltshire
Dalemain, Cumbria
Dunrobin Castle, Sutherland (3)
Eastnor Castle, Herefordshire
Euston Hall, Norfolk
Glamis Castle, Angus
Godinton Park, Kent
Haddon Hall, Derbyshire
Heale House, Wiltshire
Hever Castle, Kent
Hodnet Hall, Shropshire
Holker Hall, Cumbria
Hopetoun House, Lothian
How Caple Court, Herefordshire
Iford Manor, Wiltshire
Kingstone Lisle Park, Oxfordshire
Littlecote House, Wiltshire
Longleat House, Wiltshire
Luton Hoo, Bedfordshire
Lyme Park, Cheshire
Manderston, Berwickshire
Mapperton House, Dorset
Melbourne Hall, Derbyshire
Mellerstain House, Berwickshire
Mount Ephraim, Kent
Nunwell House, Isle of Wight
The Owl House, Kent
Painswick Rococo Gardens, Gloucestershire (to be restored)
Parham House, West Sussex
Parnham, Dorset
Pencarrow, Cornwall
Penshurst Place, Kent
Somerleyton Hall, Suffolk
Spetchley Park, Worcestershire

Stanway House, Gloucestershire
Sudeley Castle, Gloucestershire
Syon Park, Middlesex
Tatton Park, Cheshire
Torosay Castle, Argyllshire
Traquair House, Peeblesshire
Warwick Castle, Warwickshire
Wilton House, Wiltshire

## Lakes

Arbigland, Dumfries
Barford Park, Somerset
Barton Manor, Isle of Wight
Batsford Arboretum, Gloucestershire
Benington Lordship, Hertfordshire
Blairquhan, Ayrshire
Blenheim Palace, Oxfordshire
Bowood House, Wiltshire
Bryn Bras Castle, Gwynedd
Burton Constable Hall, North Humberside
Castle Howard, Yorkshire
Chiddingstone Castle, Kent
Chilham Castle, Kent
Chillingham Castle, Northumberland
Chillington Hall, Staffordshire
Cholmondeley Castle, Cheshire
Combe Sydenham, Somerset
Corsham Court, Wiltshire
Dorfold House, Cheshire
Eastnor Castle, Herefordshire
Elsham Hall, South Humberside (2)
Elton Hall, Cambridgeshire
Euston Hall, Norfolk
Firle Place, East Sussex
Forde Abbey, Somerset
Grimsthorpe Castle, Lincolnshire
Hammerwood Park, West Sussex
Harewood House, Yorkshire
Hever Castle, Kent
The Hirsel, Berwickshire
Hodnet Hall, Shropshire
Kingstone Lisle Park, Oxfordshire (3)
Knebworth House, Hertfordshire
Leeds Castle, Kent
Longleat, Wiltshire
Lyme Park, Cheshire
Manderston, Berwickshire
Mannington Hall, Norfolk
Melbourne Hall, Derbyshire
Mellerstain House, Berwickshire
Minterne Gardens, Dorset
Mount Ephraim, Kent
Newick Park, Sussex
The Owl House, Kent
Parnham, Dorset
Pencarrow, Cornwall
Penshurst Place, Kent
Powderham Castle, Devon
Raby Castle, Durham
Ragley Hall, Warwickshire
Rainthorpe Hall, Norfolk
Ripley Castle, Yorkshire
Spains Hall, Essex
Spetchley Park, Worcestershire
Squerryes Court, Kent
Stanton Harcourt, Oxfordshire
Syon Park, Middlesex
Tatton Park, Cheshire

Thorp Perrow Arboretum, Yorkshire
Torosay Castle, Argyllshire
Weston Park, Shropshire
Woburn Abbey, Bedfordshire

## Lily Ponds

Arley Hall, Cheshire
Athelhampton, Dorset
Barnsley House, Gloucestershire
Berkeley Castle, Gloucestershire
Bodrhyddan Hall, Clwyd
Bramham Park, Yorkshire
Bryn Bras Castle, Gwynedd
Castle Howard, Yorkshire
Chenies Manor, Buckinghamshire
Cholmondeley Castle, Cheshire
Clapton Court, Somerset
Dorfold Hall, Cheshire
Easton Grey House, Wiltshire
Elton Hall, Cambridgeshire
Euston Hall, Norfolk
Finchcocks, Kent
Forde Abbey, Somerset
Godinton Park, Kent
Goodnestone Park, Kent
Great Dixter, East Sussex
Heale House, Wiltshire
Hergest Croft, Herefordshire
The High Beeches, West Sussex
Hodnet Hall, Shropshire
Holdenby House, Northamptonshire (2)
Holker Hall, Cumbria
How Caple Court, Herefordshire
Iford Manor, Wiltshire (several)
Kingstone Lisle Park, Oxfordshire
Knebworth House, Hertfordshire
Lamport Hall, Northamptonshire
Littlecote House, Wiltshire
Luton Hoo, Bedfordshire
Mapperton House, Dorset
Melbourne Hall, Derbyshire
Mellerstain House, Berwickshire
Mount Ephraim, Kent
Newby Hall, Yorkshire
Norton Conyers, Yorkshire
Nunwell House, Isle of Wight
The Owl House, Kent
Parham House, West Sussex
Parnham, Dorset
Penshurst Place, Kent
Raby Castle, Durham
Rainthorpe Hall, Norfolk
Rotherfield Park, Hampshire
St Osyth's Priory, Essex
Somerleyton Hall, Suffolk
Tatton Park, Cheshire
Torosay Castle, Argyllshire
Warwick Castle, Warwickshire

## Moats

Benington Lordship, Hertfordshire (dry)
Berkeley Castle, Gloucestershire
Bickleigh Castle, Devon
Broughton Castle, Oxfordshire (3 acres)
Chillingham Castle, Northumberland (dry)
Eccleshall Castle, Staffordshire (dry)

Helmingham Hall, Suffolk
Hever Castle, Kent
Hodnet Hall, Shropshire (dry)
Kentwell Hall, Suffolk
Kingston House, Oxfordshire (dry)
Leeds Castle, Kent
Loseley Park, Surrey
Mannington Hall, Norfolk
Michelham Priory, East Sussex
Otley Hall, Suffolk
Rockingham Castle, Leicestershire
Spetchley Park, Worcestershire
Stanton Harcourt, Oxfordshire
Sudeley Castle, Gloucestershire

## Rivers, Streams, Other Water Features

Adlington Hall, Cheshire. River Dean
Ardtornish House, Argyllshire. Streams
Beaulieu Abbey, Hampshire. Mill pond
Benington Lordship, Hertfordshire. Rock
garden pools
Blairquhan, Ayrshire
Bryn Bras Castle, Gwynedd. Stream, pools,
swimming pool/lakelet
Castle Howard, Yorkshire. Waterfall
Cawdor Castle, Nairn. Burn
Chatsworth House, Derbyshire. Grotto
pond, willow-tree fountain
Chiddingstone Castle, Kent. Water tower
Chillingham Castle, Northumberland, Burn,
river
Clapton Court, Somerset. Stream and ponds
in woodland glades
Corby Castle, Cumbria. River Eden
Dalemain, Cumbria. Dacre Beck
Doddington Hall, Lincolnshire. Stream
Dorfold Hall, Cheshire. Stream
Easton Grey House, Wiltshire. River Avon
Eccleshall Castle, Staffordshire. Mere
Haddon Hall, Derbyshire. River
Hammerwood Park, West Sussex. Stream
with pools leading to lake
Heale House, Wiltshire. River Avon
Hergest Croft, Herefordshire. Woodland
pond
How Caple Court, Herefordshire. Pools
Levens Hall, Cumbria. River Kent
The High Beeches, West Sussex. Streams
Houghton Lodge, Hampshire. River, well
Melbourne Hall, Derbyshire. Wishing well
at natural spring with inscription by Lady
Caroline Lamb
Moccas Court, Hereford. River Wye
Muncaster Castle, Cumbria. Duck ponds
Newby Hall, Yorkshire. River Ure
Painswick Rococo Gardens,
Gloucestershire. Stream, plunge pool,
dipping pond
The Priory, Lavenham, Suffolk. Pond
Rousham, Oxfordshire. River Cherwell
Syon Park, Middlesex. River Thames
Torosay Castle, Argyllshire
Warwick Castle, Warwickshire. River Avon
West Dean Gardens, West Sussex.
Winterbourne
Wilton House, Wiltshire. River Nadder

# Garden Centres/Plant Sales

Arley Hall, Cheshire
Barnsley House, Gloucestershire. Plants from the garden, garden furniture
Barton Manor, Isle of Wight. Specialities, vines, kniphofias, watsonias
Batsford Arboretum, Gloucestershire. Garden centre
Belvoir Castle, Lincolnshire. Mainly spring bedding and summer pot plants
Benington Lordship, Hertfordshire. Foliage shrubs, unusual herbaceous plants
Bickleigh Castle, Devon. Plant sales: mainly dwarf conifers
Blenheim Palace, Oxfordshire. Garden centre
Bowood House, Wiltshire. Garden centre
Bramdean House, Hampshire
Broadleas, Wiltshire. Plant sales: rare plants from the garden
Broughton Castle, Oxfordshire. Plant sales, specially herbaceous plants
Brympton d'Evercy, Somerset
Castle Howard, Yorkshire. Garden centre, many unusual plants
Chatsworth House, Derbyshire
Chenies Manor, Buckinghamshire. Culinary herbs
Cholmondeley Hall, Cheshire. Plant sales
Clapton Court, Somerset. Rare plants, trees, shrubs, fuchsias, pelargoniums
Combe Sydenham, Somerset
Crarae Glen, Argyllshire. Shrubs and trees
Dalemain, Cumbria. Herbs, shrub roses, Himalayan blue poppies
Deans Court, Dorset. Plant sales: organically grown herbs
Docwra's Manor, Hertfordshire. Unusual herbaceous plants, shrubs, Mediterranean plants
Earlshall Castle, Fife
Edmondsham House, Dorset. Plant sales, also organic composts

Elsham Hall, South Humberside
Exbury Gardens, Hampshire. Ericaceous and other plants
Forde Abbey, Somerset
Gaulden Manor, Somerset. Plants sales, specially herbs, bog plants
Goodnestone Park, Kent
Great Dixter, East Sussex. Plant sales, specially clematis
Hammerwood Park, West Sussex (opening soon)
Harewood House, Yorkshire
Heale House, Wiltshire
Helmingham Hall, Suffolk. Herbaceous plants, vegetables
Hergest Croft, Herefordshire. Unusual trees, shrubs, herbaceous plants and alpines
Hever Castle, Kent
Hodnet Hall, Shropshire. Rhododendrons, azaleas, alpines, herbs
Holdenby House, Northamptonshire. Herbs, perennials, house plants
Holker Hall, Cumbria. Unusual plants
Hopetoun House, Lothian. Unusual plants, specially hardy perennials
Houghton Lodge, Hampshire. Plant sales, specially fuchsias (over 100 kinds)
How Caple Court, Herefordshire. English and old shrub roses, unusual herbaceous plants and shrubs
Kingston House, Oxfordshire. Plant stall
Kingstone Lisle Park, Oxfordshire. Plant sales, forestry nursery
Leeds Castle, Kent
Levens Hall, Cumbria. Plant sales: shrubs, herbaceous, tender perennials
Littlecote House, Wiltshire. Shrubs, alpines, herbs, herbaceous
Longleat, Wiltshire. Garden shop
Loseley Park, Surrey

Manderston, Berwickshire. Specializing in hebes
Mannington Hall, Norfolk. Roses
Mapperton House, Dorset (from 1990)
Michelham Priory, East Sussex. Plant sales: herbs and herbaceous plants
Misarden Park, Gloucestershire
Muncaster Castle, Cumbria
Newby Hall, Yorkshire
Newick Park, East Sussex. Herbs, cottage-garden plants, old roses
Norton Conyers, Yorkshire. Old-fashioned and unusual hardy plants
The Owl House, Kent. Plant sales
Parham House, West Sussex. Plants sold in shop
Pencarrow, Cornwall. Plant sales: rare conifers, rhododendrons, camellias, geraniums, pelargoniums, fuchsias
Powderham Castle, Devon. Plant sales, specially lavender
Prideaux Place, Cornwall
Rainthorpe Hall, Norfolk. Garden centre
Ripley Castle, Yorkshire
Riverhill House, Kent
Rodmarton Manor, Gloucestershire. Plant sales
Smedmore House, Dorset. Plant sales: herbaceous, small conifers, clematis
Spetchley Park, Worcestershire. Plant sales
Stansted Park, Hampshire. Plant sales
Sudeley Castle, Gloucestershire. Plant sales, specially old roses
Syon Park, Middlesex. Garden centre
Tatton Park, Cheshire
West Dean Gardens, West Sussex. Nursery: trees, shrubs, old roses, unusual herbaceous plants
Whatton House, Leicestershire
Wilton House, Wiltshire

# Specialities

Barford Park, Somerset. Lilies, candelabra primulas
Bramdean House, Hampshire. Herbaceous, chalk-loving plants
Brympton d'Evercy, Somerset. Vineyard, labour-saving plants
Castle Howard, Yorkshire. Roses, rhododendrons
Chenies Manor, Buckinghamshire. Culinary herbs
Cholmondeley Castle, Cheshire. Rhododendrons, azaleas, magnolias, cornus
Clapton Court, Somerset. Rare trees, shrubs, plants
Crarae Glen, Argyllshire. Nothofagus spp.
Dalemain, Cumbria. Meconopsis
Deans Court, Dorset. Organic gardening

Doddington Hall, Lincolnshire. Old-fashioned and rambler roses, flag irises, old-fashioned pinks
Earlshall Castle, Fife. Herbaceous plants
Edmondsham House, Dorset. Organically grown vegetables, spring bulbs
Elsham Hall, South Humberside. Spring bulbs and blossom, snowdrops
Exbury Gardens, Hampshire. Ericaceous plants
Haddon Hall, Derbyshire. Roses, clematis, wild flowers, alpines in walls
Harewood House, Yorkshire. Rhododendrons, hostas, astilbes
Heale House, Wiltshire. Old roses
Helmingham Hall, Suffolk. Old roses, herbaceous plants, vegetables
Hodnet Hall, Shropshire. Acid-loving

plants, magnolias, camellias, cornus, stewartia, heaths, lilacs
Holdenby House, Northamptonshire. Herbs, fragrant plants
Holker Hall, Cumbria. Magnolias, cornus, rhododendrons
Houghton Lodge, Hampshire. Fuchsias
Kentwell Hall, Suffolk. Plants of the Tudor period
Iford Manor, Wiltshire. Acanthus
Layer Marney Hall, Essex. Roses, lilacs
Manderston, Berwickshire. Hebes
Mertoun, Roxburghshire. Azaleas
Michelham Priory, East Sussex. Medicinal herbs
Minterne Gardens, Dorset. Rhododendrons
Muncaster Castle, Cumbria. Rhododendrons, camellias, azaleas, magnolias

Pencarrow, Cornwall. Rare conifers, rhododendrons, camellias
Powderham Castle, Devon. Roses
The Priory, Lavenham, Suffolk. Herbs
Rainthorpe Hall, Norfolk. Bamboos

Ripley Castle, Yorkshire. Herbaceous and alpine plants
Riverhill House, Kent. Rhododendrons
Sheldon Manor, Wiltshire. Old-fashioned roses in grass, sorbus

Smedmore House, Dorset. Hydrangeas, fuchsias, tender shrubs and climbers
Tatton Park, Cheshire. Japanese, Chinese and North American plants
West Dean Gardens, West Sussex. Horse chestnuts, tulip trees

## NCCPG National Collections

Acer: Hergest Croft, Herefordshire
Betula: Hergest Croft, Herefordshire
Cornus: Newby Hall, Yorkshire
Euonymus: Broadleas, Wiltshire
Kniphofia: Barton Manor, Isle of Wight

Monarda: Leeds Castle, Kent
Nepeta: Leeds Castle, Kent
Primula (candelabra and sikkimensis): Newick Park, East Sussex

Pyrethrum: Lamport Hall, Northamptonshire
Stewartia: The High Beeches, West Sussex
Watsonia: Barton manor, Isle of Wight
Zelkova: Hergest Croft, Herefordshire

# Acknowledgements

I would like to thank Lady Ashbrook, Mr and Mrs Charles Clive-Ponsonby-Fane, Mr Robin Compton, Mr and the Hon Mrs A Heber-Percy, Major David and Lady Anne Rasch and Mrs Rosemary Verey for giving up so much of their time to show me their gardens, and for their kind hospitality; Simon McBride for taking so much trouble over his superb photographs of the award-winning gardens; and Victoria Merrill at the Historic Houses Association for co-ordinating the project with such cheerful efficiency.

Filling in forms is a time-consuming and tedious chore, and I am most grateful to the owners of gardens listed in the gazetteer for completing our questionnaires so thoughtfully and informatively, and for returning them so promptly.

Above all, I must thank Christie's and the Historic Houses Association for giving me such a pleasurable assignment.

# Index

Page numbers in *italics* refer to illustrations.

In the listings (pages 141–57) only the plants have been indexed as the listings are already in alphabetical order under the various categories.